WITHDRAWN

H E HAD IT coming if ever a man did, and I could
have killed him then and nobody the wiser. If he
had been man enough, we could have gone off on the
dock and slugged it out, and everything would have been
settled either way the cat jumped. There's nothing like a
sock on the chin to sort of clean things up. It saves hard
feelings and time wasted in argument. But Duggs was the
chief mate, and he wasn't man enough to whip me and
knew it.

Bilge water, they say, is thicker than blood, and once
men have been shipmates, no matter how much they hate
each other's guts, they stand together against the world.
That's the way it is supposed to be, but it certainly wasn't
going to be that way with Duggs and me. I decided that
in a hurry.

From the hour I shipped on that freighter, Duggs made
it tough for me, but it wasn't only me but the whole crew.
You don't mind so much if a really tough guy makes you
like it, but when a two-by-twice scenery bum like Duggs
rubs it into you just because he has the authority, it just
naturally hurts.

If we'd gone off on the dock where it was man to man,
I'd have lowered the boom on his chin and left him for the
gulls to pick over. But we were aboard ship, and if you
sock an officer aboard ship, it's your neck.

—From "Thicker Than Blood"

Bantam Books by Louis L'Amour

YONDERING

STORIES

Louis L'Amour

Postscript by Beau L'Amour

BANTAM BOOKS

NEW YORK

2018 Bantam Books Mass Market Edition

Published in the United States by Bantam Books,
an imprint of Random House, a division of
Penguin Random House LLC, New York.

BANTAM and the HOUSE colophon are registered trademarks of
Penguin Random House LLC.

The July 6, 1939, *Tulsa Tribune* column "The Rambler,"
by Roger Devlin, is reprinted by permission of BH Media Group Inc.

Originally published in the United States by Bantam Books,
an imprint of Random House, a division of
Penguin Random House LLC, in 1954.

ISBN 978-0-525-62110-2
Ebook ISBN 978-0-525-62111-9

Printed in the United States of America

randomhousebooks.com

2 4 6 8 9 7 5 3 1

Bantam Books mass market edition: November 2018

To Marc Jaffe . . .
a good friend
and a fine gentleman
from New York
whom I met in a saloon
in Elko, Nevada

CONTENTS

INTRODUCTION

I N THE BEGINNING there was a dream, a young boy's dream, a dream of far lands to see, of oceans to cross, and somewhere at the trail's end, a girl. *The girl.*

More than all else I wanted to tell stories, stories that people could read or hear, stories to love and remember. I had no desire to write to please those who make it their business to comment but for the people who do the work of the world, who live on the land or love the land, people who make and bake and struggle to make ends meet, for the people who invent, who design, who build, for the people who do. And if somewhere down the line a man or woman can put a finger on a line and say, "Yes, that is the way it was. I was there," then I would be amply repaid.

I have never scoffed at sentiment. Cynicism is ever the outward face of emptiness.

What, after all, is romance? It is the music of those who make the world turn, the people who make things happen. Romance is the story of dreams that could come true and so often do.

Why do men ride the range? Go to sea? Explore the polar ice caps? Why do they ride rockets to unknown worlds? It is because of romance, because of the stories they have read and the stories they have dreamed.

Some have said this is the age of the nonhero, that the day of the hero is gone. That's nonsense. When the hero is gone, man himself will be gone, for the hero is our future, our destiny.

These are some of the stories of a writer trying to find his way, trying to find the truth of what he has seen, to understand the people, to learn a little more about telling a story.

The people whom I have met and with whom I worked in those earlier years were not always nice people, but each in his own way was strong, or he could not survive. Of course, there were some who did not, some who could not survive. For one reason or another, nature weeded them out and cast them aside, just as happened on our frontier during the westward movement.

Some of these stories are from my own life; some are from the lives of people I met along the way.

Somewhere my love lay sleeping
    Behind the lights of a far-off town;
So I gave my heart to a bend in the road,
    And off I went, a-yondering.

YONDERING

DEATH, WESTBOUND

In those days there was a large drifting population of itinerant workers, and they were absolutely essential to the welfare of the country. They had to have men to work the harvest, for example, and some fellows would start harvesting wheat in Texas and they'd work all the way up state by state 'til they got into Canada. By the time they finished that, they had quite a stake. Some would go on to college then, some would go back to bumming, and some would look for jobs in other places. But there was a large body of itinerant workers around; they were necessary to the economy.

The Depression hadn't come yet but it was about to and all the things that brought it about were happening. People who were hoboing or itinerant workers of one kind or another knew it was going to happen before they did on Wall Street. The whole situation began to tighten up. People who had jobs didn't quit, they held on to them.

I T WAS NEARLY dark when the westbound freight pulled out of the yards, and two 'boes, hurrying from behind a long line of empties, scrambled into one of the open doors of a boxcar about halfway between the caboose and the locomotive.

There were two more men in the car when they crawled in after their bundles. One of these was sitting at one side of the door where he could see without being seen, a precaution against any shack that might drift along or be standing beside the track. Joe had had experience with shacks, and much worse, with railroad dicks; he knew their kind. Sometimes the shacks were pretty good guys, but a railroad dick is always a louse.

The other occupant of the car lay in the shadow, apparently sleeping.

The newcomers, two hard-faced young fellows carrying bundles, looked around.

Joe's curiosity got the better of him. "Westbound, fellas?"

"Yeah—you?"

"Uh-uh. L.A., if we can make it."

"We?"

"Yeah, me an' the kid over there."

"Chee, I never even see 'im. S'matter, 's he asleep?"

"Naw, he's sick I guess. We been on this train t'ree nights now, an' he's been sick all the while. I don't know what's the matter. He coughs a lot—maybe he's a lunger."

"Chee, that's kinda tough, ain't it? Sick as a goddam drag when the bulls is all gettin' tough."

"The Santy Fe is the toughest line of 'em all. 'Member hearin' 'bout Yermo Red?"

"Aw hell, Yermo was on the U.P. I made it thru there once on the bum with a coupla Polacks. He was plenty tough, that guy."

"Naw, he just t'ought he was tough. Them guys is mostly yellow when there is a showdown."

Joe walked over to look at the kid. The boy's face was damp with perspiration and he looked bad. One of the others, a flat-nosed young fellow with heavy shoulders, walked over.

"Cheesus, he looks bad, don't he? 'At kid should oughta have a doctor!"

"Yeah."

The other young fellow walked over. "S'matter, Heavy? Is he bad off?" Then seeing the kid's face, he murmured: "Gawah!"

All three returned to a spot near the door. A heavy silence had descended upon the group. Joe rolled a cigarette and complied in silence to the others' dumb request for the makin's.

Heavy looked glumly out at the night. "Cheesus, that's a helluva place to get sick in! Wonder if he'll croak."

The slight youngster with the pale face who answered to the name of Slim grunted: "Naw, he'll pull t'ru. A guy that has to live like this is too tough to die like anybody else."

Heavy looked at Joe and with a jerk of his head toward the kid: "Known him long?"

"Two weeks I guess. He had a coupla bucks and split 'em with me when I was bad off. He's a good kid. We been hunting jobs ever since, but this Depression finished the work. Seems like they ain't nothing left to do anymore."

"Wait'll we get a new president. What's Hoover care for us laborin' stiffs?"

Slim snorted derisively: "The next one won't be a bit better. One way or the other we get it in the neck!"

Heavy moved into a corner of the car and, carefully arranging a roll of newspapers to form a place to lie, he lay down and drew his coat over his head to sleep. A few minutes later his snores gave ample proof of his success.

Slim jerked his head toward the sleeper: "Will he bother the kid, d'ye think?"

Joe shook his head: "Naw, the kid's out of his head; I guess he's about all in. When this train stops I'll try and find somebody to give him some dope or somethin'."

They lapsed into silence broken only by the steady pound and rattle of the swiftly moving freight train and the snores of the sleeper. At intervals the kid would move and talk indistinctly for a minute or so and then once more fall into silence. Outside the car the night was quite moonlit and they could see the fields flickering by in monotonous rotation. The countless cracks in the old car made it cold and dismal. Slim dozed off against the door, knees drawn up to his chin. Joe sat silent, watching the fields outside and thinking.

It had been over a year since he had worked more than a few hours at a time, over a year of living in boxcars, cheap flophouses, and any dump he could find to crawl into. But after all, what had it been before? Just a round of jobs, a few months and then a long drunk, or maybe a short one, if he got himself rolled in some bawdy house. The kid here, he'd been the only pal he'd ever had that played square, an' now he was sicker'n hell. Life didn't mean much to a guy when he was just a workin' stiff. Sure, he'd boozed a lot, but what th' hell? Didn't he have a right to have a little fun? Well, maybe it wasn't fun, but at least a guy wasn't thinkin' about the next shift or how much ore he had to get out.

Joe dozed off, but came to with a start as a red light flashed by and the freight began to slow for a station.

Slim and Heavy both woke up with the awareness that a hobo acquires when traveling.

"What kind of a burg is this we're comin' into, Joe? Looks like a damned jerkwater!"

"Yeah—I know the place. Just a water tank and a general store. Better keep outta sight from now on—there's a bad bull in this next town if I remember right!"

The long drag slowly pulled to a bumping, groaning stop, and Slim, watching his chance when the shack was at the other end, dropped off.

Up ahead they could hear the shouts of the train crew as they worked about the engine, and once a shack went by, his lantern bobbing along beside the train. He just casually flashed it into the door as he passed, and as all three were out of sight, they were passed unnoticed.

A whistle up forward, more groaning and bumping and jarring, and the train slowly gathered momentum.

Heavy's forehead wrinkled anxiously: "Wonder what's become o' Slim? He should've made it by now!"

And a minute later, as the train gathered speed in the shadow of several oil tanks, he did make it, swinging into the car with a dark object in his hand.

"Whatcha got, Slim?" Heavy leaned forward curiously.

"Aw, pull in your neck, Hefty, I just grabbed the kid a cuppa java an' a orange at that lunch counter!"

"But Cheesus, Slim, you only had a nickel!"

"Sure, I got the guy to gimme a cuppa java for the nickel and I swiped the orange when the lunch-counter girl wasn't lookin'. If he wants his cup back he'll have to pick it up in the next town!"

Joe rolled the kid over on his back and slowly raised him to a sitting position: "Here, kid, it's a cuppa coffee. Try an' get it down, it'll do you good."

The kid tried to drink, but ended in a coughing spell that left flecks of blood on his lips. Joe laid him back on the floor and returned to the others near the door.

Slim looked helplessly at the orange: "Cheesus, guess he couldn't tackle this. He seems pretty far gone." He raised his hand as if to throw the orange away and then on second thought shoved it into his coat pocket.

Once more the train bumped along. The moon had gone down now and the night was black outside the door. Heavy was once more asleep, and Slim, chin resting on his knees, was dozing off. Joe still sat looking out into the night, his face grimy from cinders and dust, his beard graying in spots. At last he too dozed off into a half-sleep.

The freight was slowing for the next town when a swiftly bobbing flashlight awakened them. Joe was the first to comprehend.

"Cheesus, guys, we're sunk—it's that railroad dick!"

Heavy cursed and jumped for the door to swing out when a harsh voice broke in: "All right, 'bo, stay where y'are or I'll shoot yer guts out! Come on, you—all of ya! Get 'em up in the air!

"All right, pile out on the ground an' less look you guys over. Keep 'em up, now!" The railroad dick's voice was harsh and his face ugly in the half-light. His companion, a weasel-faced fellow, glided up and started frisking them with the question: "Got anythin' on ya bigger'n a forty-five?"

Slim spoke aggrievedly: "Aw, why don't you guys leave us alone? We're just huntin' a place to work. What would we be doin' packin' rods!"

The big fellow stepped forward belligerently: "Shut up, bum. I'll do the talkin' an' you'll answer when yer spoken to, get me?"

Slim said nothing. The weasel-faced man pulled their personal effects from their pockets, smirking over the few odds and ends a man carries about. A couple of jack-knives, a piece of soiled string, a dirty handkerchief or two, a pocketbook containing a pair of poll tax receipts,

a card for a hod carriers union two years old, a few letters. The weasel-faced man read the letters with an occasional glance at Slim's angry face. Finally from one of
them he extracted a picture of a girl, which he held out
for the big man to see with an insulting remark.

Slim's eyes swiftly calculated the distance. He jumped
and struck viciously, his fist striking Weasel-face on the
point of the chin, knocking him flat. The big man side-
stepped and struck with the gun barrel, felling Slim to the
ground. Then stepping toward Heavy and Joe, he snapped:
"Got tough, did he? Well, suppose you guys try it. I killed
a couple of guys fer tryin' to get tough with me!"

Joe's tired voice spoke slowly: "Uh-uh, I heard 'bout
that—both of 'em unarmed. You said they got tough;
some people said they had thirty bucks on 'em."

"What was that?" The big man whirled toward Joe.
"What d'you say?"

"Me? I didn't say nothin', just clearin' my throat."

"Well, ya better be careful, get me? Or I'll slam you like
I did him!" He waved his hand toward Slim's fallen figure.

He called to Weasel-face: "Look in that damned car—
maybe they left some junk in there worth lookin' over!"

"Okay, boss!"

Weasel-face scrambled into the car. Then: "Hey, boss,
here's another bum in here sleepin'!"

"D'hell there is! Well, roll the bastard out an' less look
him over."

Voice from the car: "Come on, you, crawl outta that! Hey,
what's the matter? Get up or I'll boot the hell outta ya!"

A moment later, Weasel-face dragged the kid to the
door and dumped him out to the ground.

"Here he is, boss, playin' sleepy on us!"

The boss walked up determinedly and kicked the kid forcibly in the ribs. Joe's shout halted him, a frown on his face.

"Hey, skipper, watch yerself, the kid's sick; he's got the consumption or somethin'!"

"He won't play sick with me; I'll boot his head off. Get up, d'ye hear?" He grabbed the kid by the shoulder and jerked him to his feet, where the kid hung in a slump. For a moment the boss gazed into his face, his own growing white: "God! The son-of-a-bitch is dead!" He dropped the kid and turned around.

In the moment of detachment following his discovery, unable to help the kid, the remaining two, supporting the now conscious Slim, had slipped off into the surrounding darkness, leaving the two dicks behind and the crumpled form of the kid lying beside the freight, which, slowly moving, was once more westbound.

DEAD-END DRIFT

I came into Kingman, Arizona, wearing a pin-striped suit with a straw hat and carrying a Malacca walking stick. It's a wonder they didn't shoot me walking into town like that, and I know they took me for a real tenderfoot. But after I'd been in town a few days, I got a job in the Katherine Mine. The Katherine is out on the Colorado about three quarters of a mile, as I recall, back from the Colorado bank. At the time they were employing about 160 men. They had a company store there, bunkhouses, a boardinghouse. I moved into one of the bunkhouses and went to work as a mucker. A mucker is a guy who uses a shovel, loads cars with muck and wheels, then dumps them. They usually expect about sixteen tons of ore a day out of somebody, and I'd usually do sixteen or eighteen, something like that, because I was young and husky and could do it. That really was my first experience in a mine.

The Katherine Mine where I worked had what we called a Big Stope. You run a tunnel into a mine and then you run up a raise and begin hollowing out, cutting out the ore and chuting it down into chutes so you can pull it out. There was good ore up there and there wasn't too much good ore in this mine, so the stope began to get bigger and bigger and bigger and it finally got so you couldn't see the roof of the thing at all.

Some miners would come down and take one look at it and go up top and quit. I worked the graveyard shift there for a while, and there weren't too many men working at that hour. You'd go down in the mine and you could hear the timbers groan and creak with the weight they were taking.

———

THE TRICKLE OF sand ceased, and there was silence. Then a small rock dropped from overhead into the rubble beneath, and the flat finality of the sound put a period to the moment.

There was a heavy odor of dust, and one of the men coughed, the dry, hacking cough of miner's consumption. Silence hung heavily in the thick, dead air.

"Better sit still." Bert's voice was quiet and unexcited. "I'll make a light." They waited, listening to the miner fumbling with his hand lamp. "We might dislodge something," he added, "and start it again."

They heard his palm strike the lamp, and he struck several times before the flint gave off the spark to light the flame. An arrow of flame leaped from the burner. The sudden change from the impenetrable darkness at the end of the tunnel to the bright glare of the miner's lamp left them blinking. They sat very still, looking slowly around, careful to disturb nothing. The suddenness of the disaster had stunned them into quiet acceptance.

Frank's breathing made a hoarse, ugly sound, and when their eyes found him, they could see the dark, spreading stain on his shirtfront and the misshapen look of his broken body. He was a powerful man, with blond, curly hair above a square, hard face. There was blood on the rocks near him and blood on the jagged rock he had rolled from his body after the cave-in.

There was a trickle of blood across Bert's face from a

scalp wound, but no other injuries to anyone. Their eyes evaded the wall of fallen rock across the drift, their minds filled with awareness.

"Hurt bad?" Bert said to Frank. "Looks like the big one hit you."

"Yeah." Frank's voice was low. "Feels like I'm stove up inside."

"Better leave him alone," Joe said. "The bleeding seems to be letting up, and there's nothing we can do."

Frank stared down at his body curiously. "I guess I'm hurt bad."

He turned his head deliberately and stared at the muck pile. The cave-in had left a slanting pile of broken rock that reached toward them along the drift, cutting them off completely from the outside world, from light and air. Behind them was the face of the drift where Rody had been drilling. From the face of the drift to the muck pile was a matter of a few feet. Frank touched his dry lips with his tongue, remembering what lay beyond the cave-in.

It could scarcely have been the tunnel alone. Beyond it was the Big Stope. He reached over and turned out the light. The flame winked, and darkness was upon them.

"What's the idea?" Joe demanded.

"Air," Frank said. "There's four of us, and there isn't going to be enough air. We may be some time in getting out."

"If we get out," Joe said.

Rody shifted his weight on the rock slab where he was sitting, and they heard the rasp of the coarse denim. "How far do you reckon she caved, Frank?"

"I don't know." Then he said what they all feared. "Maybe the Big Stope went."

"If it did," Rody commented, "we might as well fold

our cards and toss in our hands. Nobody can open that stope before the air gives out. There's not much air in here for four men."

"I warned Tom about that stope," Joe said. "He had no right to have men working in here. That stope was too big in the first place. Must be a hundred feet across and no pillars, and down below there was too much weight on the stulls. The posts were countersunk into the laggin' all of two inches, like a knife in butter."

"The point is," Frank said, "that we're here. No use talking about what should have been. If any part of the stope went, it all went. There's a hundred feet of tunnel to drive and timber, and workin' in loose muck isn't going to help."

No one spoke. In the utter blackness and stillness of the drift, they waited. There was no light, no sound. All had been cut off from them. Joe wiped the sweat from his brow with the back of his hand.

The blackness of a mine, the complete darkness, had always bothered him. At night in the outer world, no matter how clouded the sky, there is always some light, and in time the eyes will adjust, and a man can see—a little, at any rate. Here there was no light, and a man was completely blind.

And there was no sound. Only two hundred feet to the surface, yet it might as well have been two thousand. Two hundred feet of rock between them and the light, and that was the shortest route. By the drift or tunnel it was a quarter of a mile to the shaft where the cage could take them to the surface.

Above them was the whole weight of the mountain, before them the solid wall where they had been drilling, behind them the mass of the cave-in, thousands of tons of broken rock and broken timbers.

On the surface there would be tense, frightened men, frightened not for themselves but for those entombed below—and they could not know that anyone was alive.

The skip would be coming down now, bringing men to attack that enormous slide. On top men would be girding for the struggle with the mountain. Around the collar of the shaft men and equipment would be gathered to be sent below. Near the warehouse men would be standing, and some women, tense and white, wondering about those below. And the men who were buried alive could only wait and hope.

"Got a chew, Bert?" Joe asked.

"Sure." Bert pushed his hand into the darkness, feeling for Joe's. Their hands were steady. Joe bit off a chew, then passed the plug back, their hands fumbling in the dark again.

"We ain't got a chance!" Rody exclaimed suddenly. "She might have caved clear to the station. Anyway, there's no way they can get through in time. We ain't got the air to last five hours even if they could make it that quick."

"Forget it," Joe said. "You wouldn't do nothing but blow your money on that frowzy blonde in Kingman if you got free."

"I was a sap for ever coming to work in this lousy hole," Rody grumbled. "I was a sap."

"Quit crabbing," Bert said mildly. "We're here now, and we've got to like it."

There was a long silence. Somewhere the mountain creaked, and there was a distant sound of more earth sliding.

"Say"—Frank's voice broke into the silence—"any of you guys work in Thirty-seven?"

"You mean that raise on the Three Hundred?" Bert asked. "Sure, I put in a couple of shifts there."

"Aren't we right over it now?"

"Huh?" Joe moved quickly. "How high up were they?"

"Better than ninety feet." Frank's tone was tight, strained. He held himself, afraid to breathe deep, afraid of the pain that would come. He was not sure what had happened to him. Part of his body was numb, but there was a growing pain in his belly as the shock wore off. He knew he was in deep trouble, and that the chances of his getting out alive were small. He dreaded the thought of being moved, doubted if he would survive it.

"If that raise was up ninety feet"—Joe spoke slowly, every word standing alone—"then it ain't more than ten feet below us. If we could dig down—"

"Ten feet? In that kind of rock?" Rody sneered. "You couldn't dig that with a pick. Not in a week. Anyway, Thirty-seven ain't this far along. We're thirty yards beyond at least."

"No," Frank said, "I think we're right over it. Anyway, it's a chance. It's more than we've got now."

There was a long silence while they turned the idea over in their minds. Then Joe said, "Why a raise here? There's no ore body here. That's supposed to be further along."

"Air," Bert said. "They wanted some circulation."

He got up, and they heard him fumbling for a pick. They heard the metallic sound as it was dragged toward him over the rock. "Better move back against the muck pile," he said. "I'm digging."

"You're a sap," Rody said. "You've got no chance."

"Shut up!" Joe's tone was ugly. "If you ain't willing to try, you can go to hell. I want out of here."

"Who're you tellin' to shut up?" They heard Rody rise suddenly. "I ain't never had no use for you, you—"

"Rody!" Frank's tone was harsh. "I've got a pick handle, and I know where you are. You go back where you were and keep your mouth shut. This is a hell of a time to start something."

A light flared in Frank's hand, and he hitched himself a little higher to see better. "That's right, Bert. Start right there. Some of that top stuff will just flake off."

Sweat beaded his strained white face. One big hand clutched a pick handle. Slowly, as if he had difficulty in moving them, his eyes shifted from face to face. He stared at Rody the longest. Rody's stiff black hair curled back from a low forehead. He was almost as broad as Frank but thicker.

The sodden blows of the pick became the ticking clock of the passing time. It was a slow, measured beat, for the air was already thickening, and the blows pounded with the pulse of their blood. The flame of the carbide light ate into their small supply of air, burning steadily.

Bert stopped, mopping his face. "She's damn hard, Frank. It's going to take the point off this pick in a hurry."

"We've got four of them," Frank said. The whole front of him was one dark stain now. "I always carry a pick in a mine."

Bert swung again, and they watched as the point of the pick found a place and broke back a piece of the rock. The surface had been partly shattered by the explosions as the drift was pushed farther into the mountain. It would be harder as they got down farther.

Frank's big hands were relaxed and loose. He watched

the swing of the pick, and when Joe got up to spell Bert, he asked him, "Anybody on top waitin' for you?"

"Uh-huh." Joe paused, pick in hand. "A girl."

Rody started to speak but caught Frank's eye and settled back, trying to move out of reach of the pick handle.

"My wife's up there," Bert said. "And I've got three kids." He took off his shirt and mopped his body with it.

"There's nobody waitin' for me," Frank said. "Nobody anywhere."

"What d'you suppose they're doing out there?" Bert said. "I'd give a lot to know."

"Depends on how far it caved." Joe leaned on the pick handle, gasping for breath. "Probably they are shoring her up with timbers around the station or at the opening into the Big Stope."

He returned to work. He swung the pick, and a fragment broke loose; a second time and another fragment. Bert sat with his elbows on his knees, head hanging, breathing heavily. Frank's head was tipped back against the rock, his white face glistening like wet marble in the faint light that reached him.

It was going to be a long job, a hard job, and the air was growing worse. Being active, they were using it more rapidly, but it was their only chance; nobody could get through to them in time. As Joe worked, the sweat streamed from his body, running into his eyes and dripping from his chin. Slowly and methodically he swung the pick, deadened to everything but the shock of the blows. He no longer noticed what progress he made; he had become an automaton. Bert started up to relieve him, but Joe shook his head. He was started now, and it was like an infection in his blood. He needed the pick. He clung to it as to a lifeline.

At last he did give way to Bert. He dropped on the rocks, his chest heaving, fighting for air. He tried to keep from remembering Mary, but she was always with him, always just beyond the blows of his pick. Probably she did not yet know what had happened to them, what this sudden thing was that had come into their lives.

She would be at work now, and as the mine was forty miles from town, it might be hours before she knew of the cave-in and even longer before she knew who was trapped below. It would be her tragedy as well as his. Joe cursed. Tomorrow they would have gone to the doctor. He was reliable, Frank had told him, a good man and not a quack.

Big Frank knew about Mary. He knew that with every drive of the pick it would be a closer thing for her. There were but four of them here, underground, but outside were Mary and Bert's wife and kids. It would be a close thing, any way it was looked at. He, Joe, could take it. He had never done anything else, but Mary was in a strange town with no friends, and unless they got to the doctor—

They were fools to have gone ahead when they knew they were taking a chance, but nobody expected anything like this. He had worked in mines most of his life and no trouble until now, and then the roof fell in. The whole damned mountain came down—or so it seemed. When he heard the crash, his first thought was for Mary. He was trapped here, but she was trapped out there, and she was alone.

"Better take a rest," Frank said. "We've got some time."

Joe sat down, and Bert looked across at him. "We could work in the dark," he suggested. "That flame eats up air."

Frank shook his head. "If you can't see, there's too

much waste effort. You've got to see where the pick goes. Try it with the light a little longer."

Joe's eyes went to Frank. The big man lay tense and still, gripping the rock under his hand. He was in agony; Joe knew it and hated it. Frank was his friend.

"Will we make it, Frank?" He was thinking of Mary. What would she do? What could she do? How could she handle it alone? It wasn't as if they were married. "Think we'll make it?"

"We'll make it," Frank said. "We'll make it, all right."

"Listen!" Bert sat up eagerly. "I think I hear them! Wasn't that the sound of a pick?"

They listened, every muscle tense. There was no sound. Then, far away, some muck shifted. Frank doused the light, and darkness closed in, silent and heavy like the dead, dead air. There was no vibrancy here, no sense of living.

They heard Joe get up, heard the heavy blows of the pick. He worked on and on, his muscles aching with weariness. Each blow and each recovery was an effort. Then Bert spoke, and they heard them change places. Standing once more, Bert could feel the difference. It was much harder to breathe; his lungs labored, and his heart struggled against the walls of his chest, as if to break through. Once he stopped and held a hand over it, frightened.

Long since they had thrown the first two picks aside, their points worn away. They might have to return to them, but now they were using another, sharper pick. They were standing in a hole now. Once a flake of rock fell, and Bert held himself, expecting a crash. It did not come.

Rody moved suddenly. Frank lit the light with a brush of his palm. Rody looked at him, then reached for the pick. "Let me have it," Rody said. "Hell, it's better than sittin' there suckin' my thumb. Give me the pick."

Bert passed it to him; then he staggered to the muck pile and fell, full length, gasping with great throat-rasping gasps.

Rody swung the pick, attacking the bottom of the hole savagely. Sweat ran into his eyes, and he swung, attacking the rock as if it were a flesh-and-blood enemy, feeling an exultant fury in his blows.

Once he stopped to take five, and looking over at Frank, he said, "How goes it, big boy?"

"Tolerable," Frank said. "You're a good man, Rody."

Rody swelled his chest, and the pick swung easily in his big hands. All of them were lying down now because the air was better close to the muck.

"Hear anything?" Bert asked. "How long will it take them to reach us, Frank?"

"Depends on how much it caved." They had been over this before, but it was hope they needed, any thread of it. Even talking of rescue seemed to bring it nearer. The numbness was all gone now, and his big body throbbed with pain. He fought it, refusing to surrender to it, trying to deny it. He held the pain as though it were some great beast he must overcome.

Suddenly Joe sat up. "Say! What became of the air line for the machine?"

They stared at each other, shocked at their forgetting. "Maybe it ain't busted," Bert said.

Stumbling in his eagerness, Joe fell across the muck, bumping Frank as he did so, jerking an involuntary grunt from him. Then Joe fell on his knees and began clawing rocks away from where the end of the pipe should be, the pipe that supplied compressed air for drilling. He found the pipe and cleared the vent, unscrewing the broken hose to the machine. Trembling, he turned the valve. Cool air shot into the room, and as they breathed deeply, it slowly died away to nothing.

"It will help," Joe said. "Even if it was a little, it will help."

"Damned little," Rody said, "but you're right, Joe. It'll help."

"How deep are you?" Frank asked. He started to shift his body and caught himself with a sharp gasp.

"Four feet—maybe five. She's tough going."

Joe lay with his face close to the ground. The air was close and hot, every breath a struggle. When he breathed, he seemed to get nothing. It left him gasping, struggling for air. The others were the same. Light and air were only a memory now, a memory of some lost paradise.

How long had they been here? Only Frank had a watch, but it was broken, so there was no way of calculating the time. It seemed hours since that crash. Somehow it had been so different from what he had expected. He had believed it would come with a thundering roar, but there was just a splintering sound, a slide of muck, a puff of wind that put their lights out, then a long slide, a trickling of sand, a falling stone. They had lacked even the consolation of drama.

Whatever was to come of it would not be far off now. Whatever happened must be soon. There came no sound, no breath of moving air, only the thick, sticky air and the heat. They were all panting now, gasping for each breath.

Rody sat down suddenly, the pick slipping from his fingers.

"Let me," Joe said.

He swung the pick, then swung it again.

When he stopped, Bert said, "Did you hear something?"

They listened, but there was no sound.

"Maybe they ain't tryin'," Rody said. "Maybe they think we're dead.

"Can you imagine Tom Chambers spendin' his good money to get us out of here?" Rody said. "He don't care. He can get a lot of miners."

Joe thought of those huge, weighted timbers in the Big Stope. Nothing could have held that mass when it started to move. Probably the roof of the Big Stope had collapsed. Up on top there would be a small crowd of waiting people now. Men, women, and children. Still, there wouldn't be so many as in Nevada that time. After all, Bert was the only one down here with children.

But suppose others had been trapped? Why were they thinking they were the only ones?

The dull thud of the pick sounded again. That was Rody back at work; he could tell by the power. He listened, his mind lulled into a sort of hypnotic twilight where there was only darkness and the sound of the pick. He heard the blows, but he knew he was dying. It was no use. He couldn't fight it any longer.

Suddenly the dull blows ceased. Rody said, "Hey! Listen!" He struck again, and it was a dull sound, a hollow sound.

"Hell!" Rody said. "That ain't no ten feet!

"Let's have some light over here," Rody said. "Frank—?"

He took the light from Frank's hand. The light was down to a feeble flicker now, no longer the proud blade of light that had initially stabbed at the darkness.

Rody peered, then passed the lamp back to Frank.

"There should be a staging down there." Frank's voice

was clear. "They were running a stopper off it to put in the overhead rounds."

Rody swung, then swung again, and the pick went through. It caught him off balance, and he fell forward, then caught himself. Cool air was rushing into the drift end, and he took the pick and enlarged the hole.

Joe sat up. "God!" he said. "Thank God!"

"Take it easy, you guys, when you go down," Frank said. "That ladder may have been shaken loose by blasting or the cave-in. The top of the ladder is on the left-hand side of the raise. You'll have to drop down to the staging, though, and take the ladder from there. It'll be about an eight- or nine-foot drop."

He tossed a small stone into the hole, and they heard it strike against the boards down below. The flame of the light was bright now as more air came up through the opening. Frank stared at them, sucking air into his lungs.

"Come on, Rody," Joe said. "Lend a hand. We've got to get Frank to a doctor."

"No." Frank's voice was impersonal. "You can't get me down to that platform and then down the ladder—I'd bleed to death before you got me down the raise. You guys go ahead. When they get the drift opened up will be time enough for me. Or maybe when they can come back with a stretcher. I'll just sit here."

"But—" Joe protested.

"Beat it," Frank said.

Bert lowered himself through the opening and dropped. "Come on!" he called. "It's okay!"

Rody followed. Joe hesitated, mopping his face, then looked at Frank, but the big man was staring sullenly at the dark wall.

"Frank—" Joe stopped. "Well, gee . . ."

He hesitated, then dropped through the hole. From the platform he said, "Frank? I wish—"

His boots made small sounds descending the ladder.

The carbide light burned lower, and the flame flickered as the fuel ran low. Big Frank's face twisted as he tried to move; then his mouth opened very wide, and he sobbed just once. It was all right now. There was no one to hear. Then he leaned back, staring toward the pile of muck, his big hands relaxed and empty.

"Nobody," he muttered. "There isn't anybody, and there never was."

OLD DOC YAK

I came into Los Angeles hitchhiking on a truck and went down to San Pedro wanting to get a ship heading for the Far East. At the time there were about seven hundred seamen on the beach and all of them broke. It was very tough to get a ship of any kind but I registered at the Marine Service Bureau, which we used to call Fink Hall or the Slave Market. That was where you had to register and wait your turn to get a ship. Meanwhile, you had to live some way or other, and during the next three months I slept in empty boxcars and lumber piles, got along as best I could.

During those three months, fellows were living it any way they possibly could. If you had two dimes in your pocket you'd better hold them together—if they rattled, somebody would roll you for them.

At one point we got a little cash ahead, several of us, and we rented a shack up on the side of a hill. At that time there were several places: Mexican Hollywood was one of them and there was a place called Happy Valley and then there were a few scattered outside of that. There were shacks that you could rent for eight to twelve dollars a month. Well, a couple of other fellows and myself rented a shack up on the side of the hill. It was two rooms and a small kind of cubbyhole that did a job as a kitchen and we had a cot and a full-sized bed and a mattress on the floor and we would rent out space to other people to come in and sleep for ten cents a night. And with that we

*would try to accumulate money enough to pay the rent
the next time it came around.*

*Then we decided that we would do our own cooking,
so we'd send a sailor down to the docks to help the Japanese fishermen hoist the fish up from the boats and the
Japanese would usually give the man a fish for this and
we'd send others down to a wholesale grocery and vege-
table place where they would help clean out and sweep
up and they'd pick up some extra onions and potatoes
and carrots and whatnot and bring those home and then
we'd send other guys down to bum bread from some of
the ships. The result was that we were doing pretty well
there for a while.*

H E WAS A man without humor. He seemed somehow aloof, invulnerable. Even his walk was pompous and majestic. He strode with the step of kings and
spoke with the voice of an oracle, entirely unaware that
his whole being was faintly ludicrous, that those about
him were always suspended between laughter and amazed
respect.

Someone began calling him Old Doc Yak for no apparent reason, and the name stayed with him. He was a large
man, rather portly, wearing a constantly grave expression
and given to a pompous manner of speech. His most simple remark was uttered with a sense of earthshaking im-
port, and a listener invariably held his breath in sheer
suspense as he began to speak, only to suffer that sense of
frustration one feels when an expected explosion fails to
materialize.

His conversation was a garden of the baroque in which
biological and geological terms flowered in the most un-

expected places. Jim commented once that someone must have thrown a dictionary at him and he got all the words but none of the definitions. We listened in amused astonishment as he would stand, head slightly tilted to one side, an open palm aslant his rather generous stomach, which he would pat affectionately as though in amused approbation of his remarks.

Those were harsh, bitter days. The waterfronts were alive with seamen, all hunting ships. One theme predominated in all our conversations, in all our thoughts, perhaps even in the very pulsing of our blood—how to get by.

No normal brain housed in a warm and sheltered body could possibly conceive of the devious and doubtful schemes contrived to keep soul and body together. Hunger sharpens the wits and renders less effective the moral creeds and codes by which we guide our law-abiding lives. Some of us who were there could even think of the philosophical ramifications of our lives and of our actions. The narrow line that divides the average young man or woman from stealing, begging, or prostitution is one that has little to do with religion or ethics but only with such simple animal necessities as food and shelter. We had been talking of that when Old Doc Yak ventured his one remark.

"I think," he said, pausing portentously, "that any man who will beg, who will so demean himself as to ask for food upon the streets, will stoop to any abomination, no matter how low."

He arose, and with a finality that permitted of no reply, turned his back and walked away. It was one of the few coherent statements I'd ever heard him make, and I watched his broad back, stiff with self-righteousness, as he walked away. I watched, as suddenly speechless as the others.

There was probably not a man present who had not at some time panhandled on the streets. They were a rough, freehanded lot, men who gave willingly when they had it and did not hesitate to ask when in need. All were men who worked, who performed the rough, hard, dangerous work of the world, yet they were men without words, and no reply came to their lips to answer that broad back or the bitter finality of that remark. In their hearts they felt him wrong, for they were sincere men, if not eloquent.

Often after that I saw him on the streets. Always stiff and straight, he never unbent so far as to speak, never appeared even to notice my passing. He paid his way with a careful hand and lived remote from our lonely, uncomfortable world. From meal to meal we had no idea as to the origin of the next, and our nights were spent wherever there was shelter from the wind. Off on the horizon of our hopelessness there was always that miracle—a ship—and endlessly we made the rounds in search of work. Shipping proceeded slowly, and men struggled for the few occasional jobs alongshore. Coming and going on my own quest, I saw men around me drawn fine by hunger, saw their necks become gaunt, their clothing more shabby. It was a bitter struggle to survive in a man-made jungle.

The weeks drew on, and one by one we saw the barriers we had built against hunger slowly fall away. By that time there were few who had not walked the streets looking for the price of a cup of coffee, but even the ready generosity of a seaport town had been strained, and shipping seemed to have fallen off.

One morning a man walked into the Seaman's Institute and fainted away. We had seen him around for days, a quiet young man who seemed to know no one, to have no contacts, too proud to ask for food and too backward to find other means. And then he walked in that morning and crumpled up on the floor like an empty sack.

It was a long moment before any of us moved. We stood staring down at him, and each of us was seeing the specter of his own hunger.

Then Parnatti was arrested. He had been hungry before, and we had heard him say, "I'm going to eat. If I can make it honest, I'll make it, but I'm going to eat regardless." We understood his feelings, although the sentiments were not ours. Contrary to opinion, it is rarely the poor who steal. People do not steal for the necessities but for the embellishments, but when the time came, Parnatti stole a car from a parking lot and sold it. We saw the item in the paper without comfort and then turned almost without hope to the list of incoming ships. Any one of them might need a man; any one of them might save us from tomorrow.

Old Doc Yak seemed unchanged. He came and went as always; as always his phrases bowed beneath a weight of words. I think, vaguely, we all resented him. He was so obviously not a man of the sea, so obviously not one of us. I believe he had been a steward, but stewards were rarely popular in the old days on the merchant ships. Belly robbers, they called them.

Glancing over the paper one afternoon, searching for a ship that might need men, I looked up accidentally just in time to see Old Doc Yak passing a hand over his face. The hand trembled.

For the first time, I really saw him. Many times in the past few days we had passed each other on the street, each on his way to survival. Often we had sat in the main room at the Institute, but I had paid little attention. Now, suddenly, I was aware of the change. His vest hung a little slack, and the lines in his face were deeper. For the moment even his pompous manner had vanished. He looked old and tired.

In the ugly jungle of the waterfront, the brawl for existence left little time for thinking of anything except the immediate and ever-present need for shelter and food for the body. Old Doc Yak had been nothing more than another bit of waterfront jetsam discarded from the whirl of living into the lazy maelstrom of those alongshore. Now, again, as on that other night, he became an individual, and probably for the first time I saw the man as he was and as he must have seen himself.

Tipped back against the wall, feeling the tightness of my leather jacket across my shoulders, I rubbed the stubble on my unshaved chin and wondered about him. I guess each of us has an illusion about himself. Somewhere inside of himself he has a picture of himself he believes is true. I guess it was that way with Doc. Aloof from those of us who lived around him, he existed in a world of his own creation, a world in which he had importance, a world in which he was somebody. Now, backed into a corner by economic necessity, he was a little puzzled and a little helpless.

Some of us had rented a shack. For six dollars a month we had shelter from the wind and rain, a little chipped crockery, a stove, and a bed. There was a cot in the corner where I slept, and somebody had rustled an old mattress that was stretched out on the deck—floor, I should say. For a dime or perhaps three nickels, if he was good for them, a man could share the bed with three or four others. For a nickel a man got an armful of old newspapers with which he could roll up on the floor. And with the money gathered in such a way we paid another month's rent.

It wasn't much, but it was a corner away from the wind, a place of warmth, and a retreat from the stares of the police and the more favored. Such a place was needed, and never did men return home with more thankfulness than we returned to that shack on its muddy hillside. Men came and went in the remaining weeks of our stay, the strange, drifting motley of the waterfront, men good, bad, and indifferent. Men were there who knew the ports and rivers of a hundred countries, men who knew every sidetrack from Hoboken to Seattle. And then one night Old Doc Yak walked up the path to the door.

There was rain that night, a cold, miserable rain, and a wind that blew it against our thin walls. It was just after ten when the knock came at the door, and when Copper opened it, Old Doc walked in. For a moment his small blue eyes blinked against the light, and then he looked about, a slow distaste growing on his face. There was a sailor's neatness about the place, but it was crude and not at all attractive.

He looked tired, and some of his own neatness was lacking. He might have been fifty-five, but he looked older this night; yet his eyes were still remote, unseeing of us, who were the dregs. He looked around again, and we saw his hesitation, sensed the defeat that must have brought him, at last, to this place. But our shack was warm.

"I would like," he said ponderously, "a place to sleep."

"Sure," I said, getting up from the rickety chair I'd tipped against the wall. "There's room in the double bed for one more. It'll cost you a dime."

"You mean," he asked abruptly, and he actually looked at me, "that I must share a bed?"

"Sorry. This isn't the Biltmore. You'll have to share with Copper and Red."

He was on the verge of leaving when a blast of wind and blown rain struck the side of the house, sliding around under the eaves and whining like a wet saw. For an instant he seemed to be weighing the night, the rain, and the cold against the warmth of the shack. Then he opened his old-fashioned purse and lifted a dime from its depths.

I say "lifted," and so it seemed. Physical effort was needed to get that dime into my hand, and his fingers released it reluctantly. It was obviously the last of his carefully hoarded supply. Then he walked heavily into the other room and lay down on the bed. It was the first time I had ever seen him lie down, and his poise seemed suddenly to evaporate, all his stiff-necked righteousness seemed to wilt, and his ponderous posturing with words became empty and pitiful. Lying on the bed with the rain pounding on the roof, he was only an old man, strangely alone.

Sitting in the next room with a fire crackling in the stove and the rattling of rain on the windows, I thought about him. Youth and good jobs were behind him, and he was facing a question to which all the ostentatious vacuity of his words gave no reply. The colossal edifice he had built with high-sounding words, the barriers he had attempted to erect between himself and his doubt of himself were crumbling. I put another stick in the stove, watched the fire lick the dampness from its face, and listened to the rain beating against the walls and the labored breathing of the man on the bed.

In the washroom of the Seaman's Institute weeks before we had watched him shave. It had been a ritual lacking only incense. The glittering articles from his shaving kit, these had been blocks in the walls of his self-esteem. The careful lathering of his florid cheeks, the application of shaving lotion, these things had been steps in a ritual that never varied. We who were disciples of Gillette and dull blades watched him with something approaching reverence and went away to marvel.

Knowing what must have happened in the intervening weeks, I could see him going to the pawnshop with first one and then another of his prized possessions, removing bit by bit the material things, those glittering silver pieces that shored up his self-vision. Each time his purse would be replenished for a day or two, and as each article passed over the counter into that great maw from which nothing ever returns, I could see some particle of his dignity slipping away. He was a capitalist without capital, a conqueror without conquests, a vocabulary without expression. In the stove the fire crackled; on the wide bed the old man muttered, stirring in his sleep. It was very late.

He did not come again. Several times the following night I walked to the door, almost hoping to see his broad bulk as it labored up the hill. Even Copper looked uneasily out of the window, and Slim took a later walk than usual. We were a group that was closely knit, and though he had not belonged, he had for one brief night been one of us, and when he did not return, we were uneasy.

It was after twelve before Slim turned in. It had been another wet night, and he was tired. He stopped by my chair, where I sat reading a magazine.

"Listen," he said, flushing a little, "if he comes—Old Doc, I mean—I'll pay if he ain't got the dime. He ain't such a bad guy."

"Sure," I said. "Okay."

He didn't come. The wind whined and snarled around the corners of the house, and we heard the tires of a car whine on the wet pavement below. It is a terrible thing to see a man's belief in himself crumble, for when one loses faith in one's own illusion, there is nothing left. Even Slim understood that. It was almost daybreak before I fell asleep.

Several nights drifted by. There was food to get, and the rent was coming due. We were counting each dime, for we had not yet made the six dollars. There was still a gap, a breach in our wall that we might not fill. And outside was the night, the rain, and the cold.

The *Richfield,* a Standard tanker, was due in. I had a shipmate aboard her, and when she came up the channel, I was waiting on the dock. They might need an AB.

They didn't.

It was a couple of hours later when I climbed the hill toward the shack. I didn't often go that way, but this time it was closer, and I was worried. The night before I'd left the money for the rent in a thick white cup on the cupboard shelf. And right then murder could be done for five bucks. I glanced through the window. Then I stopped.

Old Doc Yak was standing by the cupboard, holding the white cup in his hand. As I watched, he dipped his fingers in and drew out some of our carefully gleaned nickels, dimes, and quarters. Then he stood there letting those shining metal disks trickle through his thick fingers and back into the cup. Then he dipped his fingers again, and I stood there, holding my breath.

A step or two and I could have stopped him, but I stood there, gripped by his indecision, half guessing what was happening inside him. Here was money. Here, for a little while, was food, a room, a day or two of comfort. I do not think he considered the painstaking effort to acquire those few coins or the silent, bedraggled men who had trooped up the muddy trail to add a dime or fifteen cents to the total of our next month's rent. What hunger had driven him back, I knew. What helplessness and humiliation waited in the streets below, I also knew.

Slowly, one by one, the coins dribbled back into the cup, the cup was returned to the shelf, and Old Doc Yak turned and walked from the door. For one moment he paused, his face strangely gray and old, staring out across the bleak, rain-washed roofs toward the gray waters of the channel and Terminal Island just beyond.

Then he walked away, and I waited until he was out of sight before I went inside, and I, who had seen so much of weariness and defeat, hesitated before I took down the cup. It was all there, and suddenly I was a little sorry that it was.

Once more I saw him. One dark, misty night I came up from the lumber docks, collar turned up, cap pulled low, picking my way through the shadows and over the railroad ties, stumbling along rails lighted only by the feeble red and green of switch lights. Reaching the street, I scrambled up the low bank and saw him standing in the light of a streetlamp.

He was alone, guarded from friendship as always by his icy impenetrability but somehow strangely pathetic with his sagging shoulders and graying hair. I started to speak, but he turned up his coat collar and walked away down a dark street.

IT'S YOUR MOVE

The Seaman's Institute in San Pedro was a place like a YMCA but for sailors. They had beds which you could get for fifty cents a night. They had showers and whatnot and they also had a library there and a big room where there were a lot of checker tables, and we had some of the finest checker players, I think, there ever was anywhere would come into that room.

OLD MAN WHITE was a checker player. He was a longshoreman, too, but he only made his living at that. Checker playing was his life. I never saw anybody take the game like he took it. Hour after hour, when there was nobody for him to play with, he'd sit at a table in the Seaman's Institute and study the board and practice his moves. He knew every possible layout there could be. There was this little book he carried, and he would arrange the checkers on the board, and then move through each game with an eye for every detail and chance. If anybody ever knew the checkerboard, it was him.

He wasn't a big man, but he was keen-eyed, and had a temper like nobody I ever saw. Most of the time he ignored people. Everybody but other checker players. I mean guys that could give him a game. They were few enough, and with the exception of Oriental Slim and MacCready, nobody had ever beat him. They were the best around at the time, but the most they could do with the old man was about one out of ten. But they gave him a game and that was all he wanted. He scarcely noticed anybody else, and you couldn't get a civil word out of him. As a rule he never opened his face unless it was to talk the game with somebody who knew it.

Then Sleeth came along. He came down from Frisco and began hanging around the Institute talking with the guys who were on the beach. He was a slim, dark fellow with a sallow complexion, quick, black eyes, and he might have been anywhere from thirty to forty-five.

He was a longshoreman, too. That is, he was then. Up in Frisco he had been a deckhand on a tugboat, like me. Before that he had been a lot of things, here and there. Somewhere he had developed a mind for figures, or maybe he had been born with it. You could give him any problem in addition, subtraction, or anything else, and you'd get the answer just like that, right out of his head. At poker he could beat anybody and was one of the best pool shots I ever saw.

We were sitting by the fireplace in the Institute one night when he came in and joined us. A few minutes later, Old Man White showed up wearing his old pea jacket as always.

"Where's MacCready?" he said.

"He's gone up to L.A., Mr. White," the clerk said. "He won't be back for several days."

"Is that other fellow around? That big fellow with the pockmarked face?"

"Slim? No, he's not. He shipped out this morning for Grays Harbor. I heard he had some trouble with the police."

Trouble was right. Slim was slick with the cards, and

he got himself in a game with a couple of Greeks. One of the Greeks was a pretty good cheat himself, but Oriental Slim was better and cashing in from the Greek's roll. One word led to another, and the Greek went for a rod. Well, Oriental Slim was the fastest thing with a chiv I ever saw. He cut that Greek, then he took out.

Old Man White turned away, growling something into his mustache. He was a testy old guy, and when he got sore that mustache looked like a porcupine's back.

"What's the matter with that guy?" Sleeth said. "He acts like he was sore about something."

"It's checkers," I said. "That's Old Man White, the best checker player around here. Mac and Slim are the only two who can even make it interesting, and they're gone. He's sour for a week when he misses a game."

"Hell, I'll play with him!"

"He won't even listen to you. He won't play nobody unless they got some stuff."

"We'll see. Maybe I can give him a game."

Sleeth got up and walked over. The old man had his book out and was arranging his men on the board. He never used regular checkers himself. He used bottle tops, and always carried them in his pocket.

"How about a game?" Sleeth said.

Old Man White growled something under his breath about not wanting to teach anybody; he didn't even look up. He got the checkers set up, and pretty soon he started to move. It seems these guys that play checkers have several different openings they favor, each one of them named. Anyway, when the old man started to move, Sleeth watched him.

"The Old Fourteenth, huh? You like that? I like the Laird and Lady best."

Old Man White stopped in the middle of a move and looked up, frowning. "You play checkers?" he said.

"Sure, I just asked you for a game!"

"Sit down, sit down. I'll play you three games."

Well, it was pitiful. I'm telling you it was slaughter. If the old man hadn't been so proud, everything might have been different, but checkers was his life, his religion; and Sleeth beat him.

It wasn't so much that he beat him; it was the way he beat him. It was like playing with a child. Sleeth beat him five times running, and the old man was fit to be tied. And the madder he got, the worse he played.

Dick said afterward that if Sleeth hadn't talked so much, the old man might have had a chance. You see, Old Man White took plenty of time to study each move, sometimes ten minutes or more. Sleeth just sat there gabbing with us, sitting sideways in the chair, and never looking at the board except to move. He'd talk, talk about women, ships, ports, liquor, fighters, everything. Then, the old man would move and Sleeth would turn, glance at the board, and slide a piece. It seemed like when he looked at the board, he saw all the moves that had been made, and all that could be made. He never seemed to think; he never seemed to pause; he just moved.

Well, it rattled the old man. He was sort of shoved off balance by it. All the time, Sleeth was talking, and sometimes when he moved, it would be right in the middle of a sentence. Half the time, he scarcely looked at the board.

Then, there was a crowd around. Old Man White being beat was enough to draw a crowd, and the gang all liked Sleeth. He was a good guy. Easy with his dough, always having a laugh on somebody or with somebody, and just naturally a right guy. But I felt sorry for the old man. It meant so much to him, and he'd been king bee around the docks so long, and treating everybody with contempt if they weren't good at checkers. If he had even been able to make it tough for Sleeth, it would have been different, but he couldn't even give him a game. His memory for moves seemed to desert him, and the madder he got and the harder he tried, the more hopeless it was.

It went on for days. It got so Sleeth didn't want to play him. He'd avoid him purposely, because the old man was so stirred up about it. Once Old Man White jumped up in the middle of a game and hurled the board clear across the room. Then he stalked out, mad as a wet hen, but just about as helpless as an Armenian peddler with both arms busted.

Then he'd come back. He'd always come back and insist Sleeth play him some more. He followed Sleeth around town, cornering him to play, each time sure he could beat him, but he never could.

We should have seen it coming, for the old man got to acting queer. Checkers was an obsession with him. Now he sometimes wouldn't come around for days, and when he did, he didn't seem anxious to play anymore. Once he played with Oriental Slim, who was back in town, but Slim beat him, too.

That was the finishing touch. It might have been the one game out of ten that Slim usually won, but it hit the old man where he lived. I guess maybe he figured he couldn't play anymore. Without even a word, he got up and went out.

A couple of mornings later, I got a call from Brennan to help load a freighter bound out for the Far East. I'd quit my job on the tug, sick of always going out but never getting anyplace, and had been longshoring a little and waiting for a ship to China. This looked like a chance to see if they'd be hiring; so I went over to the ship at Terminal Island, and reported to Brennan.

The first person I saw was Sleeth. He was working on the same job. While we were talking, another ferry came over and Old Man White got off. He was running a steam winch for the crew that day, and I saw him glance at Sleeth. It made me nervous to think of those two guys on the same job. In a dangerous business like longshoring— that is, a business where a guy can get smashed up so easy—it looked like trouble.

It was after four in the afternoon before anything happened. We had finished loading the lower hold through No. 4 hatch, and were putting the strong-backs in place so we could cover the 'tween-decks hatchway. I was on deck waiting until they got those braces in place before I went down to lay the decking over them. I didn't want to be crawling down a ladder with one of those big steel beams swinging in the hatchway around me. Old Man White was a good hand at a winch, but too many things can happen. We were almost through for the day, as we weren't to load the upper hold 'til morning.

A good winch-driver doesn't need signals from the hatch-tender to know where his load is. It may be out of sight down below the main deck, but he can tell by the feel of it and the position of the boom about where it is. But sometimes on those old winches, the steam wouldn't come on even, and once in a while there would be a surge of power that would make them do unaccountable things without a good hand driving. Now, Old Man White was a good hand. Nevertheless, I stopped by the hatch coaming and watched.

It happened so quick that there wasn't anything anyone could have done. Things like that always happen quick, and if you move, it is usually by instinct. Maybe the luckiest break Sleeth ever got was he was light on his feet.

The strong-back was out over the hatch, and Old Man White was easing it down carefully. When it settled toward the 'tween-decks hatchway, Sleeth caught one end and Hansen the other. It was necessary for a man to stand at each end and guide the strong-back into the notch where it had to fit to support the floor of the upper hold. Right behind Sleeth was a big steel upright, and as Old Man White began to lower away, I got nervous. It always made me nervous to think that a wrong move by the winch-driver, or a wrong signal from the hatch-tender spotting for him, and the man with that post at his back was due to get hurt.

Sleeth caught the end of the strong-back in both hands and it settled gradually, with the old winch puffing along easy-like. Just then I happened to glance up, and something made me notice Old Man White's face.

He was as white as death, and I could see the muscles at the corner of his jaw set hard. Then, all of a sudden, that strong-back lunged toward Sleeth.

It all happened so quick, you could scarcely catch a breath. Sleeth must have remembered Old Man White was on that winch, or maybe it was one of those queer hunches. As for me, I know that in the split second when that strong-back lunged toward him, the thought flashed through my mind, "Sleeth. It's your move!"

And he did move, almost like in the checker games. It was as if he had a map of the whole situation in his mind. One moment he was doing one thing and the next . . .

He leaped sideways and the end of that big steel strong-back hit that stanchion with a crash that you could have heard in Sarawak; then the butt swung around and came within an eyelash of knocking Hansen into the hold, and I just stood there with my eyes on that stanchion thinking how Sleeth would have been mashed into jelly if he hadn't moved like Nijinsky.

The hatch-tender was yelling his head off, and slowly Old Man White took up the tension on the strong-back and swung her into place again. If it had been me, I'd never have touched that thing again, but Sleeth was there, and the strong-back settled into place as pretty as you could wish. Only then could I see that Sleeth's face was white and his hand was shaking.

When he came on deck, he was cool as could be. Old Man White was sitting behind that winch all heaped up like a sack of old clothes. Sleeth looked at him then, grinned a little, and said, sort of offhand, "You nearly had the move on me that time, Mr. White!"

AND PROUDLY DIE

Everything that's loose drifts down to the sea eventually. Driftwood and drift people, the same way.

WE WERE ALL misfits, more or less, just so much waste material thrown out casually at one of the side doors of the world. We hadn't much to brag about, but we did plenty of it, one time or another. Probably some of us had something on the ball, like Jim, for instance, who just lacked some little touch in his makeup, and that started him off down the odd streets. We weren't much to look at, although the cops used to come down now and again to give us the once-over. As a rule they just left us alone, because we didn't matter. If one of us was killed, they just figured it was a break for the community, or something. And probably they were right.

Maybe Snipe was one of us after all, but he didn't seem to fit in anywhere. He was one of those guys who just don't belong. He couldn't even find a place with us, and we had about hit rock bottom. Maybe in the end he did find a place, but if he did, it wasn't the place he wanted.

He had sort of drifted in, like all the rest. A little, scrawny guy with a thin face and a long nose that stuck out over the place where his chin should have been. His chin had slipped back against his neck like it was ashamed of itself, and he had those watery blue eyes that seemed sort of anxious and helpless, as though he was always afraid somebody was going to take a punch at him.

I don't know why he stayed, or why we let him stay. Probably he was so much of a blank cartridge nobody cared. We were a pretty tight little bunch, otherwise, and we had to be. It was a matter of survival. It was the waterfront, and times were hard. Getting by was about all a guy could do, and we did it and got along because each of us had his own line and we worked well together. Snipe didn't belong, but he seemed to like being around, and we didn't notice him very much. Whenever Sharkey and Jim would get to talking, he'd sit up and listen, but for that matter, we all did. He seemed to think Sharkey was about the last word in brains, and probably he was.

Snipe was afraid to die. Not that there's anything funny about that, only he worried about it. It was like death had a fascination for him. He was scared of it, but he couldn't stay away. And death along the waterfront is never nice. You know what I mean. A sling breaks, maybe, and a half-dozen bales of cotton come down on a guy, or maybe his foot slips when he's up on the mast, and down he comes to light on a steel deck. Or maybe a boom falls, or the swing of a strong-back mashes him. But no matter how it happens, it's never pretty. And Snipe was scared of it. He told me once he'd always been afraid to die.

Once, I'd been down along the docks looking for a live wire to hit up for the price of coffee, when I saw a crowd on the end of the wharf. Guys on the burn are all rubbernecks, so I hurried along to see what was doing. When I got closer, I could see they were fishing a stiff out of the water. You know what I mean—a dead guy.

Well, I've seen some sights in my life, and death is never

pretty along the waterfront, like I've said, but this was the worst. The stiff had been in the water about two weeks. I was turning away when I spotted Snipe. He was staring at the body like he couldn't take his eyes off it, and he was already green around the gills. For a minute I thought he was going to pull a faint right there on the dock.

He saw me then. We walked away together and sat down on a lumber pile. Snipe rolled a smoke from a dirty-looking sack of Bull Durham, and I tossed little sticks off the dock, watching them float lazily on the calm, dark water.

Across the channel one of the Luckenbach boats was loading cargo for her eastern trip, and the stack of a GP tanker showed over the top of a warehouse on Terminal. It was one of those still, warm afternoons with a haze of heat and smoke hanging over Long Beach. Another tanker was coming slowly upstream, and I sat there watching it, remembering how I'd burned my knees painting the white S on the stack of a tanker like it. I sat there watching, kind of sleepy-like, and wishing I was coming in with a payoff due instead of kicking my heels in the sun wishing for two bits. But all the time, way down deep, I was thinking of Snipe.

I felt in my pockets hoping for a dime I'd overlooked, but I'd shook myself down a dozen times already. Out of the corner of my eye I could see Snipe staring out over the channel, that limp-looking fag hanging from his lip, and his damp, straw-colored hair plastered against his narrow skull. His fingers were too long, and the nails always dirty. I felt disgusted with him and wondered what he wanted to live for. Maybe he wondered, too.

"That stiff sure looked awful, didn't it?" he said.

"None of them look so good t' me."

"I'd hate to look like that. Seawater is nasty stuff. I never did like it."

I grunted. A shore boat was heading for the Fifth Street landing, and I watched it as the wake trailed out in a widening V, like the events that follow the birth of a man. Then we could hear the slap of water under the dock.

"I'd sure hate to die like that," Snipe said. "If a guy could die like a hero now, it wouldn't be so bad. I wonder what Sharkey meant the other night when he said when it was no longer possible to live proudly, a man could always die proudly."

"What the hell difference does it make how you die? A corpse is a corpse, no matter how it got that way. That stuff about a life after death is all hooey. Like Sharkey said, it was an invention of the weak to put a damper on the strong. The little fellow thinks that if the big guy is worried about the hereafter, he'll play it fair in this one, see? A dead man don't mean anything, no more than a rotten potato. He just was something, that's all!"

"But what became of the life that was in him? Where does that go?"

"Where does the flame go when the fire goes out? It's just gone. Now, forget it, and let's find the gang. I'm fed up talking about stiffs."

We started for the shack. A few clouds had rolled up, and it was starting to drizzle. Out on the channel the ripples had changed to little waves with ruffles of white riding the crests. There was a tang in the air that smelled like a blow. I looked off toward the sea and was glad I was ashore. It wasn't going to be any fun out there tonight. Snipe hurried along beside me, his breath wheezing a little.

"I'm a good swimmer," he said, reaching for a confidence I could tell he didn't have.

"Well, a pretty good swimmer."

Where did a runt like him ever get that hero idea? From Sharkey, I guess. Probably nobody ever treated him decent before. Looking at him, I wondered why it was some guys draw such tough hands. There was Sharkey, as regular a guy as ever walked, a big, fine-looking fellow with brains and nerve, and then here was Snipe, with nothing. Sharkey had a royal flush, and Snipe was holding nothing but deuces and treys in a game that was too big for him.

His frayed collar was about two sizes too large, and his Adam's apple just grazed it every time he swallowed. He didn't have a thing, that guy. He was bucking a stacked deck, and the worst of it was, he knew it.

You see a lot of these guys along the waterfronts. The misfits and the also-rans, the guys who know too much and those who know too little. Everything loose in the world seems to drift toward the sea and usually winds up on the beach somewhere. It's a sort of natural law, I guess. And here was Snipe. It wouldn't have been so tough if he'd been the dumb type that thought he was a pretty swell guy. But Snipe wasn't fooled. Way down inside he had a feeling for something better than he was, and every time he moved he knew it was him, Snipe, that was moving.

You could see him seeing himself. It gave you kind of a shock, sometimes. I had never quite got it until then, but I guess Sharkey had from the first. You could see that Snipe knew he was Snipe, just something dropped off the merry-go-round of life that didn't matter.

Instead of going on with me, he turned at the corner

and walked off up the street, his old cap pulled down over his face, his funny, long shoes squidging on the sloppy walk.

It was warm and cheery inside the shack. Sharkey had had the guys rustle up some old papers and nail them over the walls as insulation. When you couldn't do anything else, you could read the latest news of three months back or look at pictures of Mae West or Myrna Loy, depending if you liked them slim or well upholstered. Most of them looked at Mae West.

The big stove had its belly all red from the heat, and Tony was tipped back in a chair reading the sports. Deek was playing sol at the table, and Jim was standing by in the kitchen watching Red throw a mulligan together. Sharkey had his nose in a book as usual, something about the theory of the leisure class. I had to grin when he showed it to me. We sure were a leisure class, although there wasn't one of us liked it.

It was nice sitting there. The heat made a fellow kind of drowsy, and the smell of mulligan and coffee was something to write home about. I sat there remembering Snipe walking off up the street through that first spatter of rain, and how the wind whipped his worn old coat.

He was afraid of everything, that guy. Afraid of death, afraid of cops, scared of ship's officers, and of life, too, I guess. At that, he was luckier than some, for he had a flop. It would be cold and wet on the streets tonight, and there would be men sleeping in boxcars and lumber piles, and other guys walking the streets, wishing they had lumber piles and boxcars to sleep in. But we were lucky, with a shack like this, and we only kept it by working together. In that kind of a life, you got to stick together. It's the only answer.

Windy Slim was still out on the stem. He never came in early on bad nights, it being easier to pick up a little change when the weather is wet and miserable. Copper was out somewhere, too, and that was unusual, him liking the rain no better than a cat. The drizzle had changed now to a regular downpour, and the wind was blowing a gale.

We all knew what it would be like at sea, with the wind howling through the rigging like a lost banshee and the decks awash with black, glassy water. Sometimes the shack sagged with the weight of the wind, and once Sharkey looked up and glanced apprehensively at the stove.

Then, during a momentary lull, the door jerked open and Slim stomped in, accompanied by a haze of wind and rain that made the lamp spit and almost go out. He shook himself and began pulling off his coat.

"God have pity on the poor sailors on such a night as this!" Jim said, grinning.

"Say—" Slim stopped pulling off his wet clothes and looked at Sharkey. "Brophy and Stallings picked up Copper tonight!"

"The devil they did!" Sharkey put down his book. "What happened?"

"Copper, he bums four bits from some lug down on the docks where he used to work an' goes to the Greek's for some chow. He has a hole in his pocket but forgets it. After he eats he finds his money is gone. The Greek hollers for a bull, an' Brophy comes running, Cap Stallings with him.

"Snipe, he was with Copper when he raised the four bits, but when the bull asks him did Copper have any money, the little rat is so scared he says he don't know nothing about it. He always was scared of a cop. So they took Copper an' throwed him in the can."

"The yellow rat!" Tony said. "An' after all the feeds Copper staked him to!"

"Why have him here, anyway?" Red said. "He just hangs around. He ain't any good for anything!"

Me, I sat there and didn't say anything. There wasn't anything you could say. Outside the wind gathered and hurled a heavy shoulder against the house, the lamp sputtered and gulped, and everybody was quiet. Everybody was thinking what I was thinking, I guess, that Snipe would have to go, but there wasn't anyplace for him to go. I tried to read again, but I couldn't see anything but that spatter of falling rain and Snipe walking away up the street. Red was right, he wasn't any good for anything, not even himself.

The door opened then, and Snipe came in. It was all in his face, all the bitter defeat and failure of him. That was the worst of it. He knew just what he'd done, knew just what it would mean to that tough, lonely bunch of men who didn't have any friends but themselves and so had to be good friends to each other. He knew it all, knew just how low he must have sunk, and only felt a little lower himself.

Sharkey didn't say anything, and the rest of us just sat there. Then Sharkey took a match out of his pocket and handed it to Snipe. Everybody knew what that meant. In the old days on the bum, when the crowd didn't like a fellow, they gave him a match as a hint to go build his own fire.

Sharkey picked up the poker then and began to poke at the fire. Out in the kitchen everything was quiet. Snipe stood there, looking down at Sharkey's shoulders, his face white and queer. Then he turned and went out. The sound of the closing door was loud in the room.

The next morning Sharkey and a couple of us drifted down to the big crap game under the PE trestle. Everybody was talking about the storm and the ferry to Terminal Island being rammed and sunk during the night. About a dozen lives lost, somebody said.

"Say, Sharkey," Honolulu said, looking up from the dice. "One of your crowd was on that ferry. That little guy they called Snipe. I saw him boarding her at the landing."

"Yeah?"

"Yeah."

Sharkey looked down at the dice and said nothing. Slim was getting the dice hot and had won a couple of bucks. The lookout got interested, and when all at once somebody hollered "Bull," there were the cops coming up through the lumberyard.

Two or three of our boys were in the inner circle, and when the yell came, everybody grabbed at the cash. Then we all scattered out, running across the stinking tide flat east of the trestle. I got a fistful of money myself, and there was a lot left behind. I glanced back once, and the cops were picking it up.

The tide wasn't out yet, and in some places the water was almost knee-deep, but it was the only way, and we took it running. I got all wet and muddy but had to laugh, thinking what a funny sight we must have made, about twenty of us splashing through that water as fast as we could pick 'em up and put 'em down.

I was some little time getting back to the shack, and when I did get there, Sharkey was sitting on the steps talking to Windy and Jim. They looked mighty serious, and when I came up, they motioned me to come along and then started back for the trestle.

Thinking maybe they were going back after the money, I told them about the cops getting it, but Slim merely shrugged and said nothing. He had a slug of chewing in his jaw and looked serious as hell.

Finally we got to the mudflat, and though it was still wet, Sharkey started picking his way across. We hadn't gone far before I could see something ahead, partly buried in the gray mud. It looked like an old sack, or a bundle of dirty clothes. When we got closer I could see it was a body—probably washed in by the tide.

It sort of looked as if the man had been walking in and, when the mud on his feet got too heavy, just lay down. Even before Sharkey stooped to turn his head over, I could see it was Snipe. He had on that old cap of his, and I couldn't have missed it in a million.

He looked pretty small and pitiful, lying there in the mud mingled with the debris left by an outgoing tide. Once in a while even yet, I think of how he looked, lying there on that stinking mudflat under a low, clouded sky, with a background of lumberyard and trestle. There was mud on the side of his face, and a spot on his nose. His long fingers were relaxed and helpless, but somehow there wasn't a thing about him that looked out of place. We stood there looking at him a minute, and none of us said anything, but I was thinking: "Well, you were afraid of it, and here it is—now what?"

We left him there and said nothing to anybody. Later, Red saw them down there picking him up but didn't go near, so we never knew what the coroner thought of it, if anything. I often wonder what happened when that ferry went down. She was hit hard and must have sunk like a rock, with probably fifty or sixty people aboard. It was Snipe's big chance to be a hero, him being such a good swimmer. But there he was.

As I said to Sharkey, it was a hell of a place to be found dead.

SURVIVAL

There on the waterfront, you met all kinds and types of people. It was definitely an education and I learned a lot about getting along, because you had to respect the other man's individuality and the other man's pride and his person as much as you wanted yourself to be respected. Ninety percent of them, I would say, were really good, solid characters.

Tex Worden was a seaman, a really tough, hard-boiled man. He was not a man you'd choose for an evening's company by any means. He got drunk a lot of times, he fought a lot of times, but he was a first-rate seaman.

T EX WORDEN SHOVED his way through the crowd in the Slave Market and pushed his book under the wicket.

The clerk looked up, taking in his blistered face and swollen hands. "What'll you have, buddy? You want to register?"

"Naw, I'm here to play a piano solo, what d'you think?"

"Wise guy, eh?"

Tex's eyes were cold. "Sure, and what about it?"

"You guys all get too smart when you get ashore. I'm used to you guys, but one of these days I'm going to come out from behind here and kick hell out of one of you!"

"Why not now?" Worden said mildly. "You don't see me out there running down the street, do you? You just come out from behind that counter, and I'll lay you in the scuppers."

At a signal from the man behind the wicket a big man pushed his way through the crowd and tapped Tex Worden on the shoulder. "All right, buddy, take it easy. You take it easy, or you get the boot."

"Yeah?"

"Yeah!"

Tex grinned insultingly and turned his back, waiting for the return of his book. The clerk opened it grudgingly, then looked up, startled.

"You were on the *Raratonga!*"

"So what?"

"We heard only one of the crew was saved!"

"Who the hell do you think I am? Napoleon? And that 'saved' business, that's the bunk. That's pure malarkey. I saved myself. Now come on, get that book fixed. I want to get out of here."

The plainclothesman was interested. "No kiddin', are you Tex Worden?"

"I am."

"Hell, man, that must have been some wreck. The papers say that if it wasn't for you none of them would have gotten back. Dorgan was on that boat, too!"

"Dorgan?" Tex turned to face him. "You know Dorgan?"

"*Knew* him? I should say I did! A tough man, too. One of the toughest."

Worden just looked at him. "How tough a man is often depends on where he is and what he's doing." He was looking past the plainclothesman, searching for a familiar face. In all this gathering of merchant seamen hunting work, he saw no one.

Times were hard. There were over seven hundred seamen on the beach, and San Pedro had become a hungry town. Jobs were scarce, and a man had to wait his turn. And he didn't have eating money. Everything he had had gone down with the *Raratonga*. He had money coming to him, but how long it would be before he saw any of it was a question.

Near the door he glimpsed a slight, bucktoothed seaman in a blue pea jacket whose face looked familiar. He edged through the crowd to him. "Hi, Jack, how's about staking a guy to some chow?"

"Hey? Don't I know you? Tex, isn't it?"

"That's right. Tex Worden. You were on the *West Ivis* when I was."

"Come on, there's a greasy spoon right down the street." When they were outside, he said, "I don't want to get far from the shipping office. My number's due to come up soon."

"How long's it been?"

"Three months. Well, almost that. Times are rough, Tex." He looked at Worden. "What happened to you?"

"I was on the *Raratonga*."

The sailor shook his head in awe. "*Jee-sus!* You were the only one who came back!"

"Some passengers made it. Not many but some."

"How's it feel to be a hero? And with Hazel Ryan yet. And Price! The actress and the millionaire! You brought them back alive."

"Me an' Frank Buck. If this is how it feels to be a hero, you can have it. I'm broke. There's a hearing today, and maybe I can hit up the commissioner for a few bucks."

The other seaman thrust out a hand. "I'm Conrad, Shorty Conrad. Paid off a ship from the east coast of

South America, and I lied to you: It didn't take me three months, because I've got a pal back there. I'll say a word for you, and maybe you can get a quick ship-out."

They ordered coffee and hamburger steaks. "This is a tough town, man. No way to get out of this dump unless you can take a pierhead jump or get lucky. If you know a ship's officer who'll ask for you, you got a better chance."

"I don't know nobody out here. I been shipping off the east coast."

A burly Greek came along behind the counter. He stared hard at them. "You boys got money? I hate to ask, but we get stiffed a lot."

"I got it." Shorty showed him a handful of silver dollars. "Anyway, this is Tex Worden. He was on the *Raratonga*."

"You got to be kiddin'."

The Greek eyed him with respect. "That where you got blistered?" He motioned toward Worden's hands. "What happened to them?"

"Knittin'," Tex said. "Them needles get awful heavy after a while."

He was tired, very, very tired. The reaction was beginning to set in now. He was so tired he felt he'd fall off the stool if he wasn't careful, and he didn't even have the price of a bed. If he hit the sack now, he'd probably pass out for a week. His shoulders ached, and his hands were sore. They hurt when he used them, and they hurt just as much when he didn't.

"It was a nasty blow, Shorty. You never saw wind like that."

"She went down quick, eh? I heard it was like fifteen minutes."

"Maybe. It was real quick. Starb'rd half door give way,

and the water poured in; then a bulkhead give way, and the rush of water put the fires out. No power, no pumps— it was a madhouse."

They were silent, sipping their coffee and eating the greasy steaks. Finally Shorty asked, "How long were you out there?"

"Fifteen days, just a few miles off the equator. It rained once—just in time."

Faces of men he knew drifted by the door. He knew some of them but could not recall their names. They were faces he'd seen from Hong Kong to Hoboken, from Limehouse to Malay Street in Singapore or Grant Road in Bombay, Gomar Street in Suez, or the old American Bar on Lime Street in Liverpool. He'd started life as a cowboy, but now he'd been at sea for fifteen years.

It was a rough crowd out there on Beacon Street; if he did not know them all, he knew their kind. There were pimps and prostitutes, thieves and drunks. There were seamen, fishermen, longshoremen, and bums, but they were all people, and they were all alive, and they were all walking on solid ground.

"Maybe I'll save my money," he said aloud, "buy myself a chicken ranch. I'd like to own a chicken ranch near Modesto."

"Where's Modesto?"

"I don't know. Somewhere north of here. I just like the sound of it."

Tex Worden looked down at his hands. Under the bandages they were swollen with angry red cracks where the blisters had been and some almost raw flesh that had just begun to heal. In the mirror he saw a face like a horror mask, for tough as his hide was, the sun had baked it to an angry red that he could not touch to shave. He looked frightening and felt worse. If only he could get some sleep!

He did not want to think of those bitter, brutal days when he rowed the boat, hour after hour, day after day, rowing with a sullen resignation, all sense of time forgotten, even all sense of motion. There had been no wind for days, just a dead calm, the only movement being the ripples in the wake of the lifeboat.

He got up suddenly. "I almost forgot. I got to stop by the commissioner's office. They want to ask me some questions. Sort of a preliminary inquiry, I guess."

Shorty stole a quick look at him. "Tex—you be careful. Be real careful. These aren't seamen. They don't know what it's like out there. They can't even imagine."

"I'll be all right."

"Be careful, I tell you. I read something about it in the papers. If you ain't careful they'll crucify you."

THERE WERE SEVERAL men in business suits in the office when they entered. They all looked at Tex, but the commissioner was the only one who spoke. "Thank you, son. That was a good job you did out there."

"It was my job," Tex said. "I done what I was paid for."

The commissioner dropped into a swivel chair behind his desk. "Now, Worden, I expect you're tired. We will not keep you any longer than we must, but naturally we must arrive at some conclusions as to what took place out there and what caused the disaster. If there is anything you can tell us, we'd be glad to hear it."

Shorty stole a glance at the big man with the red face. A company man, here to protect its interests. He knew the type.

"There's not much to tell, sir. I had come off watch about a half hour before it all happened, and when I went below, everything seemed neat and shipshape. When the ship struck, I was sitting on my bunk in the fo'c's'le taking off my shoes.

"The jolt threw me off the bench, an' Stu fell off his bunk on top of me. He jumped up an' said, 'What the hell happened?' and I said I didn't know, but it felt like we hit something. He said, 'It's clear enough outside, and we're way out to sea. Must be a derelict!' I was pulling on my shoes, and so was he, an' we ran up on deck.

"There was a lot of running around, and we started forward, looking for the mate. Before we'd made no more than a half-dozen steps, the signal came for boat stations, and I went up on the boat deck. Last I saw of Stu he was trying to break open a jammed door, and I could hear people behind it.

"We must have hit pretty hard because she was starting to settle fast, going down by the head with a heavy list to starb'rd. I was mighty scared because I remembered that starb'rd half door, and—"

"What about the half door, Worden? What was wrong with it?"

"Nothing at all, Commissioner," the company man interrupted. "The company inspector—"

"Just a minute, Mr. Winstead." The commissioner spoke sharply. "Who is conducting this inquiry?"

"Well, I—"

"Proceed with your story, Worden."

"The half door was badly sprung, sir. Somebody said the ship had been bumped a while back, and I guess they paid no mind to repairs. Anyway, it wasn't no bother unless they was loaded too heavy, and—"

"What do you mean, Worden? Was the ship over-loaded?"

Winstead scowled at Worden, his lips drawing to a thin, angry line.

"Well, sir, I guess I ain't got no call to speak, but—"

"You just tell what happened at the time of the wreck, Worden. That will be sufficient!" Winstead said, interrupting.

"Mr. Winstead! I will thank you not to interrupt this man's story again. I am conducting this inquiry, and regardless of the worth of what Worden may have to say, he is the sole remaining member of the crew. As a seafaring man of many years' experience, he understands ships, and he was there when it happened. I intend to hear *all*—let me repeat, *all*—he has to say. We certainly are not going to arrive at any conclusions by concealing anything. If your vessel was in proper condition, you have nothing to worry about, but I must say your attitude gives rise to suspicion." He paused, glancing up at the reporters, who were writing hurriedly. "Now, Worden, if you please. Continue your story."

"Well, sir, I was standing by number three hatch waiting for the last loads to swing aboard so's I could batten down the hatch, an' I heard Mr. Jorgenson—he was the mate—say to Mr. Winstead here that he didn't like it at all. He said loading so heavy with that bad door was asking for trouble, and he went on to mention that bad bulkhead amidships.

"I don't know much about it, sir, except what he said and the talk in the fo'c's'le about the bulkhead between hatches three and four. One of the men who'd been chipping rust down there said you didn't dare chip very hard or you'd drive your hammer right through, it was that thin. When I was ashore clearing the gangway, I saw she was loaded down below the Plimsoll marks."

"Weren't you worried, Worden? I should think that knowing the conditions you would have been."

"No, sir. Generally speaking, men working aboard ship don't worry too much. I've been going to sea quite a while now, and it's always the other ships that sink, never the one a fellow's on. At least that's the way it is until something happens. We don't think about it much, and if she sinks, then she sinks, and that's all there is to it."

"I see."

"Yes, sir. There was trouble with that half door before we were three days out. Me an' a couple of others were called to help Chips caulk that half door. You know—it's a door in the ship's side through which cargo is loaded. Not all ships have 'em. That door had been rammed some time or another, and it didn't fit right. In good weather or when she carried a normal load it was all right.

"But three days out we had a spot of bad weather; some of that cargo shifted a mite, and she began to make water, so we had to recaulk that door.

"To get back to that night, sir. When I got to my boat station, I saw one of the officers down on the deck with his head all stove in. I don't know whether he got hit with something or whether it was done by the bunch of passengers who were fighting over the boat. Ever'body was yellin' an' clawin', so I waded in an' socked a few of them and got them straightened out.

"I told them they'd damn well better do what they were told because I was the only one who knew how to get that lifeboat into the water. After that they quieted down some. A couple of them ran off aft, hunting another boat, but I got busy with the lifeboat cover.

"All of a sudden it was still, so quiet it scared you. The wind still blowing and big waves all around but ghostly still. You could hear a body speak just like I'm speakin' now. It was like everything quieted down to let us die in peace. I could tell by the feel of her that we hadn't long. She was settlin' down, and she had an ugly, heavy feel to her.

"Mister, that was a tryin' time. All those people who'd been yellin' an' fightin' stood there lookin' at me, and one little fellow in a gray suit—he had a tie on, an' everything. He was Jewish, I think. He asked me what he could do, and I told him to get to the other end of the boat, to loose the falls and lower away when I did.

"I got the boat cover off, and we got the boat into the water, and the ship was down so far and canted over— a bad list to her—that it was no problem gettin' those few folks into the lifeboat.

"I took a quick look around. The boat 'longside was already in the water, and there were two ABs with it, Fulton an' Jaworski, it was. They had maybe thirty people in that boat, and I saw one of the stewards there, too. There was nobody else in sight, but I could hear some yelling forward.

"Just then she gave a sort of shudder, and I jumped into the boat and told the Jew to cast off. He had trouble because she was rising and falling on the water, but a woman helped him. I didn't know who she was then, but later I found out it was that actress, Hazel Ryan.

"We shoved off, and I got oars into the water, and we started looking for others. When we got out a ways, I could see Sparks—one of them, anyway, in the radio shack.

"Then the ship gave a kind of lunge and went down by the head. She just dipped down and then slid right away, going into the water on her beam ends with all the port-side boats just danglin' there, useless, as they couldn't be got into the water. At the last minute, as she went under, I saw a man with an ax running from boat to boat cutting the falls. He was hoping they'd come up floating, and two or three of them did.

"All of a sudden I see a man in the water. He was a pleasant-looking man with gray hair, and he was swimming. He looked so calm I almost laughed. 'Cold, isn't it?' he says, and then he just turns and swims away, cool as you please. You'd have thought the beach wasn't fifty feet away.

"It's things like that fairly take your wind, sir, and there I was, trying to pull the lifeboat away from the ship and hopin' for the best.

"I turned my head once and looked back. Mostly I was trying to guide the boat through wreckage that was already afloat. When I looked back—this was just before she went under—I glimpsed somebody standin' on the bridge, one arm through the pilothouse window to hang on, and he was lighting his pipe with his free hand.

"It just didn't seem like it could be happening. There I was just minutes before, a-comin' off watch, all set for a little shut-eye, and now here I was in a lifeboat, and the ship was goin' down.

"There must have been nearly a hundred people in the water, and not a whisper out of any of them. Like they was all in shock or somethin' of the kind. Once a guy did yell to somebody else. Then something exploded underwater—maybe the boilers busted; I wouldn't know. Anyway, when it was over, a lot of those folks who'd been in the water were gone. I fetched the bow of my boat around and rowed toward something white floating in the water. It was a woman, and I got her into the boat."

"Was that Hazel Ryan?" a reporter asked.

"No, it was Lila, a stewardess. Then I held the boat steady whilst another man climbed in. He pointed out three people clingin' to a barrel. I started for them.

"The sea was rough, and folks would disappear behind a wave, and sometimes when you looked, they weren't there anymore. Those people were havin' a time of it, tryin' to hang to that barrel, so I got to them first, and folks helped them aboard. The Ryan woman was one of them.

"I'll give her this. First moment she could speak, she asked if there was anything she could do, and I said just to set quiet and try to get warm, if I needed help I'd ask for it.

"It was funny how black everything was, yet you could see pretty well for all of that. You'd see a white face against the black water, and by the time you got there, it was gone.

"One time I just saw an arm. Woman's, I think it was. She was right alongside the boat, and I let go an oar an' grabbed for her, but her arm slipped right through my fingers, and she was gone.

"Some of those we'd picked up were in panic and some in shock. That little Jewish fellow with the necktie and all, he didn't know a thing about the sea, but he was cool enough. We moved people around, got the boat trimmed, and I got her bow turned to meet the sea and started to try to ride her out."

"What about the radio?"

"We didn't think about that for long. At least I didn't. There hadn't been much time, and the chances were slim that any message got off. It all happened too fast.

"Sparks was in there, and he was sending. I am sure of that, but he hadn't any orders, and most shipmasters don't want any Mayday or SOS goin' out unless they say. If he sent it, he sent it on his own, because the old man never made the bridge."

"The man you saw lighting his pipe?"

"Jorgenson, I think. He was watch officer, but they were changing watch, so I don't know. He wasn't heavy enough for the old man.

"Anyway, I'd no time to think of them. The sea was making up, and I was havin' the devil's own time with that boat. She'd have handled a lot easier if we'd had a few more people aboard.

"Lila, she was hurting. Seemed like she was all stove up inside, and the shock was wearing off. She was feeling pain, turning and twisting like, and the Ryan woman was trying to help. She and that little Jew, they worked over her, covering her with coats, trying to tuck them under so she'd ride easier. The rest just sat and stared."

"No other boats got off?"

"I don't know—except that boat with Fulton and Jaworski. They were good men, and they'd do what could be done. The ship had taken a bad list, so I don't think many of the boats on the topside could be launched at all."

"How was the weather?"

"Gettin' worse, sir. There was nobody to spell me on the oars because nobody knew anything about handling a boat in a heavy sea. I shipped the oars and got hold of the tiller, which made it a mite easier.

"Lila had passed out; spray was whipping over the boat. I was hanging to that tiller, scared ever' time a big one came over that it would be the last of us. There was no way to play. You just had to live from one sea to the next."

"How long did the storm last?"

"About two days. I don't rightly remember because I was so tired everything was hazy. When the sea calmed down enough, I let Schwartz have the tiller. I'd been gripping it so hard and so long I could hardly let go."

"You were at the tiller forty-eight hours without relief?"

"Yes, sir. Maybe a bit more. But after that she began to settle down, and the sun came out."

"The boat was provisioned according to regulations?"

"Yes, sir. We'd some trouble about water later but not much."

"How about the crew and the officers? Were they efficient, in your opinion?"

"Sure. Yes, they were okay. I've been going to sea quite a spell, and I never have seen any seaman or officer shirk his job. It ain't bravery nor lack of it, just that he knows his job and has been trained for it.

"Sometimes you hear about the crew rushing the boats or being inefficient. I don't believe it ever happens. They're trained for the job, and it is familiar to them. They know what they are to do, and they do it.

"Passengers are different. All of a sudden everything is different. There's turmoil an' confusion; there's folks runnin' back and forth, and the passengers don't know what's going on.

"Sometimes one of them will grab a crewman and yell something at him, and the crewman will pull loose and go about his business. The passenger gets mad and thinks they've been deserted by the crew when chances are that seaman had something to do. Maybe his boat station was elsewhere. Maybe he'd been sent with a message for the engineer on watch below.

"Maybe those crewmen you hear about rushing the boats are just getting there to get the boat cover off and clear the falls. This wasn't my first wreck, and I've yet to see a crewman who didn't stand by."

"How long before she sank?"

"Fifteen minutes, give or take a few. It surely wasn't more, though. It might have been no more than five. We'd made quite a bit of water before the cargo shifted and she heeled over. With that half door underwater—well, I figure that door gave way and she just filled up and sank."

"Mr. Commissioner?" Winstead asked. "I'd like permission to ask this man a few questions. There are a few matters I'd like to clear up."

"Go ahead."

"Now, my man, if you'd be so kind. How many were in the boat when you got away from the scene of the wreck?"

"Eight."

"Yet when you were picked up by the *Maloaha* there were but three?"

"Yes."

"How do you account for that?"

"Lila—she was the stewardess—she died. Like I said, she'd been hurt inside. She was a mighty good woman, and I hated to see her go. Clarkson—he went kind of screwy. Maybe he didn't have all his buttons to start with. Anyway, he got kind of wild and kept staring at a big shark who was following us. One night he grabbed up a boat hook and tried to get that shark. It was silly. That shark was just swimmin' along in hopes. No use to bother him. Well, he took a stab at that shark and fell over the side.

"Handel, he just sat an' stared. Never made no word for anybody, just stared. He must've sat that way for eight or nine days. We all sort of lost track of time, but he wouldn't take water, wouldn't eat a biscuit. He just sat there, hands hanging down between his knees.

"I'd rigged a sort of mast from a drifting stick and part of a boat cover. The mast this boat should have carried was missing. Anyway, the little sail I rigged gave us some rest, and it helped. Late one day we were moving along at a pretty fair rate for us when I saw a squall coming. She swept down on us so quick that I gave the tiller to Schwartz and stumbled forward to get that sail down before we swamped. With the wind a-screaming and big seas rolling up, I'd almost reached the sail when this Handel went completely off his course. He jumped up and grabbed me, laughing and singing, trying to dance with me or something.

"Struggling to get free, I fell full length in the boat, scrambled up and pulled that sail down, and when I looked around, Handel was gone."

"Gone?" Winstead said.

"You mean—over the side?" the commissioner asked.

"That's right. Nearest thing I could figure out was that when I fell, he fell, too. Only when I fell into the bottom, he toppled over the side.

"Rain and blown spray was whipping the sea, and we couldn't see him. No chance to turn her about. We'd have gone under had we tried.

"For the next ten hours we went through hell, just one squall after another, and all of us had to bail like crazy just to keep us afloat."

"So," Winstead said, "you killed a passenger?"

"I never said that. I don't know what happened. Whatever it was, it was pure accident. I'd nothing against the man. He was daffy, but until that moment he'd been harmless. I figure he didn't mean no harm then, only I had to get free of him to save the boat."

"At least, that is your story?"

"Mister, with a ragin' squall down on us there was no time to coddle nobody. I didn't have a straitjacket nor any way to get him into one. It was save the boat or we'd all drown."

"Yet even with your small sail up, you might have lasted, might you not?"

Worden considered the matter, then he shrugged. "No way to tell. I was the only seaman aboard, and it was my judgment the sail come down. I'd taken it down."

"All right. We will let that rest for the moment. That accounts for three. Now what became of the other two?"

"The Jew—Schwartz, he come to me in the night a few days later. We were lyin' in a dead calm, and most of our water was gone. Sky was clear, not a cloud in sight, and we'd a blazin' hot day ahead. He told me he was goin' over the side, and he wanted me to know because he didn't want me to think he was a quitter.

"Hell, that little kike had more guts than the whole outfit. I told him nothing doing. Told him I needed him, which was no lie. It was a comfort just to have him there because what he didn't know he could understand when I told him. He wouldn't accept the fact that I needed him.

"It even came to the point where I suggested I toss a

coin with him to see who went over. He wouldn't listen to that, and we both knew I was talkin' nonsense. I was the only seaman. The only one who could handle a boat. It was my job to bring that boat back with as many people as possible. I ain't goin' for any of that hero stuff. That's all baloney. Sure, I wanted to live as much as any man, but I had a job to do. It was what I signed on to do. At least when I signed on, it was to do a seaman's job. I ain't done nothing I wouldn't do again."

"I see. And what became of the other man?"

"He was a big guy, and he was tough. He tried to take charge of the boat. There's a lot happens in an open boat like that when everybody is close to shovin' off for the last time. People just ain't thinkin' the way they should. This big guy, he had more stamina than the rest of them. Most of them tried to take a hand in rowin' the boat.

"We'd no wind, you see, and I was hopin' we could get out of the calm into the wind again, but he wouldn't do anything. He just sat. He said I was crazy, that I was goin' the wrong way. He said I drank water at night when they were all asleep. Twice when I passed water forward for somebody else, he drank it.

"Then one night I woke up with him pourin' the last of our water down his damn throat. The Ryan woman, she was tuggin' at his arm to try to stop him, but hell, it was too late.

"It was her callin' to me that woke me up, and I went at him. He emptied the cask and threw it over the side. I tried to stop him, and we had it out, right there. He was some bigger than me and strong, but there was no guts to him. I smashed him up some and put him between the oars. I told him to row, that he'd live as long as he rowed. First we had to circle around and pick up the cask."

"An empty cask?" Winstead asked incredulously. "What in God's world did you do that for?"

"Mister, it's only in the movies where some guy on the desert an' dyin' of thirst throws away a canteen because it's empty. Shows how little some of those screenwriters know. Supposin' he finds water next day? How's he goin' to carry it?

"You throw away an empty canteen in the desert an' you're committin' suicide. Same thing out there. We might get a rain squall, and if we did, we'd need something to hold water. So we circled and picked up that cask."

"And what happened to Dorgan?"

Tex Worden's face was bleak. "He quit rowin' twenty-four hours before we got picked up."

Winstead turned to the commissioner. "Sir, this man has admitted to killing one passenger; perhaps he killed two or three. As to his motives—I think they will appear somewhat different under cross-examination.

"I have evidence as to this man's character. He is known along the waterfronts as a tough. He frequents houses of ill fame. He gets into drunken brawls. He has been arrested several times for fighting. His statements here today have cast blame upon the company. I intend to produce evidence that this man is not only a scoundrel but an admitted murderer!"

Tex sat up slowly.

"Yes, I've been arrested for fighting. Sometimes when I come ashore after a long cruise I have a few too many, and sometimes I fight, but it's always with my own kind. After a trip on one of those louse-bound scows of yours, a man has to get drunk. But I'm a seaman. I do my job. There's never a man I've worked with will deny that. I'm sorry you weren't in that boat with us so you could have seen how it was.

"You learn a lot about people in a lifeboat. Me, I never claimed to be any psalm singer. Maybe the way I live isn't your way, but when the time comes for the men to step out, I'll be there. I'll be doin' my job.

"It's easy to sit around on your fat behinds and say what you'd have done or what should have been done. You weren't there.

"Nobody knows what he'd do until he's in the spot. I was the only guy in that boat knew a tiller from a thwart. It was me bring that boat through or nobody. I'd rather lose two than lose them all. I wasn't doin' it because it was swell of me or because they'd call me a hero. I was bringin' them in because it was my job.

"Handel now. He wasn't responsible. Somethin' happened to him that he never expected. He could have lived his life through a nice, respected man, but all of a sudden it isn't the same anymore. There's nobody to tell to do something or to even ask. He's caught in a place he can't see his way out of. He'd never had just to *endure,* and there was nothing in him to rise to the surface and make him stand up. It sort of affected his mind.

"Hazel Ryan? She has moxie. When I told her it was her turn to row, she never hesitated, and I had to make her quit. She wasn't all that strong, but she was game. A boatload like her an' I could have slept halfway back.

"Dorgan was a bad apple. The whole boat was on edge because of him. He'd been used to authority and was a born bully. He was used to takin' what he wanted an' lettin' others cry about it. I told him what he had to do, and he did it after we had our little set-to."

"Who did you think you were, Worden? God? With the power of life and death?"

"Listen, mister"—Worden leaned forward—"when I'm the only seaman in the boat, when we have damn' little water, an' we're miles off the steamer lanes, when there's heat, stillness, thirst, an' we're sittin' in the middle of a livin' hell, you can just bet I'm Mister God as far as that boat's concerned.

"The company wasn't there to help. You weren't there to help, nor was the commissioner. Sure, the little fat guy prayed, an' Clarkson prayed. Me, I rowed the boat."

He lifted his hands, still swollen and terribly lacerated where the blisters had broken to cracks in the raw flesh. "Forty hours," he said, "there at the end I rowed for forty hours, tryin' to get back where we might be picked up. We made it.

"We made it," he repeated, "but there was a lot who didn't."

The commissioner rose, and Winstead gathered his papers, his features set and hard. He threw one quick, measuring glance at Worden.

"That will be all, gentlemen," the commissioner said. "Worden, you will remain in port until this is straightened out. You are still at the same address?"

"Yes, sir. At the Seaman's Institute."

Shorty glanced nervously out the window, then at Winstead. Tex turned away from the desk, a tall, loose figure in a suit that no longer fit. Winstead left, saying nothing, but as Worden joined Shorty, the commissioner joined them.

"Worden?"

"Yes, sir?"

"As man to man—and I was once a seaman myself—

Mr. Winstead has a lot of influence. He will have the best attorney money can hire, and to a jury off the shore things do not look the same as in a drifting lifeboat.

"The *Lichenfield* docked a few minutes ago, and she will sail after refueling. I happen to know they want two ABs. This is unofficial, of course. The master of the vessel happens to be a friend of mine."

They shook hands briefly.

There was a faint mist falling when they got outside. Tex turned up his coat collar. Shorty glanced toward Terminal Island. "You got an outfit? Some dungarees an' stuff?"

"I'd left a sea bag at the Institute." He touched the blue shirt. "This was in it. I can draw some gear from the slop chest."

"They got your tail in a crack, Tex. What's next, the *Lichenfield?*"

"Well," he said shortly, "I don't make my living in no courtroom."

SHOW ME THE WAY
TO GO HOME

IT WAS THE night the orchestra played "Show Me the Way to Go Home," the night the fleet sailed for Panama. The slow drizzle of rain had stopped, and there was nothing but the play of searchlights across the clouds, the mutter of the motors from the shore boats, and the spatter of grease where the man was frying hamburgers on the Fifth Street landing. I was standing there with a couple of Greek fishermen and a taxi driver, watching the gobs say good-bye to their wives and sweethearts.

There was something about the smell of rain, the sailors saying good-bye, and the creak of rigging that sort of got to you. I'd been on the beach for a month then.

A girl came down to the landing and leaned on the rail watching the shore boats. One of the gobs waved at her, and she waved back, but didn't smile. You could see that they didn't know each other; it was just one of those things.

She was alone. Every other girl was with somebody, but not her. She was wearing a neat, tailored suit that was a little worn, but she had nice legs and large, expressive eyes. When the last of the shore boats was leaving she was still standing there. Maybe it wasn't my move, but I was lonely, and when you're on the beach you don't meet many girls. So I walked over and leaned on the rail beside her.

"Saying good-bye to your boyfriend?" I asked, though I knew she wasn't.

"I said good-bye to him a long time ago."

"He didn't come back?"

"Do they ever?"

"Sometimes they want to and can't. Sometimes things don't break right."

"I wonder."

"And sometimes they do come back and things aren't like they were, and sometimes they don't come back because they are afraid they won't be the same, and they don't want to spoil what they remember."

"Then why go?"

"Somebody has to. Men have always gone to sea, and girls have waited for them."

"I'm not waiting for anybody."

"Sure you are. We all are. From the very beginning we wait for somebody, watch for them long before we know who they are. Sometimes we find the one we wait for, sometimes we don't. Sometimes the one we wait for comes along and we don't know it until too late. Sometimes they ask too much and we are afraid to take a chance, and they slip away."

"I wouldn't wait for anyone. Especially him. I wouldn't want him now."

"Of course not. If you saw him now, you'd wonder why you ever wanted him. You aren't waiting for him, though—you're waiting for what he represented. You knew a sailor once. Girls should never know men who have the sea in their blood."

"They always go away."

"Sure, and that's the way it should be. All the sorrow and tragedy in life come from trying to make things last too long."

"You're a cynic."

"All sentimentalists are cynics, and all Americans are sentimentalists. It's the Stephen Foster influence. Or too many showings of 'Over the Hill to the Poorhouse' and 'East Lynne.' But I like it that way."

"Do people really talk like this?"

"Only when they need coffee. Or maybe the first time a girl and a man meet. Or maybe this talk is a result of the saying-good-bye influence. It's the same thing that makes women cry at the weddings of perfect strangers."

"You're a funny person." She turned to look at me.

"I boast of it. But how about that coffee? We shouldn't stand here much longer. People who lean on railings over water at night are either in love or contemplating suicide."

We started up the street. This was the sort of thing that made life interesting,—meeting people. Especially attractive blondes at midnight.

Over the coffee she looked at me. "A girl who falls in love with a sailor is crazy."

"Not at all. A sailor always goes away, and then she doesn't have time to be disillusioned. Years later she can make her husband's life miserable telling him what a wonderful man so-and-so was. The chances are he was a fourteen-carat sap, only he left before the new wore off."

"Is that what you do?"

"Very rarely. I know all the rules for handling women. The trouble is that at the psychological moment I forget to use them. It's depressing."

"It's getting late. I'm going to have to go home."

"Not alone, I hope."

She looked at me again, very coolly. "You don't think I'm the sort of girl you can just pick up, do you?"

"Of course not," I chuckled. "But I wished on a star out there. You know that old gag."

She laughed. "I think you're a fool."

"That cinches it. Women always fall in love with fools."

"You think it is so easy to fall in love as that?"

"It must be. Some people fall in love with no visible reason, either material, moral, or maternal. Anyway, why should it be so complicated?"

"Were you ever in love?"

"I think so. I'm not exactly sure. She was a wonderful cook, and if the way to a man's heart is through his stomach, this was a case of love at first bite."

"Do you ever take anything seriously?"

"I'm taking you seriously. But why not have a little fun with it? There's only one thing wrong with life: people don't love enough, they don't laugh enough—and they are too damned conventional. Even their love affairs are supposed to run true to form. But this is spontaneous. You walk down where the sailors are saying good-bye to their sweethearts because you said good-bye to one once. It has been raining a little, and there is a sort of melancholy tenderness in the air. You are remembering the past, not because of him, because his face and personality have faded, but because of the romance of saying good-bye, the smell of strange odors from foreign ports, the thoughts the ocean always brings to people—romance, color, distance. A sort of vague sadness that is almost a happiness. And then, accompanied by the sound of distant music and the perfume of frying onions, I come into your life!"

She laughed again. "That sounds like a line."

"It is. Don't you see? When you went down to the landing tonight you were looking for me. You didn't know who I was, but you wanted something, someone. Well, here I am. The nice part of it is, I was looking for you."

"You make it sound very nice."

"Why not? A man who couldn't make it sound nice while looking at you would be too dull to live. Now finish your coffee and we'll go home."

"Now listen, I . . ."

"I know. Don't say it. But I'll just take you to the door, kiss you very nicely, and close it."

THERE HAD BEEN another shower, and the streets were damp. A fog was rolling from the ocean, the silent mist creeping in around the corners of the buildings, encircling the ships to the peaks of their masts. It was a lonely, silent world where the streetlights floated in ghostly radiance.

"You were wondering why men went to sea. Can't you imagine entering a strange, Far Eastern port on such a night as this? The lights of an unknown city—strange odors, mysterious sounds, the accents of a strange tongue? It's the charm of the strange and the different, of something new. Yet there's the feeling around you of something very old. Maybe that's why men go to sea."

"Maybe it is, but I'd never fall in love with another sailor."

"I don't blame you."

We had reached the door. She put her key in the lock, and we stepped in. It was very late, and very quiet. I took her in my arms, kissed her good night, and closed the door.

"I thought you said you were going to say good night, and then go?" she protested.

"I said I was going to kiss you goodnight, and then close the door. I didn't say on which side of it I'd be."

"Well . . ."

The hell of it was, my ship was sailing in the morning.

THICKER THAN BLOOD

I had to go into the Seaman's Institute one night. It was raining and I didn't want to get out there to sleep any sooner than I had to, so I was in the Seaman's Institute later than usual. There was a fellow sitting in front of the fireplace and I got to talking to him. He said he had a job, that he was going to ship out on a ship off the docks at Wilmington; they had wired ahead for a couple of seamen. I said, "Well geez, I wish I was that lucky." He said, "Why don't you come along, they might need another man." So just on the chance I went with him, and we had to walk from the Seaman's Institute, from San Pedro around to Wilmington. And so we walked around there. It was two o'clock in the morning, or just before two and it was real dirty, dense fog. We sat on the dock and waited and waited and waited. The ship didn't get in 'til almost four, and when it did it came up through the fog, you couldn't see it 'til it was right on top of you. It tied up at the dock and I went aboard and signed on in the mate's cabin, with just a small light burning over his desk, and went off to the Far East.

H E HAD IT coming if ever a man did, and I could have killed him then and nobody the wiser. If he had been man enough, we could have gone off on the dock and slugged it out, and everything would have been settled either way the cat jumped. There's nothing like a sock on the chin to sort of clean things up. It saves hard feelings and time wasted in argument. But Duggs was the chief mate, and he wasn't man enough to whip me and knew it.

Bilgewater, they say, is thicker than blood, and once men have been shipmates, no matter how much they hate each other's guts, they stand together against the world. That's the way it is supposed to be, but it certainly wasn't going to be that way with Duggs and me. I decided that in a hurry.

From the hour I shipped on that freighter, Duggs made it tough for me, but it wasn't only me but the whole crew. You don't mind so much if a really tough guy makes you like it, but when a two-by-twice scenery bum like Duggs rubs it into you just because he has the authority, it just naturally hurts.

If we'd gone off on the dock where it was man to man, I'd have lowered the boom on his chin and left him for the gulls to pick over. But we were aboard ship, and if you sock an officer aboard ship, it's your neck.

Sometimes I think he laid awake nights figuring ways to be nasty, but maybe he didn't have to go to that much effort. I suspect it just came naturally. He made it rough for all of us, but particularly me. Not that I didn't have my chances to cool him off. I had three of them. The first was at sea, the second in Port Swettenham, and the third— well, you'll hear about that.

Every dirty job he could find fell to Tony or me, and he could think of more ways to be unpleasant without trying than you could if you worked at it. Unless you have been at sea, you can't realize how infernally miserable it can become. There are a thousand little, insignificant things that can be done to make it miserable. Always something, and it doesn't have to be anything big. Often it is the little things that get under your skin, and the longer it lasts, the worse it gets.

Of course, the food was bad, but that was the steward's fault. Curry and rice and fried potatoes for three straight weeks. That was bad enough, but Duggs kept finding work for us to do after we were off watch. Emergencies, he called them, and you can't refuse duty in an emergency. There were men aboard that ship who would have killed Duggs for a Straits dollar. Me, I'm an easygoing guy, but it was getting to me.

One morning at four o'clock I was coming off watch. It was blowing like the bull of Barney, and a heavy sea running. Duggs had just come on watch, and he calls to me to go aft with him and lend a hand. The log line was fouled. Back we went, and the old tub was rolling her scuppers under, with seas breaking over her that left you gasping like a fish out of water, they were that cold.

We reeled in the log line, hand over hand, the wind tearing at our clothes, the deck awash. He did help some, I'll give him that, but it was me who did the heavy hauling, and it was me who cleared the little propeller on the patent log of seaweed and rope yarns.

Right there was the perfect opportunity. Nobody would have been surprised if we'd both been washed over the side, so it would have been no trick to have dumped him over the rail and washed my hands of him. Duggs had on sea boots and oilskins, and he would have gone down quick.

I finished the job, tearing skin from my hands and getting salt into the raw wounds, the ship plunging like a crazy bronco in a wild and tormented sea. Then, in the moment when I could have got him and got him good, he leaned over and shouted to be heard above the wind, "There! I'm sure glad I managed to get that done!"

And I was so mad I forgot to kill him.

The next time was in Port Swettenham. Duggs knew I had a girl in Singapore, but instead of letting me go ashore, he put me on anchor watch. All night long I stood by the rail or walked the deck, looking at the far-off lights of town and cussing the day I shipped on a barge with a louse-bound, scupper-jumping, bilge-swilling rat for mate. And my girl was ashore expecting me—at least, I hoped she was.

We sailed from Singapore, called at Belawan and Penang, and finally we crawled up the river to Port Swettenham.

It was hot and muggy. Keeping cool was almost impossible, and I had only two changes of clothes for working. One of them I managed to keep clean to wear off watch; the other was stiff with paint and tar. When time allowed I'd wash the one set and switch. The mate deliberately waited one day until I'd changed into clean clothes, and then he called me.

We were taking on some liquid rubber, and down in the empty fuel-oil tank in the forepeak was a spot of water about as big as a pie plate. He told me to climb down fifteen feet of steel ladder covered with oil slime and sop up that water. Aside from being a complete mess before I'd reached the bottom, there was almost an even chance I'd slip and break a leg.

Forward we went together, then down in the forepeak, and stopped by the manhole that let one into the tank. He held up his flashlight, pointing out that dime's worth of water. I had a steel scraper in my hand, and when he leaned over that manhole, I thought what a sweet setup that was.

I could just bend that scraper over his head, drop him into the tank, put the hatch cover on, then go on deck and give them the high sign to start pumping rubber. There'd be a fuss when the mate turned up missing, but they'd never find him until they emptied the tank, and if I knew the old man, I knew he'd never pump the rubber out of that tank for a dozen mates. And just then Chips stuck his head down the hatch and yelled for Duggs.

Time passed, and we tied up in Brooklyn. I drew my pay and walked down the gangway to the dock. Then I turned and looked back.

From beginning to end that voyage had been plain, un-adulterated hell, yet I hated to leave. When a guy lives on a ship that long, it begins to feel like home no matter how rough it is, and I had no other.

Six months I'd sailed on that packet, good weather and bad. Around the world we'd gone and in and out of some of the tiniest, dirtiest ports in the Far East. I'd helped to paint her from jackstaff to rudder and stood four hours out of every twenty-four at her wheel across three oceans and a half-dozen seas. She was a scummy old barge, but as I stood there looking back, I had to cuss just to keep from feeling bad. Then I walked away.

After that there were other ships and other ports, some good and some bad, but I never forgot Duggs and swore the first time I found him ashore, I'd beat the hell out of him. Every time I'd see that company flag—and they had thirty-odd ships—I'd go hunting for Duggs. I knew that someday I'd find him.

One day in Portland I was walking along with a couple of guys, and I glimpsed that house flag over the top of a warehouse at the dock. Thinks I, now's my chance to get that mug; this will be him.

Sure enough, when I walked down the dock, there he was, giving the last orders before casting off and standing right at the foot of the gangway ready to board. It was now or never. I walked up, all set to cop a Sunday on his chin, and I say, "Remember me?"

He sized me up. "Why, sure! You're Duke, aren't you?" There'd been a time they called me that—among other things.

"That's me. And you—!"

"Well, well!" He was grinning all over. "What do you know about that? We were just talking about you the other day, and we were wondering what had become of you!

"Remember Jones? He's skipper on the *Iron Queen* now, and Edwards—he was third, you'll remember—he's with the Bull Line. They're all scattered now, but that was a good crew, and we came through a lot together. I'll never forget the night you hit that Swede in the Dato Keramat Gardens in Penang! Man, what a wallop that was! I'll bet he's out yet!

"Well," he says then, "I wish we could talk longer. It's like old times to see somebody from the old ship, and we came through, didn't we? We came through some of the roughest weather I ever did see, but we made it! And they say bilgewater is thicker than blood. Well, so long, Duke, and good luck!"

Then Duggs stuck out his mitt, and I'll be damned if I didn't shake hands with him!

THE ADMIRAL

When I was in Shanghai, China, there were a lot of what they called the boat people over there who live on boats all the time. Hundreds of thousands of families that never came ashore at all. They lived on boats, on sampans usually, sometimes on junks, but usually a family would be on a sampan, which is like a small rowboat sculled by one oar in the stern. Usually one part of the boat is covered over. Well, there were a lot of those boats around, they'd come around to the ships begging for food, begging for bamboo, which was wood which they could take and sell. There was one particular boat that we formed an attachment for. There were two women on it, and this little fellow I guess he was about four or five years old. He was a very fat little fellow, kind of pompous, and we got to calling him the Admiral because he always stood in the sampan like he was the commander, like he was in charge.

A FTER I FINISHED painting the hatch-combing, I walked back aft to the well deck where Tony and Dick were standing by the rail looking down into the Whangpoo. The sampan was there again, and the younger woman was sculling it in closer to the ship's side. When she stopped, the old woman fastened a net on the end of a long stick and held it up to the rail, and Tony put some bread and meat into it.

Every day they came alongside at about the same time, and we were always glad to see them, for we were lonely men. The young woman was standing in the stern as always, and when she smiled, there was something pleasant and agreeable about it that made us feel better. The old woman gave the kids some of the bread and meat, and we stood watching them.

Probably they didn't get meat very often, and bread must have been strange to them, but they ate it very seriously. They were our family, and they seemed to have adopted us just as we adopted them when they first came alongside at Wayside Pier. They had come to ask for "bamboo," which seemed to mean any kind of lumber or wood, and for "chow-chow," which was food, of course. The greatest prize was "soapo," but although most of the Chinese who live like that sell the soap or trade it, our family evidently used it—or some of it.

That was one reason we liked them, one reason they had become our family, because they were clean. They wore the faded blue that all the Chinese of that period seemed to wear, but theirs was always newly washed. We had thrown sticks of dunnage to them or other scrap lumber and some that wasn't scrap, but then the mate came by and made us stop.

There were five of them, the two women and three young ones, living in a sampan. Tony had never seen the like, nor had I, but it was old stuff to Dick, who had been out to the Far East before.

He told us lots of the Chinese lived that way, and some never got ashore from birth to death. There is no room for them on China's crowded soil, so in the seemingly ramshackle boats they grow up, rear families, and die without knowing any other home. There will be a fish net on the roof of the shelter of matting, and on poles beyond the roof the family wash waves in the wind. Sometimes the younger children have buoys fastened to their backs so they will float if they fall over the side.

Two of the children in our family were girls. I have no idea how old they were. Youngsters, anyway. We never saw them any closer than from our rail to the sampan. They were queer little people, images of their mother and the old woman but more serious. Sometimes we'd watch them play by the hour when not working, and they would never smile or laugh. But it was the Admiral who was our favorite. We just called him that because we didn't know his name. He was very short and very serious. Probably he was five years old, but he might have been older or younger. He was a round-faced little tyke, and he regarded us very seriously and maybe a little wistfully, for we were big men, and our ship was high above the water.

We used to give them things. I remember when Tony came back from a spree and brought some chocolate with him. While he was painting over the side on a staging, he dropped it to the Admiral, who was very puzzled. Finally he tasted it and seemed satisfied. After that he tasted everything we dropped to him.

Tony had a red silk handkerchief he thought the world of, but one day he gave it to the Admiral. After that, whenever we saw the Admiral, he was wearing it around his head. But he was still very serious and maybe a little prouder.

Sometimes it used to scare me when I thought of them out there on the Whangpoo in the midst of all that shipping. Partly it was because the Chinese had a bad habit: they would wait till a ship was close by and then cut across her bows real sharp. Dick said they believed they could cut off evil spirits that were following them.

There were wooden eyes painted white with black pupils on either side of the bow of each sampan or junk. They were supposed to watch for rocks or evil spirits. Those eyes used to give me the willies, always staring that way, seeming to bulge in some kind of dumb wonder. I'd wake up at night remembering those eyes and wondering where the Admiral was.

But it got Tony more than me. Tony was a hard guy. He was said to have killed a cop in Baltimore and shipped out to get away. I always thought the old man knew, but he never said anything, and neither did the rest of us. It just wasn't any of our business, and we knew none of the circumstances. Something to do with payoffs, we understood.

Tony took to our family as if they were his own flesh and blood. I never saw a guy get so warmed up over anything. He was a tough wop, and he'd always been a hard case and probably never had anybody he could do for. That's what a guy misses when he's rambling around— not somebody to do something for him but somebody to think of, to work for.

One day when we were working over the side on a staging, the sampan came under us, and Tony turned to wave at the Admiral. "Lookit, Duke," he says to me, "ain't he the cute little devil? That red silk handkerchief sure sets him off."

It was funny, you know? Tony'd been a hard drinker, but after our family showed up, he began to leave it alone. After he gave that red silk handkerchief to the Admiral, he just quit drinking entirely, and when the rest of us went ashore, he'd stay aboard, lying in his bunk, making something for the Admiral.

Tony could carve. You'd have to see it to believe how good he was. Of course, in the old days of sail, men aboard ship carved or created all sorts of things, working from wood, ivory, or whatever came to hand. Tony began to carve out a model of our own ship, a tramp freighter from Wilmington. That was the night we left for Hong Kong and just a few hours after the accident.

We had been painting under the stern, hanging there on a plank staging, and it was a shaky business. The stern is always the worst place to paint because the stage is swinging loose underneath, and there isn't a thing to lay hold of but the ropes at either end.

Worse still, a fellow can't see where the ropes are made fast to the rail on the poop deck, and those coolies are the worst guys in the world for untying every rope they see knotted. One time at Taku Bar I got dropped into the harbor that way. But this time it was no trouble like that. It was worse.

We were painting almost overhead when we heard somebody scream. Both of us turned so quickly we had to grab the ropes at either end to keep from falling, and when we got straightened around, we saw the Admiral in the water.

Our family had been coming toward our ship when somehow the Admiral had slipped and fallen over the side, and now there he was, buoyed up by the bladder fastened to his shoulders, the red handkerchief still on his head. Probably that had happened a dozen times before, but this time a big Dollar liner was coming upstream, and she was right abeam of us when the Admiral fell.

And in a minute more he'd be sucked down into those whirling propeller blades.

Then the plank jerked from under my feet, and I fastened to that rope with both hands, and I felt my heart jump with sudden fear. For a minute or so I had no idea what had happened, and by the time I could pull myself up and get my feet on the staging again, Tony was halfway to the Admiral and swimming like I'd seen nobody swim before.

It was nip and tuck, and you can believe it when I say I didn't draw a breath until Tony grabbed the Admiral just as the big liner's stern hove up, the water churning furiously as she was riding high in the water. Tony's head went down, and both he and the Admiral disappeared in the swirl of water that swept out in a wake behind the big liner.

There was a moment there when they were lost in the swirl of water behind the steamer, and then we saw them, and Tony was swimming toward the sampan towing the Admiral, who had both hands on Tony's shoulder.

That night when we slipped down the Whangpoo for Hong Kong, Tony started work on his boat. For we were coming back. We had discharged our cargo and were heading south to pick up more, and by the time we returned, there would be cargo in Shanghai for us.

You'd never guess how much that boat meant to us. All the time we were gone, we thought about our family, and each of us picked up some little thing in Hong Kong or Kowloon to take back to them. But it was the carving of the boat that occupied most of our time. Not that we helped, because we didn't. It was Tony's job, and he guarded it jealously, and none of us could have done it half so well.

We watched him carve the amidships house and shape the ventilators, and we craned our necks and watched when he fastened a piece of wire in place as the forestay. When one of us would go on watch, the mate would ask how the boat was coming. Everybody on the ship from the old man to the black cook from Georgia knew about the ship Tony was carving, and everyone was interested.

Once the chief mate stopped by the fo'c's'le to examine it and offer a suggestion, and the second mate got to telling me about the time his little boy ran his red fire engine into the preacher's foot. Time went by so fast it seemed no time at all till we were steaming back up the Whangpoo again to anchor at Wayside Pier. We were watching for our family long before they could have seen us.

The next morning the boat was finished, and Chips took it down to the paint locker and gave it a coat of paint and varnish, exactly like our own ship; the colors were the same and everything. There wasn't much of a hold, but we had stuffed it with candy. Then we watched for the sampan.

Dick was up on the cross-tree of the mainmast when he saw it, and he came down so fast it was a crying wonder he didn't break a leg. When he hit the deck, he sprinted for the rail. In a few minutes we were all standing there, only nobody was saying anything.

It was the sampan. Only it was bottom up now and all stove in. There wasn't any mistaking it, for we'd have known that particular sampan anywhere even if it hadn't been for the red silk handkerchief. It was there now, a little flag, fluttering gallantly from the wreckage.

THE MAN WHO STOLE SHAKESPEARE

Without any question of doubt, the most exciting city in the world in my lifetime was Shanghai, China. Thirteen flags were flying over Shanghai at that time. I went into a nightclub one night and we counted the uniforms of twenty-nine different armies and navies on the floor at once. The major part of town was called Frenchtown but there was an international section also and there were wonderful nightclubs there and a lot of very fine hotels and some of the best food in the world. You could get a good meal for six cents and you could also get one for six hundred dollars and that was in a time when things were a lot cheaper than they are now. Everybody there was making money. Everybody was on the take.

WHEN I HAD been in Shanghai but a few days, I rented an apartment in a narrow street off Avenue Edward VII where the rent was surprisingly low. The door at the foot of the stairs opened on the street beside a money changer's stall, an inconspicuous place that one might pass a dozen times a day and never notice.

At night I would go down into the streets and wander about or sit by my window and watch people going about their varied business. From my corner windows I could watch a street intersection and an alleyway, and there were many curious things to see, and for one who finds his fellow man interesting, there was much to learn.

Late one afternoon when a drizzle of despondent rain had blown in from the sea, I decided to go out for coffee. Before I reached my destination, it began to pour, so I stepped into a bookstore for shelter.

This store dealt in secondhand books published in several languages and was a jumble of stacks, piles, and racks filled with books one never saw elsewhere and was unlikely to see again. I was hitch-reading from Sterne when I saw him.

He was a small man and faded. His face had the scholarly expression that seems to come from familiarity with books, and he handled them tenderly. One could see at a glance that here was a man who knew a good book when he saw one, with a feeling for attractive format as well as content.

Yet when I glanced up, he was slipping a book into his pocket. Quickly, with almost a sense of personal guilt, I looked toward the clerk, but he was watching the rain. The theft had passed unobserved.

Now, there is a sort of sympathy among those who love books, an understanding that knows no bounds of race, creed, or financial rating. If a man steals a necktie, he is a thief of the worst stripe. If he steals a car, nothing is too bad for him. But a man who steals a book is something else—unless it is my book.

My first thought when he slipped the book into his pocket was to wonder what book he wanted badly enough to steal. Not that there are only a few books worth stealing, for there are many. Yet I was curious. What, at the moment, had captured his interest, this small, gentle-seeming man with the frayed shirt collar and the worn topcoat?

When he left, I walked over to the place where the book

had been and tried to recall what it might have been, for I had only just checked that shelf myself. Then I remembered.

It had been a slim, one-play-to-the-volume edition of Shakespeare. He had also examined Hakluyt's *Voyages*, or at least one volume of the set, Huysmans's *Against the Grain*, and Burton's *Anatomy of Melancholy*.

This was definitely a man I wished to know. Also, I was curious. Which play had he stolen? Was it the play itself he wished to read? Or was it for some particular passage in the play? Or to complete a set?

Turning quickly, I went to the door, and barely in time. My man was just disappearing in the direction of Thibet Road, and I started after him, hurrying.

At that, I almost missed him. He was just rounding a corner a block away, so he had been running, too. Was it the rain or a feeling of guilt?

The rain had faded into a drizzle once more. My man kept on, walking rapidly, but fortunately for me, he was both older than I and his legs were not as long.

Whether he saw me, I do not know, but he led me a lively chase. It seemed scarcely possible for a man to go up and down so many streets, and he obviously knew Shanghai better than I. Yet suddenly he turned into an alley and dodged down a basement stairway. Following him, I got my foot in the door before he could close it.

He was frightened, and I could understand why. In those wilder years they found several thousand bodies on the street every year, and he perhaps had visions of adding his own to the list. Being slightly over six feet and broad in the shoulder, I must have looked dangerous in that dark passageway. Possibly he had visions of being found in the cold light of dawn with a slit throat, for such things were a common occurrence in Shanghai.

"Here!" he protested. "You can't do this!" That I was doing it must have been obvious. "I'll call an officer!"

"And have to explain that volume of Shakespeare in your pocket?" I suggested.

That took the wind out of him, and he backed into the room, a neat enough place, sparsely furnished except for the books. The walls were lined with them.

"Now see here," I said, "you've nothing to worry about. I don't intend to report you, and I'm not going to rob you. I'm simply interested in books and in the books people want enough to steal."

"You're not from the bookstore?"

"Nothing of the kind. I saw you slip the book into your pocket, and although I did not approve, I was curious as to what you had stolen and why." I held out my hand. "May I see?"

He shook his head, then stood back and watched me, finally taking off his coat. He handed me the book from his pocket, which was a copy of *Henry IV,* bound in gray cloth with a thin gold line around the edges. The book was almost new and felt good to the hands. I turned the pages, reading a line or two. "You've a lot of books," I said, glancing at the shelves. "May I look?"

He nodded, then stepped back and sat down. He certainly was not at ease, and I didn't blame him.

The first book I saw was Wells's *Outline of History.* "Everybody has that one," I commented. "Yes," he said hesitantly.

Ibsen was there, and Strindberg, Chekhov, and Tolstoy. A couple of volumes by Thomas Hardy were wedged alongside three by Dostoevsky. There were books by Voltaire, Cervantes, Carlyle, Goldoni, Byron, Verlaine, Baude-laire, Cabell, and Hume.

The next book stopped me short, and I had to look again to make sure the bookshelf wasn't kidding. It was a quaint, old-fashioned, long-out-of-date *Home Medical Advisor* by some Dr. Felix Peabody, published by some long-extinct publisher whose state of mind must have been curious, indeed.

"Where in the world did you get this?" I asked. "It seems out of place stuck in between Hegel and Hudson."

He smiled oddly, his eyes flickering to mine and then away. He looked nervous, and since then I have often wondered what went through his mind at that moment.

Scanning the shelves to take stock of what his interests were, I came upon another queer one. It was between Laurence Sterne's *Sentimental Journey* and George Gissing's *Private Papers of Henry Ryecroft*. It was *Elsie's Girlhood*.

After that I had to sit down. This man was definitely some kind of a nut. I glanced at him, and he squirmed a little. Evidently he had seen my surprise at the placement of some of the books, or the fact that he had them at all.

"You must read a lot," I suggested. "You've a lot of good books here."

"Yes," he said; then he leaned forward, suddenly eager to talk. "It's nice to have them. I just like to own them, to take them in my hands and turn them over and to know that so much that these men felt, saw, thought, and understood is here. It is almost like knowing the men themselves."

"It might be better," I said. "Some of these men were pretty miserable in themselves, but their work is magnificent."

He started to rise, then sat down again suddenly as

though he expected me to order him to stay where he was.

"Do you read a lot?" he asked.

"All the time," I said. "Maybe even too much. At least when I have books or access to them."

"My eyes"—he passed a hand over them—"I'm having trouble with my glasses. I wonder if you'd read to me sometime? That is," he added hastily "if you have the time."

"That's the one thing I've plenty of," I said. "At least until I catch a ship. Sure I'll read to you."

As a matter of fact, he had books here of which I'd heard all my life but had found no chance to read. "If you want, I'll read some right now."

It was raining outside, and I was blocks from my small apartment. He made coffee, and I read to him, starting with *The Return of the Native* for no reason other than that I'd not read it and it was close at hand. Then I read a bit from *Tales of Mean Streets* and some from Locke's *Essay Concerning Human Understanding*.

Nearly every day after that I went to see Mr. Meacham. How he made his living, I never knew. He had some connection, I believe, with one of the old trading companies, for he seemed very familiar with the interior of China and with people there.

The oddity of it appealed to some irony in my sense of humor. A few weeks before I'd been coiling wet lines on the forecastle head of a tramp steamer, and now here I was, reading to this quaint old gentleman in his ill-fitting suit.

He possessed an insatiable curiosity about the lives of the authors and questioned me about them by the hour.

That puzzled me, for a reader just naturally acquires some such knowledge just by reading the book jackets, and in the natural course of events a man can learn a good deal about the personal lives of authors. However, he seemed to know nothing about them and was avid for detail.

There was much about him that disturbed me. He was so obviously alone, seemingly cut off from everything. He wasn't bold enough to make friends, and there seemed to be no reason why anybody should take the trouble to know him. He talked very little, and I never did know where he had come from or how he happened to be in such a place as Shanghai, for he was a contradiction to everything one thinks of when one considers Shanghai. You could imagine him in Pittsburgh, St. Louis, or London, in Glasgow or Peoria, but never in such a place as this.

One day when I came in, I said, "Well, you name it. What shall I read today?"

He hesitated, flushed, then took a book from the shelf and handed it to me. It was *Elsie's Girlhood*, a book of advice to a young girl about to become a woman.

For a minute I thought he was kidding, and then I was sure it couldn't be anything else. "Not today," I said. "I'll try Leacock."

When I remembered it afterward, I remembered he had not seemed to be kidding. He had been perfectly serious and obviously embarrassed when I put him off so abruptly. He hesitated, then put the book away, and when I returned the next day, the book was no longer on the shelf. It had disappeared.

It was that day that I guessed his secret. I was reading at the time, and it just hit me all of a sudden. It left me completely flabbergasted, and for a moment I stared at the printed page from which I was reading, my mouth open for words that would not come.

Yes, I told myself, that had to be it. There was no other solution. All the pieces suddenly fell into place: the books scattered together without plan or style, with here and there books that seemed so totally out of place and unrelated.

That night I read later than ever before.

Then I got a job. Dou Yu-seng offered to keep the rent paid on my apartment (I always suspected he owned the building) while I took care of a little job up the river. I knew but little about him but enough to know of affiliations with various warlords and at least one secret society. However, what I was to do was legitimate.

Yet when I left, I kept thinking of old Mr. Meacham. He would be alone again, with nobody to read to him.

Alone? Remembering those walls lined with books, I knew he would never actually be alone. They were books bought here and there, books given him by people moving away, books taken from junk heaps, but each one of them represented a life, somebody's dream, somebody's hope or idea, and all were there where he could touch them, feel them, know their presence.

No, he would not be alone, for he would remember *Ivan Karmazov*, who did not want millions but an answer to his questions. He would remember those others who would people his memories and walk through the shadows of his rooms: *Jean Valjean, Julien Sorel, Mr. John Oakhurst*, gambler, and, of course, the little man who was *the friend of Napoleon*.

He knew line after line from the plays and sonnets of

Shakespeare and a lot of Keats, Kipling, Li Po, and *Kasidah*. He would never really be alone now.

He never guessed that I knew, and probably for years he had hidden his secret, ashamed to let anyone know that he, who was nearly seventy and who so loved knowledge, had never learned to read.

SHANGHAI,
NOT WITHOUT GESTURES

S HE CAME IN from the street and stood watching the auction, a slender girl with great dark eyes and a clear, creamy complexion. It was raining outside on Kiangse Road, and her shoes were wet. From time to time she shifted uncomfortably and glanced about. Once her eyes met mine, and I smiled, but she looked quickly away, watching the auction.

There was always an auction somewhere, it seemed. One day it might be on Range Road or somewhere along the Route Frelupt, tomorrow in Kelmscott Garden. Household effects, usually, for people were always coming or going. The worlds of international business, diplomacy, and the armed services are unstable, and there is much shifting about from station to station, often without much warning.

I knew none of these people, being an outsider in Shanghai and contented to be so, for a writer, even when a participant, must also be the observer. As yet I was not a writer, only someone wishing to be and endlessly working toward that end.

There were beautiful things to be seen: Soochow curtains, brass-topped tea tables, intricately carved chests of drawers, even sometimes swords or scimitars with jeweled hilts or the handmade guns of long ago. I used to imagine stories about them and wonder what sort of people had owned them before. It wasn't much of a pastime, but they were dark days, and it was all I could afford.

The girl interested me more. Reading or thinking stories is all right, but living them is better. This girl had obviously not come to buy. She had come to get in out of the rain, to find a place to sit down. Probably it was cold in her rooms.

Rooms? No—more likely just one room, a small place with a few simple things. Some worn slippers, a Japanese silk kimono, and on the old-fashioned dresser would be a picture—a man, of course. He would be an army or naval officer, grave and attractive.

By the way she seemed to be moving her toes inside her shoes and bit her lower lip from time to time, I knew she was tired of walking and her feet were sore.

When I tried to move closer to her, she noticed it and got up to go. I was persistent. There was a story here that I knew well. I had often lived it. When she stepped into the rain, I was beside her.

"Wet, isn't it?" I said, hoping to hear her voice, but she hurried on, turning her face away and ignoring me.

"Please," I said, "I'm not being fresh. I'm just lonely. Weren't you ever lonely?"

She started to walk slower and glanced at me. Her eyes were dark and even larger than I had thought. She smiled a little, and she had a lovely mouth. "Yes," she said, "I am often lonely."

"Would you like some coffee?" I suggested. "Or tea? What does one drink in Shanghai?"

"Almost everything," she said, and laughed a little. She seemed surprised at the laugh and looked so self-conscious I knew she was hungry. Once you have been very hungry you know the signs in someone else. It makes you feel very different. "But I would like some coffee," she admitted.

We found a little place several blocks away run by a retired French army officer and his wife. We sat down and looked across the table at each other. Her dark suit was a little shabby but neat, and she was obviously tired. I have become sensitive to such things.

There was the slightest bit of an accent in her voice that intrigued me, but I could not place it. I have heard many accents, but I was younger then, and that was the other Shanghai, before the guns of Nippon blasted Chapei into smoking ruins and destroyed the fine tempo of the life.

"You are new here?" she asked. "You don't belong here?"

"I have just come," I said, "but I belong nowhere."

"Then you must be at home. Nobody belongs in Shanghai. Everyone is either just going or just arriving."

"You?" I suggested.

She shrugged a shoulder. "I am like you. I belong nowhere. Perhaps Shanghai more than anywhere else because it is a city of passersby. Not even the Chinese belong here, because this city was started for Europeans. It was only a mudflat then."

She moved her feet under the table, and I heard them squish. She had been walking a long time, and her feet were soaked.

"I'm part Russian, but I was born in Nanking. My grandfather left Russia at the time of the Revolution, and for a time they lived in Siberia. There was an order for his arrest, and he escaped over the border with his wife and children. She was French. He met her in Paris when he was a military attaché there.

"I am told he had a little money, but he could never seem to find a place, and the money disappeared. My father was an interpreter in Peking and then in Nanking."

She sipped her coffee, and we ordered sandwiches. This time there was money enough, and for once I had more in prospect. "He knew nothing about the Revolution or the tsar's government and cared less. Everyone talked politics in Peking—all the Russians did, at least. So he came to Nanking, where I was born."

"An interesting man. I thought only grand dukes left Russia. What did he do then?"

"My grandfather died and left him whatever there was. For a time we lived very well, and my father drank."

The sandwiches came, and it was several minutes before she touched one, and then a small bite only, which she took a long time chewing. I knew the signs, for when one is hungry, it is the taste one wants. In the movies, when they portray a hungry man, he is always gulping down his food, which is entirely false. It is not at all that way, for when one has been truly hungry for some time, the stomach has shrunk, and one can eat but a little at a time. Only in the days after that first meal can one truly eat, and then there is never enough.

"What did he drink?" I asked.

"Fine old Madeira at first. And port. He would sit in the cafés and talk of Tolstoy and Pushkin or of Balzac. He was a great admirer of Balzac. Father had always wished to become a writer, but he only talked of it. He could never seem to sit down and do it."

"There are thousands like him. If one wishes to be a writer, one shouldn't talk about it, one should do it."

"Then he could not afford such wines. He drank vodka then, and finally samshu or Hanskin."

The decline and fall of a refined palate. "And then he died?"

She nodded, but I had known that it had to be. For a man to sink from fine old Madeira to Hanskin—after that there is nothing to do but die.

Our coffee was finished. I looked into the cup, made a mental calculation, and decided against ordering another. "Shall we go?" I suggested.

The rain had resolved itself into a fine mist, and street-lights were glowing through the fog that was coming in off the river. It would be this way all night. She hesitated, glanced quickly at me, and held out her hand. "I'd better go."

I took her hand. "Why not come with me? It's going to be an unpleasant night." Her eyes met mine, and she looked quickly away. "Why not?" I said. "It isn't all that much of a place, but it's warm."

"All right," she said.

We walked rapidly. It was not going to be a nasty night; it was already one. A taxi skidded around a corner, throwing a shower of spray that only just missed us. A rickshaw passed, going the other way, its curtains drawn. I was glad when we reached the door.

For myself it did not matter. Sometimes I walked for hours in the rain, but she was not dressed warm, and the rain was cold and miserable. The Shanghai streets were not a place to be at night and alone.

My place was warm. My boy was gone. I called him my "number-only" boy. I told him when he took the job he couldn't be the "number-one" boy because there would not be a number two, three, or four.

It was not just a room but a small apartment, pleasant in a way. Drifting men have a way of fixing up almost anyplace they stop to make it comfortable. Seamen often fix things up like any old maid might do and for much the same reason.

Yet the apartment was not mine. I'd been given the use of it by a Britisher who was up-country now. His name was Haig, and he came and went a good deal with no visible means of support, and I was told that he often stayed up-country months at a time. He had been an officer in one of the Scottish regiments, I believe. I had a suspicion that he was still involved in some kind of duty, although he had many weird Asiatic connections.

Some of the books were mine, and it pleased me when she went to the books immediately. It always makes a sucker out of a man who truly loves books to see someone taking a genuine interest in them.

Later, when she came out of the shower wearing my robe, her eyes were very bright. I hadn't realized she was so pretty. We sat by the fire, watching the coals.

"Lose your job?" I asked finally.

"Two weeks ago, and it came at a bad time. My rent was up last week, and there is always a demand for lodgings here. This morning they said not to come back unless I could pay."

"That's tough. What's your line?"

"I've done a lot of things. A secretary, usually. I can handle five languages very well and two others a little. I worked for Moran and Company in Tientsin, and then here for a transport firm, but lately there has been so little business, and the owner has been gambling. I don't know what I'm going to do."

Outside was China. Outside was Shanghai, the old Shanghai when it was an international city. Outside were the millions, of all nationalities: French, English, Japanese, Dutch, German, Sikh, Portuguese, Hebrew, Greek, Malay, and, of course, Chinese. Outside was the Whangpoo, a dark river flowing out of China, out of old China and into the new, then down to the sea. Outside rivers of men flowed along the dark streets, men buying and selling, fighting and gambling, loving and dying. Millions of men, women, and children, opening countless doors, going into lives of which I knew nothing, eating the food of many countries, speaking in tongues I had never heard, praying to many gods.

Listening to her as she spoke of China, I remembered the shuffle of feet in the noontime streets. There was nothing I could do. It was bad for a man to be broke but so much worse for a woman. Especially for such a girl as this.

Perhaps I was a fool, but I, too, had been hungry. Soon there would be a ship, and I would go to Bombay or Liverpool or New York, while she—

"You wouldn't have come had there been any other place to go, would you?"

"No."

A lock of her dark hair had fallen against my robe. It looked good there. So black against the soft white of her throat.

"But I am grateful. What could I have done?"

Well, what? I had a feeling I was going to make a fool of myself. Americans are a sentimental lot, and every cynic is a sentimentalist under the skin. I knew enough about women to be skeptical but had been hungry enough to be human.

A wind moaned about the eaves, and rain dashed against the window.

"Listen," I said, "this isn't quite the sporting thing, is

it? To have you come here because there was nowhere else to go and because I bought you a cup of coffee? Or maybe because of breakfast in the morning? I don't like the sound of it.

"Well, hell, I'm going to sleep on the sofa, and you can have the other room."

After the door closed, I stood looking at it. If she hadn't been so damned lovely it would have been easier to be gallant. Probably right now she was thinking what a sap I was. Well, she wouldn't be the only one.

I had a feeling I was going to be sorry for this in the morning.

OFF THE MANGROVE COAST

I have a very uneasy feeling about ever going to sea again. I don't think I ever would under any circumstances. Because every time I've gone to sea, I've run into a bad storm, a very bad one. On my first trip to sea, I went through one of the worst West India hurricanes they'd had for many, many years. Then another time I was off Florida when a hurricane hit down there and nearly destroyed Miami. I went through a couple of bad typhoons in the China Sea and that part of the world. Then coming back from France on a cruiser, I ran into the worst storm they've had in the Atlantic Ocean in over thirty years. So I'm very hesitant about going to sea anymore, because I think storms follow me.

THERE WERE FOUR of us there, at the back end of creation, four of the devil's own, and a hard lot by any man's count. We'd come together the way men will when on the beach, the idea cropping up out of an idle conversation. We'd nothing better to do, all of us being fools or worse, so we borrowed a boat off the Nine Islands and headed out to sea.

DID YOU EVER cross the South China Sea in a forty-foot boat during the typhoon season? No picnic certainly, nor any job for a churchgoing son; more for the likes of us, who mattered to no one, and in a stolen boat, at that.

Now, all of us were used to playing it alone. We'd worked aboard ship and other places, sharing our labors with other men, but the truth was, each was biding his own thoughts, and watching the others.

There was Limey Johnson, from Liverpool, and Smoke Bassett from Port-au-Prince, and there was Long Jack from Sydney, and there was me, the youngest of the lot, at loose ends and wandering in a strange land.

Wandering always. Twenty-two years old, I was, with five years of riding freights, working in mines or lumber camps, and prizefighting in small clubs in towns that I never saw by daylight.

I'd had my share of the smell of coal smoke and cinders in the rain, the roar of a freight and the driving run-and-catch of a speeding train in the night, and then the sun coming up over the desert or going down over the sea, and the islands looming up and the taste of salt spray on my lips and the sound of bow wash about the hull. There had been nights in the wheelhouse with only the glow from the compass and out there beyond the bow the black, glassy sea rolling its waves up from the long sweep of the Pacific . . . or the Atlantic.

In those years I'd been wandering from restlessness but also from poverty. However, I had no poverty of experience, and in that I was satisfied.

It was Limey Johnson who told us the story of the freighter sinking off the mangrove coast, a ship with fifty thousand dollars in the captain's safe and nobody who knew it was there anymore . . . nobody but him.

Fifty thousand dollars . . . and we were broke. Fifty thousand lying in a bare ten fathoms, easy for the taking. Fifty thousand split four ways. A nice stake, and a nice bit of money for the girls and the bars in Singapore or Shanghai . . . or maybe Paris.

Twelve thousand five hundred dollars apiece . . . if we all made it. And that was a point to be thought upon, for if only two should live . . . twenty-five thousand dollars . . . and who can say what can or cannot happen in the wash of a weedy sea off the mangrove coast? Who can say what is the destiny of any man? Who could say how much some of us were thinking of lending a hand to fate?

Macao was behind us and the long roll of the sea began, and we had a fair wind and a good run away from land before the sun broke upon the waves. Oh, it was gamble enough, but the Portuguese are an easygoing people. They would be slow in starting the search; there were many who might steal a boat in Macao . . . and logically, they would look toward China first. For who, they would ask themselves, would be fools enough to dare the South China Sea in such a boat; to dare the South China Sea in the season of the winds?

She took to the sea, that ketch, like a baby to a mother's breast, like a Liverpool Irishman to a bottle. She took to the sea and we headed south and away, with a bearing toward the east. The wind held with us, for the devil takes care of his own, and when again the sun went down we had left miles behind and were far along on our way. In the night, the wind held fair and true and when another day came, we were running under a high overcast and there was a heavy feel to the sea.

As the day drew on, the waves turned green with white beards blowing and the sky turned black with clouds. The wind tore at our sheets in gusts and we shortened sail and battened down and prepared to ride her out. Never before had I known such wind or known the world could breed such seas. Hour by hour, we fought it out, our poles bare and a sea anchor over, and though none of us were praying men, pray we did.

We shipped water and we bailed and we swore and we worked and, somehow, when the storm blew itself out, we were still afloat and somewhat farther along. Yes, farther, for we saw a dark blur on the horizon and when we topped a wave, we saw an island, a brush-covered bit of sand forgotten here in the middle of nothing.

We slid in through the reefs, conning her by voice and hand, taking it easy because of the bared teeth of coral so close beneath our keel. Lincoln Island, it was, scarcely more than a mile of heaped-up sand and brush, fringed and bordered by reefs. We'd a hope there was water, and we found it near a stunted palm, a brackish pool, but badly needed.

From there, it was down through the Dangerous Ground, a thousand-odd miles of navigator's nightmare, a wicked tangle of reefs and sandy cays, of islands with tiny tufts of palms, millions of seabirds and fish of all kinds . . . and the bottom torn out of you if you slacked off for even a minute. But we took that way because it was fastest and because there was small chance we'd be seen.

Fools? We were that, but sometimes now when the fire is bright on the hearth and there's rain against the windows and the roof, sometimes I think back and find myself tasting the wind again and getting the good old roll of the sea under me. In my mind's eye, I can see the water breaking on the coral, and see Limey sitting forward, conning us through, and hear Smoke Bassett, the mulatto from Haiti, singing a song of his island in that deep, grand, melancholy bass of his.

Yes, it was long ago, but what else have we but memories? For all life is divided into two parts: anticipation and memory, and if we remember richly, we must have lived richly. Only sometimes I think of them, and wonder what would have happened if the story had been different, if another hand than mine had written the ending?

Fools . . . we were all of that, but a tough, ruddy lot of fools, and it was strange the way we worked as a team; the way we handled the boat and shared our grub and water and no whimper from any man.

There was Limey, who was medium height and heavy but massively boned, and Long Jack, who was six-three and cadaverous, and the powerful, lazy-talking Smoke, the strongest man of the lot. And me, whom they jokingly called "The Scholar" because I'd stowed a half-dozen books in my sea bag, and because I read from them, sometimes at night when we lay on deck and watched the canvas stretch its dark belly to the wind. Smoke would whet his razor-sharp knife and sing "Shenandoah," "Rio Grande," or "High Barbaree." And we would watch him cautiously and wonder what he had planned for that knife. And wonder what we had planned for each other.

THEN ONE MORNING we got the smell of the Borneo coast in our nostrils, and felt the close, hot, sticky heat of it coming up from below the horizon. We saw the mangrove coast out beyond the white snarl of foam along the reefs, then we put our helm over and turned east again, crawling along the coast of Darvel Bay.

The heat of the jungle reached out to us across the water and there was the primeval something that comes from the jungle, the ancient evil that crawls up from the fetid rottenness of it, and gets into the mind and into the blood.

We saw a few native craft, but we kept them wide abeam, wanting to talk with no one, for our plans were big within us. We got out our stolen diving rig and went to work, checking it over. Johnson was a diver and I'd been down, so it was to be turn and turn about for us . . . for it might take a bit of time to locate the wreck, and then to get into the cabin once we'd found it.

We came up along the mangrove coast with the setting sun, and slid through a narrow passage into the quiet of a lagoon, where we dropped our hook and swung to, looking at the long wall of jungle that fronted the shore for miles.

Have you seen a mangrove coast? Have you come fresh from the sea to a sundown anchorage in a wild and lonely place with the line of the shore lost among twisting, tangling tentacle roots, strangling the earth, reaching out to the very water and concealing under its solid ceiling of green those dark and dismal passages into which a boat might make its way?

Huge columnar roots, other roots springing from them, and from these, still more roots, and roots descending from branches and under them, black water, silent, unmoving. This we could see, and beyond it, shutting off the mangrove coast from the interior, a long, low cliff of upraised coral.

Night then . . . a moon hung low beyond a corner of the coral cliff . . . lazy water lapping about the hull . . . the mutter of breakers on the reef . . . the cry of a night bird, and then the low, rich tones of Smoke Bassett, singing.

So we had arrived, four men of the devil's own choosing, men from the world's waterfronts, and below us, somewhere in the dark water, was a submerged freighter with fifty thousand dollars in her strongbox.

Four men . . . Limey Johnson—short, powerful, tough. Tattooed on his hands the words, one to a hand, *Hold— Fast.* A scar across the bridge of his nose, the tip of an ear missing . . . greasy, unwashed dungarees . . . and stories of the Blue Funnel boats. What, I wondered, had become of the captain of the sunken ship, and the others who must have known about that money? Limey Johnson had offered no explanation, and we were not inquisitive men.

And Long Jack, sprawled on the deck looking up at the stars? Of what was he thinking? Tomorrow? Fifty thousand dollars, and how much he would get of it? Or was he thinking of the spending of it? He was a thin, haggard man with a slow smile that never reached beyond his lips. Competent, untiring . . . There was a rumor about Macao that he had killed a man aboard a Darwin pearl fisher. . . . He was a man who grew red, but not tan, with a thin, scrawny neck like a buzzard, as taciturn as Johnson was talkative. Staring skyward from his pale gray eyes . . . at what? Into what personal future? Into what shadowed past?

Smoke Bassett, powerful tan muscles, skin stretched taut to contain their slumbering, restless strength. A man with magnificent eyes, quick of hand and foot . . . a dangerous man.

And the last of them, myself. Tall and lean and quiet, with wide shoulders, and not as interested in the money. Oh, yes, I wanted my share, and would fight to have it, but there was more than the money: there was getting the money; there was the long roll of the ketch coming down the China Sea; there was the mangrove coast, the night and the stars; there were the boat sounds, the water sounds . . .

a bird's wing against the wind . . . the distant sounds of
the forest . . . these things that no man can buy; these
things that get into the blood; these things that build the
memories of tomorrow, the hours to look back upon.

I wanted these more than money. For there is a time for
adventure when the body is young and the mind alert and
all the world seems there for one's hands to use, to hold,
to take. And this was my new world, this ancient world
of the Indies, these lands where long ago the Arab seamen came, and where the Polynesians may have passed,
and where old civilizations slumber in the jungles, awaiting the explorations of men. Where rivers plunge down
massive, unrecorded falls, where the lazy sea creeps under
the mangroves, working its liquid fingers into the abys-
mal darkness where no man goes or wants to go.

What is any man but the total of what he has seen?
The sum of what he has done? The strange foods, the
women whose bodies have merged with his, the smells,
the tastes, the longings, the dreams, the haunted nights?
The Trenches in Shanghai, Blood Alley, Grant Road in
Bombay, and Malay Street in Singapore . . . the worst of
it, and the best . . . the temples and towers built by lost,
dead hands, the nights at sea, the splendor of a storm,
the dancing of dust devils on the desert. These are a
man . . . and the solid thrill of a blow landed, the faint
smell of opium, rubber, sandalwood, and spice, the stink
of copra . . . the taste of blood from a split lip.

Oh, yes, I had come for things other than money, but
that evening, for the first time, no man gave another good
night.

Tomorrow there would be, with luck, fifty thousand
dollars in this boat . . . and how many ways to split it?

No need to worry until the box was aboard, or on the line, being hoisted. After that, it was every man for himself. Or was I mistaken? Would we remain friends still? Would we sail our boat into Amurang or Jesselton and leave it there and scatter to the winds with our money in our pockets?

That was the best way, but with such men, in such a place, with that amount of money . . . one lives because one remains cautious . . . and fools die young.

AT THE FIRST streaks of dawn, I was out of my blankets and had them rolled. While Smoke prepared breakfast, we got the diving outfit up to the side. We were eating when the question came.

"I'll go," I said, and grinned at them. "I'll go down and see how it looks."

They looked at me, and I glanced up from my plate and said, "How about it, Smoke? Tend my lines?"

He turned to me, a queer light flicking through his dark, handsome eyes, and then he nodded.

A line had been drawn. . . .

A line of faith and a line of doubt . . . Of the three, I had chosen Smoke Bassett, had put in him my trust, for when a man is on the bottom, his life lies in the hands of the man who tends his lines. A mistaken signal, or a signal ignored, and the diver can die.

I had given my life to Smoke Bassett, and who could know what that would mean?

JOHNSON WAS TAKING soundings, for in these waters, chart figures were not to be trusted. Many of the shores have been but imperfectly surveyed, if at all, and there is constant change to be expected from volcanic action, the growth of coral, or the waves themselves.

When we anchored outside the reef, I got into the diving dress. Limey lent me a hand, saying to me, "Nine or ten fathoms along the reef, but she drops sharp off to fifty fathoms not far out."

Careful . . . we'd have to be careful, for the enemies of a diver are rarely the shark or the octopus, but rather the deadline and constant danger of a squeeze or a blowup. The air within the suit is adjusted to the depth of the water and its pressure, but a sudden fall into deeper water can crush a man, jamming his entire body into his copper helmet. Such sudden pressure is called a squeeze.

A blowup is usually caused by a jammed valve, blowing a man's suit to almost balloon size and propelling him suddenly to the surface, where he lies helpless until rescued. While death only occasionally results from a blowup, a diver may be crippled for life by the dreaded "bends," caused by the sudden change in pressure, and the resulting formation of nitrogen bubbles in the bloodstream.

When the helmet was screwed on, Limey clapped me on the top and I swung a leg over to the rope ladder. Smoke Bassett worked the pump with one arm while he played out the hose and rope. Up—down. *Chug-chug.* A two-stroke motion like a railroad handcar. It didn't take much energy but each stroke was a pulse of oxygen . . . like a breath, or the beating of your heart. The big mulatto grinned at me as he worked the handle.

Clumsy, in the heavy shoes and weighted belt, I climbed down and felt the cool press of water rise around me. Up my body . . . past my faceplate.

It was a slow, easy descent . . . down . . . down . . . and on the bottom at sixty feet.

In the dark water, down where the slow weeds wave in the unstirring sea . . . no sound but the *chug-chug-chug* of the pump, the pump that brings the living air . . . down in a green, gray, strange world . . . cowrie shells . . . a big conch . . . the amazing wall of the reef, jagged, broken, all edges and spires . . . a stonefish, all points and poison.

Leaning forward against the weight of the water, I moved like some ungainly monster of the deep, slowly along the bottom. Slowly . . . through the weeds, upon an open sand field beneath the sea . . . slowly I walked on.

A dark shadow above me and I turned slowly . . . a shark . . . unbelievably huge . . . and seemingly uninterested . . . but could you tell? Could one ever know?

Smell . . . I'd heard old divers say that sharks acted upon smell . . . and the canvas and rubber and copper gave off no smell, but a cut, a drop of blood in the water, and the sharks would attack.

Chug-chug-chug . . . I walked on, turning slowly from time to time to look around me. And the shark moved above me, huge, black, ominous . . . dark holes in the reef where might lurk . . . anything. And then I saw . . . something.

A blackness, a vast deep, opening off to my right, away from the reef. I looked toward it, and drew back. Fifty fathoms at some places, but then deeper, much deeper. Fifty fathoms . . . three hundred feet.

A signal . . . time for me to go up. Turning, I walked slowly back and looked for the shark, but he had gone. I had failed to hold his interest . . . and I could only hope that nothing in my personality would induce him to return.

When the helmet was off, I told them. "Probably the other way. But when you go down, Limey, keep an eye open for that shark. I don't trust the beggar."

ON THE THIRD day, we found the hulk of the freighter. At the time, I was below, half asleep in my bunk. Bassett was in the galley cooking, and only Long Jack was on deck, handling the lines for Limey. Dozing, I heard him bump against the vessel's side and I listened, but there was nothing more, only a sort of scraping, a sound I could not place, as if something were being dragged along the hull.

When I heard the weighted boots on the deck, I rolled over and sat up, kicking my feet into my slippers. Johnson was seated on the rail and his helmet was off and Long Jack was talking to him. When they heard my feet on the deck, they turned. "Found it!" Limey was grinning his broken-toothed smile. "She's hanging right on the lip of the deep. She's settin' up fairly straight. You shouldn't have much trouble gettin' the box."

THERE WAS A full moon that night, wide and white, a moon that came up over the jungle, and standing by the rail, I looked out over the lagoon and watched the phosphorescent combers roll up and crash against the outer reef. When I had been standing there a long time, Smoke Bassett walked over.

"Where's Limey?"

"Fishin'," he said, "with a light."

"Tomorrow," I said, "we'll pick it up."

"Anson Road would look mighty good now. Anson Road, in Singapore . . . an' High Street. You know that, Scholar?"

"It'll look better with money in your pocket."

"Look good to me just anyway." Smoke rolled a cigarette. "Money ain't so important."

We watched the moon and listened to the breakers on the reef. "You be careful down there," Smoke Bassett told me suddenly. "Mighty careful." He struck a match and lit his cigarette, as he always did, one-handed.

Lazily, I listened to the sea talking to the reef and then listened to the surf and to the jungle beyond the line of mangroves. A bird shrieked, an unhappy, uncanny sound.

"Them two got they heads together," Smoke Bassett said. "You be careful."

Long Jack . . . a queer, silent man around whom one never felt quite comfortable. A taciturn man with a wiry strength that could be dangerous. Only once had we had words and that had been back in Macao when we first met. He had been arrogant, as if he felt he could push me around. "Don't start that with me," I told him.

His eyes were snaky, cold, there were strange little lights in them, and contempt. He just looked at me. I didn't want trouble so I told him, "You could make an awful fool of yourself, Jack."

He got up. "Right now," he said, and stood there looking at me, and I know he expected me to take water.

So, I got up, for this was an old story, and I knew by the way he stood that he knew little about fistfighting, and then a fat man, sitting in a dirty singlet and a blue dungaree coat, said, "You *are* a fool. I seen the kid fight in Shanghai, in the ring. He'll kill you."

Long Jack from Sydney hesitated and it was plain he no longer wanted to fight. He still stood there, but I'd seen the signs before and knew the moment was past.

He'd had me pegged for a kid who either couldn't or wouldn't go through.

That was all, but Long Jack had not forgotten, I was sure of that. There had been no further word, nor had we talked much on the trip down the China Sea except what was necessary. But it had been pleasant enough.

The next morning when I got into the suit, Limey came up to put on the copper helmet. There was a look in his eyes I didn't like. "When you get it out of the desk," he said, "just tie her on the line and give us a signal."

But there was something about the way he said it that was wrong. As I started into the water, he leaned over suddenly and stroked his hand down my side. I thought he wanted something and turned my faceplate toward him, but he just stood there so I started down into the water.

When I was on the deck of the freighter, I started along toward the superstructure and then saw something floating by my face. I stepped back to look and saw it was a gutted fish. An instant, I stood there staring, and then a dark shadow swung above me and I turned, stumbled, and fell just as the same huge shark of a few days before whipped by, jaws agape.

On my feet, I stumbled toward the companionway, and half fell through the opening just as the shark twisted around and came back for another try.

And then I knew why Limey Johnson had been fishing, and what he had rubbed on my arm as I went into the water. He had rubbed the blood and guts of the fish on my suit and then had dumped it into the water after me to attract the shark.

Sheltered by the companionway, I rubbed a hand at my

sleeve as far around as I could reach, trying to rub off some of the blood.

Forcing myself to composure, I waited, thinking out the situation.

Within the cabin to the right, I had already noticed that the door of the desk compartment that held the cash box stood open to the water. That meant the money was already on our boat; it meant that the bumping I'd heard along the side had been the box as it was hoisted aboard. And that letting me go down again, rubbing the blood and corruption on my sleeve had been a deliberate attempt at murder.

Chug-chug-chug . . . monotonously, reassuringly, the steady sound of the pump reached me. Smoke was still on the job, and I was still safe, yet how long could I remain so under the circumstances?

If they had attempted to kill me they would certainly attempt to kill Smoke, and he could not properly defend himself, even strong as he was, while he had to keep at least one hand on the pump. Outside, the shark circled, just beyond the door frame.

Working my way back into the passage, I fumbled in the cabin, looking for some sort of weapon. There was a fire ax on the bulkhead outside, but it was much too clumsy for use against so agile a foe, even if I could strike hard enough underwater. There was nothing. . . . Suddenly I saw on the wall, crossed with an African spear of some sort, a whaler's harpoon!

Getting it down, I started back for the door, carefully freeing my lines from any obstructions.

Chug . . . chug . . . chug . . .

The pump slowed, almost stopped, then picked up slowly again, and then something floated in the water, falling slowly, turning over as I watched, something that looked like an autumn leaf, drifting slowly down, only much larger.

Something with mouth agape, eyes wide, blood trailing a darkening streamer in the green water . . . It was Long Jack, who had seen the last of Sydney. . . . Long Jack, floating slowly down, his belly slashed and an arm cut across the biceps by a razor-edged knife.

An instant I saw him, and then there was a gigantic swirl in the water, the shark turning, doubling back over, and hurling himself at the body with unbelievable ferocity. It was my only chance; I stepped out of the door and signaled to go up.

There was no response, only the *chug-chug-chug* of the pump. Closing my valve only a little, I started to rise, but desperately as I tried, I could not turn myself to watch the shark. Expecting at any moment that he would see me and attack, I drifted slowly up.

Suddenly the ladder hung just above me, although the hull was still a dark shadow. I caught the lower step and pulled myself slowly up until I could get my clumsy feet on the step. Climbing carefully, waiting from moment to moment, I got to the surface and climbed out.

Hands fumbled at the helmet. I heard the wrench, and then the helmet was lifted off.

Smoke Bassett had a nasty wound over the eye where he had been struck by something, and where blood stained his face it had been wiped and smeared. Limey Johnson was standing a dozen feet away, only now he was drawing back, away from us.

He looked at the harpoon in my hands and I saw him wet his lips, but I said nothing at all. Bassett was helping

me out of the helmet, and I dared not take my eyes from
Johnson.

His face was working strangely, a grotesque mask of
yellowish-white wherein the eyes seemed unbelievably
large. He reached back and took up a long boat hook.
There was a driftwood club at my feet, and this must have
been what had struck Bassett. They must have rushed
him at first, or Long Jack had tried to get close, and had
come too close.

When I dropped the weight belt and kicked off the
boots, Smoke was scarcely able to stand. And I could see
the blow that had hit him had almost wrecked the side of
his face and skull. "You all right? You all right, Scholar?"
His voice was slurred.

"I'm all right. Take it easy. I'll handle it now."

Limey Johnson faced me with his new weapon, and
slowly his courage was returning. Smoke Bassett he had
feared, and Smoke was nearly helpless. It was Limey and
me now; one of us was almost through.

Overhead the sun was blazing. . . . The fetid smell of
the mangroves and the swamp was wafted to the ketch
from over the calm beauty of the lagoon. The sea was
down, and the surf rustled along the reef, chuckling and
sucking in the holes and murmuring in the deep caverns.

Sweat trickled into my eyes and I stood there, facing
Limey Johnson across that narrow deck. Short, heavy,
powerful . . . a man who had sent me down to the foulest
kind of death, a man who must kill now if he would live.

I reached behind me to the rail and took up the harpoon. It was razor-sharp.

His hook was longer . . . he outreached me by several
feet. I had to get close . . . close.

In my bare feet, I moved out away from Smoke, and

Limey began to move warily, watching for his chance, that ugly hook poised to tear at me. To throw the harpoon was to risk my only weapon, and risk it in his hands, for I could not be sure of my accuracy. I had to keep it, and thrust. I had to get close. The diving dress was some protection but it was clumsy and I would be slow.

There was no sound . . . the hot sun, the blue sky, the heavy green of the mangroves, the sucking of water among the holes of the coral . . . the slight sound of our breathing and the rustle and slap of our feet on the deck.

He struck with incredible swiftness. The boat hook darted and jerked back. The hook was behind my neck, and only the nearness of the pole and my boxer's training saved me. I jerked my head aside and felt the thin sharpness of the point as it whipped past my neck, but before I could spring close enough to thrust, he stepped back and, bracing himself, he thrust at me. The curve of the hook hit my shoulder and pushed me off balance. I fell back against the bulwark, caught myself, and he lunged to get closer. Three times he whipped the hook and jerked at me. Once I almost caught the pole, but he was too quick.

I tried to maneuver . . . then realized I had to get outside of the hook's curve . . . to move to my left, then try for a thrust either over or under the pole. In the narrow space between the low deckhouse and the rail there was little room to maneuver.

I moved left, the hook started to turn, and I lunged suddenly and stabbed. The point just caught him . . . the side of his singlet above the belt started to redden. His face looked drawn, I moved again, parried a lunge with the hook, and thrust again, too short. But I knew how to fight him now . . . and he knew, too.

He tried, and I parried again, then thrust. The harpoon point just touched him again, and it drew blood. He stepped back, then crossed the deck and thrust at me under the yard. His longer reach had more advantage now, with the deckhouse between us, and he was working his way back toward the stern. It was an instant before I saw what he was trying to do. He was getting in position to kill Bassett, unconscious against the bulwark beside the pump.

To kill . . . and to get the knife.

I lunged at him then, batting the hook aside, feeling it rip the suit and my leg as I dove across the mahogany roof of the deckhouse. I thrust at him with the harpoon. His face twisted with fear, he sprang back, stepped on some spilled fish guts staining the deck. He threw up his arms, lost hold of the boat hook, and fell backward, arms flailing for balance. He hit the bulwark and his feet flew up and he went over, taking my harpoon with him . . . a foot of it stuck out his back . . . and there was an angry swirl in the water, a dark boiling . . . and after a while, the harpoon floated to the surface, and lay there, moving slightly with the wash of the sea.

THERE'S A PLACE on the Sigalong River, close by the Trusan waters, a place where the nipa palms make shade and rustle their long leaves in the slightest touch of wind. Under the palms, within sound of the water, I buried Smoke Bassett on a Sunday afternoon. . . . Two long days he lasted, and a wonder at that, for the side of his head was curiously crushed. How the man had remained at the pump might be called a mystery . . . but I knew.

For he was a loyal man; I had trusted him with my lines, and there can be no greater trust. So when he was gone, I buried him there and covered over the grave with coral rock and made a marker for it and then I went down to the dinghy and pushed off for the ketch.

SOMETIMES NOW, WHEN there is rain upon the roof and when the fire crackles on the hearth, sometimes I will remember: the bow wash about the hull, the rustling of the nipa palms, the calm waters of a shallow lagoon. I will remember all that happened, the money I found, the men that died, and the friend I had . . . off the mangrove coast.

THE *DANCING KATE*

In one of my most interesting periods, I was down for a while in Indonesia working on a schooner. I was on the books as second mate, but actually I was functioning as supercargo as well—a seagoing bookkeeper, in other words. The captain, who also owned the ship, could barely read and write, so I used to keep track of all the sales and purchases that he made on the boat. We spent almost a year in the East Indies, moving around from place to place, usually going to all the small ports, Gorontalo and Amurang and Makassar and over to Timor and Ternate. I don't think there was anywhere in the Indies that Douglas hadn't been. It was an exciting time.

He was a man with no education, but he probably knew as much of anthropology as anybody I ever ran across. He learned it by dealing with the natives himself. For example, we went up the Fly River in New Guinea one time, left the schooner tied up, and took an outboard motor and a dugout canoe and went on up to a lake where he was doing some trading and we traded with some natives up there who had gold in quills. They'd hollow a quill and put little gold flakes in it and that was the way we'd buy it. He'd come to the East Indies when he was fifteen. He was sixty-five when I knew him and he'd had his own boat for about twenty-five years, not the one I was on but another and then this one.

I spent a lot of time with him because I'd stand the twelve-to-four watch at night and he'd usually come up

on deck part of the time, because being an officer on a
boat was a new job for me, you know, though I was an
able-bodied seaman, and we had very good native sea-
men aboard. He would stay up there and talk with me by
the hour. I used to copy information out of the logbook
and I used a lot of it in writing stories later.

———

IT WAS A strip of grayish-yellow sand caught in the
gaunt fingers of the reef like an upturned belly except
here and there where the reef had been longest above the
sea. Much of the reef was drying, and elsewhere the broken teeth of the coral formed ugly ridges flanked by a few
black, half-submerged boulders.

At one end of the bar the stark white ribs of an old
ship thrust themselves from the sand, and nearby lay the
rusting hulk of an iron freighter. It had been there more
than sixty years.

For eighteen miles in a northeast and southwest direction the reef lay across the face of the Coral Sea—at its
widest, no more than three miles but narrowing to less
than a mile, a strip of jagged coral and white water lost
in the remote emptiness of the Pacific. The long dun
swells of the sea hammered against the outer rocks, and
overhead the towering vastness of the sky became a shell
of copper with the afternoon sun.

At the near end of the bar, protected from the breaking
seas in all but a hurricane, a hollow of rock formed a
natural cistern. In the bottom were a few scant inches of
doubtful water. Beside it, he squatted in torn dungarees
and battered sneakers.

"Three days," he estimated, staring into the cistern,

eyes squinting against the surrounding glare. "Three days if I'm careful, and after that I'm washed up."

After that—thirst. The white, awful glare of the tropical sun, a parched throat, baking flesh, a few days or hours of delirium, and then a long time of lying wide-eyed to the sky before the gulls and the crabs finished the remains.

He had no doubt as to where he was. The chart had been given him in Port Darwin and was worn along the creases, but there was no crease where this reef lay, hence no doubt of his position. He was sitting on a lonely reef, avoided by shipping, right in the middle of nowhere. His position was approximately 10°45' S, 155°51' E.

The nearest land was eighty-two miles off and it might as well have been eighty-two thousand.

It started with the gold. The schooner on which he had been second mate had dropped anchor in Bugoiya Harbor, but it was not fit anchorage, so they could remain only a matter of hours. He was on the small wharf superintending the loading of some cargo when a boy approached him.

He was a slender native boy with very large, beautiful eyes. When the boy was near him, he spoke, not looking at him. "Man say you come. Speak nobody."

"Come? Come where?"

"You come. I show you."

"I'm busy, boy. I don't want a girl now."

"No girl. Man die soon. He say *please*, you come?"

Dugan looked at his watch. They were loading the last cargo now, but they would not sail for at least an hour.

"How far is it?"

"Ten minutes—you see."

A man was dying? But why come to him? Still, in these

islands odd things were always happening, and he was a curious man.

The captain was coming along the wharf, and he walked over to him. "Cap? Something's come up. This boy wants to take me to some man who is dying. Says not to say anything, and he's only ten minutes away."

Douglas glanced at the boy, then at his watch. "All right, but we've less than an hour. If we leave before you get back, we'll be several days at Woodlark or Murua or whatever they call it. There's a man in a village who is a friend of mine. Just ask for Sam. He will sail you over there."

"No need for that. I'll be right back."

Douglas glanced at him, a faint humor showing. "Dugan, I've been in these islands for fifty years. A man never knows—never."

Misima, although only about twenty miles long and four or five miles wide, was densely wooded, and the mountains lifted from a thousand to three thousand feet, and as the south side was very steep, most of the villages were along the northern shore.

The boy had walked off and was standing near a palm tree idly tossing stones into the lagoon. Taking off his cap, Dugan walked away from the wharf, wiping the sweat from his brow. He walked back from the shore and then turned and strolled toward the shade, pausing occasionally. The boy had disappeared under the trees.

At the edge of the trees Dugan sat down, leaning his back against one. After a moment a stone landed near his foot, and he glimpsed the boy behind a tree about thirty yards off. Dugan got up, stretched, and hands in his pockets, strolled along in the shade, getting deeper and deeper until he saw the boy standing in a little-used path.

They walked along for half a mile. Dugan glanced at his watch. He would have to hurry.

Suddenly the boy ducked into the brush, holding a branch aside for him. About thirty yards away he saw a small shanty with a thin column of smoke lifting from it. The boy ran ahead, leading the way.

There was a young woman there who, from her looks, was probably the boy's mother. Inside, an old man lay on an army cot. His eyes were sunken into his head, and his cheeks were gaunt. He clutched Dugan's hand. His fingers were thin and clawlike. "You must help me. You are with Douglas?"

"I am."

"Good! He is honest; everybody knows that of him. I need your help." He paused for a minute, his breathing hoarse and labored. "I have a granddaughter. She is in Sydney." He put his hand on a coarse brown sack under his cot. "She must have this."

"What is it?"

"It is gold. There are men here who will steal it when I die. It must go to my granddaughter. You take it to her, and you keep half. You will do this?"

Sydney? He was not going to Sydney; still, one could sell it and send the money to Sydney. The old man pressed a paper into his hand. "Her name and address. Get it to her—somehow. You can do it. You will do it."

"Look," he protested, "I am not going to Sydney. When I leave Douglas, I'm going to Singapore and catch a ship for home—or going on to India."

"You must! They will steal it. They have tried, and they are waiting. If they think you have it, they will rob you. I know them."

"Well." He hesitated. He had to be getting back.

Douglas's appointment at Woodlark was important to him. He would wait for no man in such a case, least of all for me, who had been with him only a few weeks, the man thought. "All right, give me the gold. I've little time."

The woman dragged the sack from under the cot, and he stooped to lift it. It was much heavier than it appeared. The old man smiled. "Gold is always heavy, my friend. Too heavy for many men to bear."

Dugan straightened and took the offered hand; then he walked out of the shack, carrying the gold.

It *was* heavy, though once aboard the schooner it would be no problem. He glanced at his watch and swore. He was already too late, and the tide—

When he reached the small harbor, it was too late. The schooner was gone!

He stood, staring. Immediately he was apprehensive. He was left on an island with about two dozen white people of whom he knew nothing and some fifteen hundred natives of whom he knew less. Moreover, there was always a drifting population, off the vessels of one kind or another that haunt Indonesian seas.

Woodlark was eighty miles away. He knew that much depended on the schooner's being there in time to complete a deal for cargo that otherwise would go to another vessel. He had been left behind. He was alone.

A stocky, bearded man approached. He wore dirty khakis and a watch cap, and the khaki coat hung loose. Did he have a gun? Dugan would have bet that he had.

From descriptions, he was sure he knew the man.

"Looks like they've gone off and left you," he commented, glancing at the sack.

"They'll be back."

"Douglas? Don't bet on it. He calls in here about once every six months. Sometimes it's a whole year."

"It's different this time," he lied. "He's spending about three months in the Louisiades and Solomons. He expects to be calling in here three or four times, so I'll just settle down and wait."

"We could make a deal," the man said. "I could sail you to the Solomons." He jerked his head. "I've got a good boat, and I often take the trip. Come along."

"Why? When he's coming back here?"

Deliberately, the man turned his back and walked away. Zimmerman—this would be Zimmerman.

At the trade store they told him where he could find Sam, and he found him, a wiry little man with sad blue eyes and thin hair. He shook his head. "I have to live here."

"Douglas said—"

"I can imagine. I like Douglas. He's one of the best men in the islands, but he doesn't live here. I do. If you get out of here, you'll do it on your own. I can tell you something else. Nobody will take the chance. You make a deal with them, or you wait until Douglas comes back."

Twice he saw the boy watching him. Dugan started back. He'd have to see the old man, and packing that gold was getting to be a nuisance.

When he got back to the shack, the woman was at the door, mashing something in a wooden dish. "He's dying," she said. "He hasn't talked since you left."

"Who is it?" The voice was very weak.

He went inside and told the old man he would have to leave his gold. The schooner was gone, and he had no way to get to Woodlark and overtake her.

"Take my boat," he said.

His eyes closed, and nothing Dugan said brought any response. And Dugan tried. He wanted to get away, but he wanted no more of his gold. From Sam's manner he knew Zimmerman was trouble, very serious trouble.

The woman was standing there. "He is dying," she said. "He has a boat?"

She pointed and he walked through the trees to the shore. It was there, tied up to a small dock. It wasn't much of a boat, and they'd make a fit pair, for he wasn't much of a sailor. His seamanship had been picked up on freighters and one tanker, and his time in sail was limited to a few weeks where somebody else was giving orders. He'd done one job of single handing with a small boat and been shot with luck. On one of the most dangerous seas he had experienced nothing but flying-fish weather all the way. Still, it was only eighty miles to Woodlark, and if the weather remained unchanged, he'd be all right. If—

The boy was there. "Three of them," he said, "three mans—very bad mans." And then he added, "They come tonight, I think."

So how much of a choice did he have? He left at dark or before dark, or he stayed and took a chance on being murdered or killing somebody himself. Anyway, the sea was quiet, only a little breeze running, and eighty miles was nothing. The best way to cope with trouble was to avoid it.

The only thing between where he was and Woodlark were the Alcesters. He had sailed by them before and would know them when he saw them.

He glanced down at the boy. "I'll leave the boat on Woodlark."

The boy shrugged. "Wherever."

He had shoved off at sundown with a good breeze

blowing, and even with his caution he made good time, or what was good time for him. He had the Alcesters abeam before daybreak, but there was a boat behind him that was coming on fast. His silhouette was low, so he lowered the sail a little to provide even less and gradually eased the helm over and slid in behind one of the Alcesters.

It was nearing daylight, but suddenly it began to grow darker, and the wind began blowing in little puffs, and there was a brief spatter of rain. He was running before the wind when the storm came, and from that time on it was sheer panic. On the second or third day—he could not remember which—he piled up on the reef, a big wave carrying the boat over into the lagoon, ripping the hull open somewhere en route.

When daylight came again, the storm was blowing itself out; the boat was gone but for a length of broken mast and a piece of the forward section that contained a spare sail, some line, and some odds and ends of canned goods. And the gold.

He had saved the gold.

Dawn was a sickly thing on that first morning, with the northern sun remote behind gray clouds. He made his way along the reef, avoiding the lacerating edges of the coral until he reached the bar.

The old freighter, one mast still standing and a gaping hole in her hull, was high and dry on the sandbar. A flock of gulls rose screaming into the air as he approached, and he walked over the soft sand into the hole.

The deck above him was solid and strong. Far down there was a hatch, its cover stove in, which allowed a little light at the forward end. Here all was secure. Sand had washed in, making a hard-packed floor. Dugan put down a tin of biscuits and the few cans he had brought along and went back outside.

It was just one hundred and fifty steps to the water of the lagoon and the hollow in the reef where rain had collected in the natural cistern. The hollow in the reef was just three feet deep and about the size of a washtub. It was half full, and the water, although fresh, was warm.

For the moment he had food, shelter, and water.

Gathering driftwood, of which there was a good bit, he built a shade over the cistern that would prevent a too rapid evaporation but could be removed when it rained.

There would be fish, shellfish, and crabs. For a time there might be eggs, and the first thing he must do would be to cover the reef, as much of it as he could reach, and see what he could find that was useful. Then he must get a fragment of that torn canvas and make a pennant to fly from the mast of the wrecked ship.

The work kept him busy. Scrambling over the reef, careful not to slip into a hole or break an ankle on the rough, often slippery rock, he gathered driftwood. Slowly the several piles grew.

At night he sat beside his fire in the hulk and ate fish and a biscuit.

After a while he lost all awareness of the sea. It was there, all around him, and it was empty. Occasionally, when his eyes strayed that way, he saw distant smoke. He rarely looked at the sack of gold.

For the first time he deliberately faced his situation. From his pocket he took the worn chart, but he did not need it to face the fact. The reef was a lonely, isolated spot in the Coral Sea, in an area where ships came but rarely. Aside from the sandbar itself there was only the ruffled water and a few black stumps of coral rising above it.

This was no place for a man. It was a place for the wind and the gulls, yet there was a little water, there was a little food, and while a man lived, there was always a chance. It was then that he looked up and saw the schooner.

It was tacking, taking a course that would bring it closer to the reef. He shouted and waved a hand, and somebody waved back. He turned and walked toward the wreck.

When the dinghy came in close to pick him up, he waded out and lifted his bag of gold into the boat. Then he climbed in. There were two men in the dinghy, and they stared at him. "My—my water—it was about gone. You came just in time."

The men stared at the sack, then at him. The place where the sack rested against the thwart had dented the sack. Only sand or flour or something of the kind would make such an impression. And the sack had been heavy. He couldn't say it was shells or clothing. They'd know he lied.

Yet it was not until he came alongside the schooner that he realized how much trouble he had bought for himself. He glanced at the schooner's name and felt a chill.

The *Dancing Kate.*

Bloody Jack Randall's schooner. Of course, he was never called Bloody Jack to his face, but behind his back they knew him by that name. He had killed a man in a saloon brawl at Port Moresby. There'd been a man shot in Kalgoorlie, but insufficient evidence released Randall. He was reported to have broken jail in New Caledonia after killing a guard.

After he was aboard, it was Randall's mate, a lean,

wiry man with haggard features, who kicked the sack. "Hey? What you got in there? It looks mighty heavy."

"Gold."

It was a sullen, heavy day with thick clouds overhead and a small sea running. Kahler's eyes went to the sack again. "Gold?" He was incredulous.

"Yes." He slid his knife into his hand, point toward them, cutting edge uppermost. "This weighs about a pound. I measured the weight by this, and it is more than they thought."

"They?"

"A man in Misima asked me to deliver it to his granddaughter in Sydney."

"What kind of a damned fool would do that?" Kahler asked.

"A man who knew who he could trust." He glanced at Randall. "Where you bound?"

Randall hesitated. "East," he said finally. "We been scouting around."

"How about Woodlark? I'll pay my passage."

"All right." Randall walked forward and gave the change of course to the Bugi seaman. There were four of the Bugis, some of the best sailors among the islands; there was Randall himself, Kahler, and the big man who rowed the boat. That would be Sanguo Pete, a half-caste.

Taking his sack, he walked forward and sat down with his back against the foremast.

Kahler came forward. "We'll have chow pretty quick. One of those Bugis is a first-rate cook." He glanced down at him. "How'd you survive on that reef? You must be tough."

"I get along."

"By this time they probably figure you're dead," Kahler said.

"Maybe."

He knew what they were thinking. If something happened to him now, no one would know any better. Well, he promised himself, nothing was going to happen. He was going to meet Douglas at Woodlark.

When they went below to eat, he let them go first. He paused for a moment near one of the Bugi seamen. His Indonesian was just marketplace talk, but he could manage. He indicated the sack. "It is a trust," he said, "from a dying man. He has a granddaughter who needs this." He gestured toward the reef. "The sea was kind," he said.

"You are favored," the Bugi replied.

"If there is trouble—?"

"We are men of the sea. The troubles of white men are the troubles of white men."

He went below. There was a plate of food at the empty place. Randall had not begun to eat. Coolly, before Randall could object, he switched plates with him.

"What's the matter?" Randall demanded. "Don't you trust me?"

"I trust nobody," he said. "Nobody, Mr. Randall."

"You know me?"

"I know you. Douglas told me about you."

They exchanged glances. "Douglas? What do you know about him?"

"I'm his second mate. I'm joining him at Woodlark. Then we'll arrange to get this"—he kicked the sack—"to that girl in Sydney."

"Why bother?" Kahler said. "A man could have himself a time with that much gold."

"And it will buy that girl an education."

"Hell! She'll get along—somehow."

The food was good, and when supper was over, he took his gold and went on deck. Randall was a very tough, dangerous man. So were the others, and it was three to one. He could have used Douglas or Hildebrand. Or Charlie—most of all, Charlie.

The sails hung slack, and the moon was out. There was a Bugi at the wheel, another on lookout in the bow. These were tricky, dangerous waters, much of them unsurveyed. He settled himself against the mainmast for a night of watching.

The storm that had wrecked his boat had blown him east, far off his course. It could be no less than a hundred miles to Misima and probably a good bit more.

The hours dragged. A light breeze had come up, and the vessel was moving along at a good clip. The moon climbed to the zenith, then slid down toward the ocean again. He dozed. The warmth of the night, the easy motion of the schooner, the food in his stomach, helped to make him sleepy. But he stayed awake. They, of course, could sleep by turns.

He was only half awake when they closed in on him. At one moment he had been thinking of what he'd heard about them, and he must have dozed off, for they closed in quickly and silently. Some faint sound of bare feet on the deck must have warned him even as they reached for him.

He saw the gleam of starlight on steel, and he ripped up with his knife. The man pulled back sharply, and his blade sliced open a shirt, and the tip of his knife drew a red line from navel to chin, nicking the chin hard as the man drew back.

Then he was on his feet. Somebody struck at him with

a marlin spike, and he parried the blow with his blade and lunged. The knife went in; he felt his knuckles come up hard against warm flesh, and he withdrew the knife as he dodged a blow at his head.

The light was bad, for them as well as for him, and one might have been more successful than three; as it was, they got in each other's way in the darkness. The man he had stabbed had gone to the deck, and in trying to crawl away, tripped up another.

He had his gun but dared not reach for it. It meant shifting the knife, and even a moment off guard would be all they would need.

One feinted a rush. The man on the deck was on his feet, and they were spreading out. Suddenly they closed in. The half-light was confusing, and as he moved to get closer to one man, he heard another coming in from behind. He tried to turn, but a belaying pin caught him alongside the skull. Only a glancing blow, but it dazed him, and he fell against the rail. He took a cut at the nearest man, missed but ripped into another. How seriously, he did not know. Then another blow caught him, and he felt himself falling.

He hit the water and went down. When he came up, the boat was swinging. The Bugi at the wheel was swinging the bow around. As the hull went away from him, the bow came to him, and there were the stays. He grabbed hold and pulled himself up to the bowsprit.

For a moment he hung there, gasping for breath. He could see them peering over the rail.

"Did you get him, Cap?"

"Get him? You damned right I did! He's a goner." He turned then. "You cut bad, Pete?"

"I'm bleedin'. I got to get the blood stopped."

"He got me, too," Kahler said. "You sure we got him?"

Randall waved at the dark water. "You don't see him, do you? We got him, all right."

After a moment they went below, and the tall yellow seaman at the wheel glanced at the foremast against the sky, lined it up with his star. His expression did not change when he saw Dugan come over the bow and crouch low.

There was no sound but the rustle of bow wash, the creak of rigging, and a murmur of voices aft. He moved aft, exchanging one glance with the Bugi, and when he was close enough, he said, "Thanks." Not knowing if the man understood, he repeated, *"Terima kasih."*

He knew the Bugi had deliberately put the rigging below the bowsprit in his way. The wonder was that even with the distraction of the fighting Randall had not noticed it.

His gun was still in the side pocket of his pants, and he took it out, struggling a bit to do so, as the dungarees were a tight fit. He put the gun in his hip pocket where it was easier of access. He did not want to use a gun, and neither did they. Bullet scars were not easy to disguise and hard to explain when found on rails or deckhouses.

Sanguo Pete loomed in the companionway and stood blinking at the change from light to darkness. There was a gash on his cheekbone that had been taped shut, and there was a large mouse over one eye. He hitched up his dungarees and started forward, a gun strapped to his hips. He had taken but two steps when he saw Dugan crouched close to the rail.

Pete broke his paralysis and yelled, then grabbed for his gun. It was too late to think about the future questions. As Pete's hand closed on the butt, Dugan shot him.

Randall loomed in the companionway, but all he saw was the wink of fire from Dugan's gun. He fell forward, half on deck.

Pete lay in the scuppers, his big body rolling slightly with the schooner.

The Bugi looked at Dugan and said, "No good mans."

"No good," Dugan agreed.

One by one he tilted them over the side and gave them to the sea.

"My ship is waiting at Woodlark Island," Dugan said.

The Bugi glanced at him. "Is Cap'n Douglas ship. I know." Suddenly he smiled. "I have two brother on your ship—long time now."

"Two brothers? Well, I'll be damned!"

Kahler was lying on the bunk when he went below. His body had been bandaged, but he had lost blood.

"We're going to Woodlark," Dugan said. "If you behave yourself, you might make it."

Kahler closed his eyes, and Dugan lay down on the other bunk and looked up at the deck overhead. The day after tomorrow—

It would be good to be back aboard, lying in his own bunk. He remembered the brief note in the Pilot Book for the area.

This coral reef, discovered in 1825, lies about 82 miles east-northeast of Rossel Island. The reef is 18 miles in length, in a northeast and southwest direction. The greatest breadth is 3 miles, but in some places it is not more than a mile wide. At the northeastern end of the reef there are some rocks 6 feet high. No anchorage is available off the reef.

Wreck. The wreck of a large iron vessel above water lies (1880) on the middle of the southeastern side of the reef.

If they wanted to know any more, they could just ask him. He'd tell them.

GLORIOUS! GLORIOUS!

I sailed some on foreign ships. Not much, but I had to get from place to place sometimes. One of my worst experiences was shipping out on a Greek ship. I shipped out of Bombay and was headed for France, for Marseilles, and I jumped ship and hid in Arabia. I either had to jump ship or kill half the crew or get killed myself so I left ship there. It was a misbegotten crew from all the ports of the world, you know, and I had a very rough time.

———

THE FOUR MEN crouched together in the narrow shadow of the parapet. The sun was setting slowly behind a curtain of greasy cloud, and the air, as always at twilight, was very clear and still. A hundred and fifty yards away was the dirty gray earth where the Riffs were hidden. The declining sun threw long fingers of queer, brassy light across the rise of the hill behind them.

On their left the trench was blown away by artillery fire; here and there a foot or a shoulder showed above the dirt thrown up by explosions. They had marched, eaten, and fought beside those men, dead now.

"Better keep your head away from that opening, kid, or you'll get it blown away."

Dugan pulled his head back, and almost on the instant a spout of sand leaped from the sandbag and splattered over his face.

Slim smiled wryly, and the Biscayan looked up from

the knife he was sharpening. He was always sharpening his knife and kept it with a razor edge. Short, thick-bodied, he had a square-jawed, pockmarked face and small eyes. Dugan was glad they were fighting on the same side.

"You got anything to eat?" Slim asked suddenly, looking over at Dugan.

"Nothing. I ate my last biscuit before that last attack," he said. "I could have eaten forty."

"You?" Slim looked at the Irishman.

Jerry shrugged. "I ate mine so long ago I've forgotten." He was bandaging his foot with a soiled piece of his shirt. A bullet had clipped the butt of his heel the day before, making a nasty wound.

Somewhere down the broken line of trenches there was a brief volley followed by several spaced rifle shots, then another brief spatter of firing.

Slim was wiping the dust from his rifle, testing the action. Then he reloaded, taking his time. "They're tough," he said, "real tough."

"I figured they'd be A-rabs or black," Jerry said, "and they ain't either one."

"North Africa was never black," Dugan said. "Nearly all the country north of the Niger is Berber country, and Berbers are white. These Riffs—there's as many redheaded ones as in Scotland."

"I was in Carthage once," Slim said. "It's all busted up—ruins."

"They were Semitic," Dugan said. "Phoenicians originally."

"How you know so much about it?" Slim asked.

"There was a book somebody left in the barracks all about this country and the Sahara."

"You can have it," Jerry said. "This country, I mean."

"Book belonged to that colonel—the fat one." Dugan moved a small stone, settled himself more comfortably. "He let it lay one time, and somebody swiped it."

"Hey!" Jerry sat up suddenly. He held the bandage tight to survey the job he was doing, then continued with it. "That reminds me. I know where there's some wine."

Slim turned his long neck. "Some *what?*"

He looked gaunt and gloomy in his dirty, ill-fitting uniform. One shoulder was stained with blood, and the threads had begun to ravel around a bullet hole. He had been hit nine times since the fighting began, but mostly they were scratches. He'd lost one shoe, and the foot was wrapped in canvas. It was a swell war.

Jerry continued to wrap his foot, and nobody said anything. Dugan watched him, thinking of the wine. Then he looked across at the neat row of men lying side by side near the far parapet. As he looked, a bullet struck one of them, and the body jerked stiffly. It did not matter. They were all dead.

"Over there in the cellar," Jerry said. He nodded his head to indicate a squat gray stone building on the peak of a conical hill about a quarter of a mile off. "The colonel found a cellar the monks had. He brought his own wine with him and a lot of canned meat and cheese. He stored it in that cellar—just like in an icebox. I helped pack some of it in not over two weeks ago. He kept me on patrol duty three days extra just for breaking a bottle. He brought in a lot of grub, too."

The Biscayan glanced up, mumbling something in Spanish. He pulled a hair from his head and tested the edge of the blade, showing his teeth when the hair cut neatly.

"What's he say?"

"He says it may still be there." Jerry shifted his rifle and glanced speculatively at the low hill. "Shall we have a look?"

"They'd blow our heads off before we could get there," Slim protested, "night or no night."

"Look," Jerry said, "we're liable to get it anyway. This is going to be like Annual, where they wiped them all out. Look how long we've been here and no relief. I think they've written us off."

"It's been seventy-five days," Dugan agreed.

"Look what happened at Chentafa. The officer in command saw they'd had it and set fire to the post; then he died with his men."

"That's more than these will do."

"Hell," Jerry said, "I think they're already dead. I haven't seen an officer in a week. Only that corporal."

"They pick them off first. Those Moors can shoot." Slim looked at Dugan. "How'd you get into this outfit, anyway?"

"My ship was in Barcelona. I came ashore and was shanghaied. I mean an army patrol just gathered in a lot of us, and when I said I was an American citizen, they just paid no attention."

"Did you get any training?"

"A week. That was it. They asked me if I'd ever fired a gun, and like a damned fool I told them I had. Hell, I grew up with a gun. I was twelve years old before I found out it wasn't part of me. So here I am."

"They wanted men, and they didn't care where or how they got them. Me, I've no excuse," Slim said. "I joined the Spanish Foreign Legion on my own. I was broke, hungry, and in a different country. It looked like an easy way out."

Far off to the left there was an outburst of firing, then silence.

"What happened to the colonel? The fat one who had all that wine brought in?"

"Killed himself. Look, they tell me there's a general for every twenty-five men in this army. This colonel had connections. They told him spend a month over there and we'll promote you to general, so he came, and then we got pinned down, and he couldn't get out. From Tetuan to Chaouen there's a whole line of posts like this one here at Seriya. There's no way to get supplies, no way to communicate."

The talk died away. It was very hot even though the sun was setting.

A big Russian came up and joined them. He looked like a big schoolboy with his close-cropped yellow hair and his pink cheeks. "They come," he said.

There was a crackle of shots, and the four climbed to their feet. Dugan lurched from weariness, caught himself, and faced about. The Russian was already firing.

A long line of Moors was coming down the opposite slope, their advance covered by a barrage of machine-gun fire from the trenches farther up the hill. Here and there a captured field gun boomed. Dugan broke open a box of cartridges and laid them out on a sandbag close at hand. Slowly and methodically, making each shot count, he began to fire.

The Biscayan was muttering curses and firing rapidly. He did not like long-range fighting. Jerry leaned against the sandbags, resting his forehead on one. Dugan could see a trickle of sweat cutting a trail through the dust.

Somewhere down the parapet one of their own machine guns opened up, the gray and white line before them melted like wax, and the attack broke. Slim grounded his rifle butt and leaned against the sandbags, fumbling for a cigarette. His narrow, cadaverous features looked yellow in the pale light. He looked around at Dugan. "How d'you like it, kid? Had enough?"

Dugan shrugged and reloaded his rifle, then stuffed his pockets with cartridges. The powder smoke made his head ache, or maybe it was hunger and the sound of guns. His cheek was swollen from the rifle stock, and his gums were sore and swollen. All of them were indescribably dirty. For seventy-five days they had held the outpost against a steady, unrelenting, consistent, energy-draining attack that seemed to take no thought of men lost. Their food was gone; only a little of the brackish water remained, and there would be no relief.

"They've written us off," Slim said. "We're dead." He was hollow-eyed and sagging, yet he was still a fighting man. He looked at Jerry. "How about that wine?"

"Let's go get it. There's a machine gun there, too, and enough ammo to fight the Battle of the Marne."

"Does the sergeant major know?"

"He did." Jerry indicated the line of dead bodies. "He's over there."

"Who's in command?" Dugan asked.

"Maybe nobody. The lieutenant was killed several days ago, shot from behind. He was a fool to hit that Turk. He slugged one guy too many."

The sun was gone, and darkness was falling over the low hills. There was no movement in the trenches across the way. The Russian stood up, then sat down abruptly, his throat shot away. He started to rise again, then just sat back down and slowly rolled over.

Slim picked him up as though he were a child and carried him to the line of bodies, placing him gently on the ground. Then he unbuckled his cartridge pouches and hung them around his own waist. Dugan looked through an opening in the sandbagged parapet at the broad shoulders of shadow along the slope. A dead Moor hung head down over the barbed wire about fifty feet away, and a slight breeze made his burnoose swell.

When it was dark, the corporal came along the trench. He looked old. His thin, haggard face was expressionless. He said what they all knew.

"There won't be any relief. I think everything behind us is wiped out, too. We wouldn't stand a chance in trying to get away. They're out there waiting, hoping we try it.

"There'll be at least one night attack, but with daybreak they'll come. There's thirty-eight of us left. Fire as long as you can, and when they get through the wire, it's every man for himself."

He looked around vacantly, then started back up the line. His shoes were broken, and one leg was bandaged. He looked tired. He stopped suddenly, looking back. "If any of you have the guts to try it, go ahead." He looked from Jerry to Slim, then at Dugan. "We're through."

Slim walked over to the dead officer and took his automatic, then the cartridges for it. He took some money, too, then dropped it into the sand. Having a second thought, he picked it up.

"If a man could get away," he said, looking over at Dugan, "this would pay a boatman. Gibraltar—that would be the place."

Dugan sat down, his back to the parapet. He glanced along the trench. Far down he could see movement.

Thirty-eight left! There had been 374 when they occupied the post. He tilted his head back and looked at the stars. They had looked the same way at home. How long ago was that?

Jerry got up. He glanced at Slim, and the Texan shrugged. "Let's go," he said. And they went.

Jerry pointed. "We'll go down that shallow place, and there's a ditch. Follow that to the right and it takes you right up to the building. If we get into that ditch, we've got it made."

There was no moon, but the stars were bright. The rear parapet had been partly knocked down by the explosion of a shell. They went over fast, Jerry first, then Dugan. Flat on their faces, they wormed across the dark ground, moving fast but silently. The ground was still hot. In the darkness his hand touched something warm. It was a gun, an automatic. He thought of Slim and felt suddenly sick; then he remembered the sergeant who had been killed out here a few days before. He took the gun but turned at right angles. The Biscayan was close behind him, his knife in his teeth, his rifle lying across his forearms.

Dugan heard a slight movement and looked up suddenly into the eyes of a Moor. For a split second they both stared, and then Dugan jerked his rifle forward, and the muzzle struck the Moor right below the eye. The Moor rolled back and then came up, very fast, with a knife. Dugan kicked him on the kneecap, then hit him with the butt and followed with the barrel. He went down, but another loomed up.

There was a scream as the Biscayan ripped one up, and then Slim broke into the fight with an automatic. Then there was a roar of shots from all along the parapet. It was the expected night attack, sooner than believed and almost successful.

Dugan came up running, saw a Moor loom up before him, and shot without lifting the rifle above his belt line. The Moor spun out of the way and fell, and Dugan fell into the ditch just one jump ahead of the Biscayan. Then Slim and Jerry joined them. Jerry was carrying three rifles and a bandoleer of cartridges.

They went along the ditch at a stumbling run. Dugan slipped once and almost fell, but when he straightened up, the stone house was looming above them. Jerry led them to the trapdoor at the end of the ditch.

The room was empty except for a desk and a couple of chairs. One chair was tipped on its side, and there were papers scattered about. The room had a musty smell, as the door and windows were heavily shuttered and barred. Both openings could be covered by rifles from the trenches below, and as the position was not a good one, the Moors had not taken it.

Jerry dragged the heavy desk aside and struck a match to find the iron ring concealed in a crack. With a heave he opened the cellar. In the flare of the match Dugan saw that Jerry's scalp was deeply lacerated and dried blood matted his hair on one side.

Slim slid into the hole and a moment later was handing up bottles. Then he sent up a magnum of champagne, and the Biscayan came up with some canned fruit and cheese.

"This guy had a taste for knickknacks," Slim said. "There's everything down here that you could get into a can."

"He took three hot ones right through the belly on the first day," Jerry said. "He was scared and crying like a baby. I don't believe he'd ever done a day's duty in his life."

Dugan took a bottle of Château Margaux and a can of the cheese. The wine tasted good. After a bit he crawled into a corner, made a pillow of some cartridge pouches, and went to sleep. When he awakened, light was filtering into the room from around the shutters. Jerry was sitting wide-legged near the cellar door, and he was drunk. Slim was at the desk.

"Kid," Slim said, "come here."

He had a map laid out. "See? If you get the chance, take the ditch to here, then down along that dry creek. It's not far to the coast, and most of those boat guys will give you a lift for money. You got any money?"

"About twenty bucks. I've been hiding it in case."

"Here." Slim took the money he'd taken from the dead officer. "You take this."

"What about you?"

"I ain't goin' to make it, kid. I got a hunch. If I do, we'll go together. If you board that boat, they may take your rifle, but you keep your sidearm, you hear? Keep it hidden. You may need it before you get across."

He turned to look at Dugan. "How old are you, kid?"

"Twenty-two," Dugan said, and he lied. He was just past sixteen.

"You look younger. Anyway, go through their pockets, whoever's dead. They won't mind, and you'll need whatever there is.

"Don't go near the army or a big town. Head for the seacoast and stay out of sight. Anybody you meet out here will try to stop you. Don't let it happen. You get away—you hear?"

Jerry lifted the bottle in a toast. "Tomorrow we die!" he said.

"Today, you mean," Slim said.

The Biscayan came up from the cellar with a machine gun. It was brand-spanking-new. He went down again and came up with several belts of ammo, then a box of them. He set the machine gun up at a shuttered window and fed a belt into it.

Dugan looked at the automatic he had picked up. It was in good shape. He found another in the cellar and several spare clips. He loaded them.

Scattered shooting broke into a steady roar. A shell exploded not too far away.

Slim had found two Spanish versions of the Colt pistols and loaded them. He strapped them on, pleased. "You know what I'm going to do? I'm going to get good and drunk, and then I'm going to open that door and show them how we do it down in Texas!"

He emptied half a bottle of the wine and looked at Dugan. "You ever been in Texas, kid?"

"I worked on a ranch there—in the Panhandle."

"I grew up on a ranch," Slim said. "Rode for a couple of outfits in New Mexico before I started out to see the world. I knew this would happen sometime. Just never figured it would be here, in a place like this."

He picked up the bottle of wine and looked at it. "What I need is some tequila. This here is a she-male's drink! Or some bourbon an' branch water."

Dugan took his rifle and walked to the window. He helped the Biscayan move the machine gun to a more advantageous position, a little closer, a little more to the left. He checked his rifle again and loaded two more and stood them close by. From a crack in the shutters he studied the route he might get a chance to take. It must be done before the whole country was overrun by the Moors.

Suddenly Jerry moved, the dried blood still caked in

his stubble of beard. He crawled on hands and knees to the edge of the trapdoor from the ditch. Then he stopped, breathing hoarsely, waiting.

Dugan had heard nothing above the occasional rattle of distant rifle fire as the Riffs began to mop up. Suddenly the trapdoor began to lift, very cautiously, then with more confidence. When it had lifted about a foot, a big Riff thrust his head up and stared into the room. All the occupants were out of his immediate range, and he lifted his head higher, peering into the semidarkness. In that instant Jerry swung the empty magnum. The solid *bop* of the blow was loud in the room, and the man vanished, the door falling into place. Jerry jerked it open, slammed it back, and leaped down into the hole. There was a brief scuffle, and then Jerry came back through the trapdoor, carrying a new rifle and a bandoleer.

Now the crescendo of firing had lifted to a loud and continuous roar, and Slim started to sing. In the tight stone room his voice boomed loudly.

Glorious! Glorious!
One keg o' beer for the four of us!
Glory be to heaven that there isn't
Ten or 'leven,
For the four of us can drink it all alone!

The Biscayan took down the bar and threw the shutters wide. Below them and away across the tawny hill the Riffian trench was suddenly vomiting up a long line of men. From behind the parapet before them a scattering fire threw a pitiful challenge at the charging line.

Dugan wiped the sweat from his eyebrows and leaned against the edge of the window. He was sagging with incredible exhaustion, and his body stank from the unwashed weeks, the sweat and the dirt. He lifted the rifle and held it against his swollen cheek and began to fire.

Behind him Jerry and Slim were singing "Casey Jones." Dugan looked down at the Biscayan, a solid chunk of man who lived to fight. Hunched behind the machine gun, he waited, watching the line as an angler watches a big fish approaching the hook.

Suddenly the firing stopped, waiting for a killing volley at close quarters.

Dugan had stopped, too. One man, a tall Moor on a fine-looking horse, had ridden out on a point a good six hundred yards away, watching the attack. He stood in his stirrups, lifting a hand to shout a command, unheard at the distance. For what seemed a long minute Dugan held his aim, then squeezed off the shot, and the man stood tall in his stirrups, then fell from the saddle to the dust and lay there. Then the Biscayan opened fire.

Dugan looked down at him, aware for the first time that the Biscayan was drunk. The gray line melted before him, and the Biscayan lifted the bottle for another drink.

The unexpected fire from the stone house, cutting a wide swath in their ranks, paralyzed the attack. Then a bunch of the Riffs broke away from the main attack and started toward the stone house. Jerry was up, firing slowly, methodically. Suddenly the machine gun swung, fired three short bursts, and the bunch of attackers melted away. From behind the parapet came a wavering cheer. Dugan winced at the few voices. So many were gone!

Dugan squinted his eyes against the sun, remembering the line of silent men beside the parapet and the big Russian with the schoolboy pink in his cheeks.

The Biscayan lifted his bottle to drink, and it shattered

in his hand, spilling wine over him. With a lurid burst of Spanish he dropped the neck of the bottle and reached for another. And he had never been a drinking man.

Slim sat on the floor, muttering. "I'm goin' to get damn good an' drunk an' go out there and show 'em how we do it down in Texas."

He started to rise and sat down hard, a long red furrow along his jaw. He swore in a dull, monotonous voice.

Dugan saw the line of Moors sweep forward and across the parapet. There was scattered shooting, some rising dust, then silence. He blinked, feeling a lump in his throat. He had known few of them, for they had been together too short a time. Only weeks had passed since he lay in his bunk aboard ship, feeling the gentle roll as it steamed west from Port Said.

The sunlight was bright and clear. Outside, except for the scattered bodies of the slain, all was quiet and peaceful under the morning sun. Dugan looked across the valley, thinking of what he would do. There was little time. Perhaps time had already run out.

The afternoon was waning before they attacked again. This time they were careful, taking advantage of the slight roll of the hill to get closer. The last hundred yards was in the open, and they seemed unaware of the ditch, which would be hidden from them until they were almost fallen into it.

Dugan's face was swollen and sore from the kick of the rifle. He was hot and tired, and he switched rifles again.

A single shot sounded, lonely against the hills, and something gasped beside him. He turned to see Jerry fall across the sill. Before he could pull him back, three more bullets chugged into his body.

"Kid," Slim said, "you better go. It's time."

He took the bar down from the door and looked down the sunlit hill. A knot of Moors was coming toward him, good men, fighting men, dangerous men. Slim stepped out with a pistol in each hand and started down toward them.

He was drunk. Magnificently, roaring drunk, and he had a pistol in either hand. "I'm a-goin' to show them how we do it down in Texas!" He opened fire, then his body jerked, and he went to his knees.

Dugan snapped a quick shot at a Moor running up with a rifle ready to fire, and then Slim got up. He had lost one gun, but he started to fire from waist level. His whole left side was bloody.

Dugan turned to yell at the Biscayan, but the man was slumped across his machine gun. He had been shot between the eyes.

Dugan pushed him away from the gun and swung it toward the front of the house. In the distance, against the pale-blue sky, above the heat waves dancing, a vulture swung in slow circles against the sky. Slim was down, all sprawled out, and the enemy was closing in.

He pointed the gun toward them and opened up, singing in a hoarse, toneless voice.

> Glorious! Glorious!
> One keg o' beer for the four of us!
> Glory be to heaven that there isn't
> Ten or 'leven,
> For the four of us can drink it all alone!

His belt went empty, and the hill was bare of all but the bodies. He got up and closed the heavy plank door.

He caught up a bandoleer and another pistol. Then he dropped through the trapdoor.

All was still. He stepped over the dead Moor and went out into the shadowed stillness of the ditch.

And then he began to run.

BY THE RUINS OF
EL WALARIEH

FROM THE HILLSIDE above the ruins of El Walarieh one could watch the surf breaking along the shore, and although the grass was sparse, thin goats grazed among the occasional clumps of brushwood high on the hill behind me. It was a strange and lonely coast, not without its own wild beauty.

Three times I had been there before the boy approached. He was a thin boy with large, beautiful eyes and smooth brown skin. He squatted beside me, his shins brown and dirty, looking curiously toward the sea, where I was looking.

"You sit here often?"

"Yes, very often."

"You look at something?"

"I look at the sea. I look at the sea and the shore, sometimes at the clouds." I shifted my position a little. "It is very beautiful."

"Beautiful?" He was astonished. "The sea is beautiful?" He looked again to be sure that I was not mildly insane.

"I like the sea, and I like to look at those ruins and to wonder who lived there, and what their lives were like."

He glanced at the ancient, time-blackened ruins. "They are no good, even for goats. The roofs have fallen in. Why do you look at the sea and not at the goats? I think the goats are more beautiful than the sea. Look at them!"

I turned my head to please him. There were at least

fifty, and they browsed or slept upon the hillside above me. They were white against the green of the hill. Yes, there was beauty there, too. He seemed pleased that I agreed with him.

"They are not my goats," he explained, "but someday I shall own goats. Perhaps as many as these. Then you will see beauty. They shall be like white clouds upon the green sky of the hillside."

He studied the camera that lay on the grass near my feet. "You have a machine," he said. "What is it for?"

"To make pictures. I want to get pictures of the sea and the ruins."

"Of the goats, too?"

To please him, I agreed. "Yes, also of the goats."

The idea seemed to satisfy him, yet he was obviously puzzled, too. There was something he did not understand. He broached the idea to me, as one gentleman to another. "You take pictures of the sea and the ruins . . . also of the goats. Why do you take these?"

"To look at them. To catch their beauty."

"But why a picture?" He was still puzzled. "They are here! You can see them without a picture. The sea is here, the sky, the ruins . . . the goats, too. They are always here."

"Yes, but I shall not always be here. I shall go away, and I want them to remember, to look at many times."

"You need the machine for that? I can remember. I can remember all of the goats. Each one of them." He paused, thinking about it. "Ah! The machine then is your memory. It is very strange to remember with a machine."

Neither of us spoke for a few minutes. "I think you have machines for many things. I would not like that."

The following day I was back on the hillside. It had not

been my plan to come again, yet somehow the conversation left me unsatisfied. I had the feeling that somehow I'd been bested. I wanted the goatherd to understand.

When he saw me sitting there, he came down the hillside. He saluted me gravely, then sat down. I handed him a cigarette, and he accepted it gravely. "You have a woman?" he asked.

"No."

"What, no woman? It is good for a man to have a woman."

"No doubt." He was, I thought, all of thirteen. "You have a woman?" I asked the question gravely.

He accepted it in the same manner. "No. I am young for a woman. And they are much trouble. I prefer the goats."

"They are no trouble?"

He shrugged. "Goats are goats."

The comment seemed to explain much. He smoked in silence, and I waited for him to speak again. "If I had a woman, I would beat her. Women are good when beaten often, but they are not so productive as goats."

It was a question I did not wish to debate. He seemed to have all the advantage in the argument. He undoubt edly knew goats, and spoke of women with profound wisdom. I knew neither goats nor women.

"If you like the hillside," he said at last, "why do you not stay? The picture will be no good. It will be the sea and the ruins only at one time, and they are not always the same. They change," he added.

"My home is elsewhere. I must go back."

"Then why do you leave? Is it not good there? I think you are very restless." He looked at me. "Have you goats at home?"

"No." I was ashamed to admit it, feeling that the confession would lower me in his esteem. "I have no goats."

"A camel?" He was giving me every chance.

"No," I confessed reluctantly, "no camel." Inspiration hit me suddenly. "I have horses. Two of them."

He considered that. "It is good to have a horse, but a horse is like a woman. It is unproductive. If you have a horse or a woman, you must also have goats."

"If one has a woman," I ventured, "one must have many goats."

He nodded. I had but stated a fact.

WHERE THERE'S FIGHTING

During World War II, at the very beginning of it, I went through Officers Training School and I began training troops down at El Campo, Texas. While I was there I was training a lot of boys from cities and farms and whatnot and I was wondering how these boys would do when they got in face-to-face with gunfire and were actually being shot at. I needn't have worried. All of them did what they had to do. There is a lot of quality in people and I dislike very much the talk about ordinary people or the common man; there is no such thing.

All men are uncommon in some respect or another. I saw men under great pressure and in all kinds of circumstances of terror and of fear and of war and of struggle. I've seen men you'd call the common man react in very uncommon and unordinary ways and some of them rise to the occasion just beautifully and you never know who that man is going to be. Sometimes many of them will. And nearly always there's somebody who emerges as sort of a leader too. . . .

THE FOUR MEN were sprawled in a cuplike depression at the top of the pass. From where the machine gun was planted it had a clear field of fire for over four hundred yards. Beyond that the road was visible only at intervals. By a careful watch of those intervals an enemy could be seen long before he was within range.

A low parapet of loose rock had been thrown up along the lip of the depression, leaving an aperture for the .30-caliber gun. Two of the men were also armed with rifles.

It was very still. The slow warmth of the morning sun soaked into their bones and ate the frost away, leaving them lethargic and pleased. The low rumble as of thunder in the far-off hills were the bombs over Serbia, miles away.

"Think they'll ever come?" Benton asked curiously.

"They'll come," Ryan said.

"We can't stop them."

"No."

"How about some coffee? Is there any left?"

Ryan nodded. "It'll be ready soon. The part that's coffee is done, the part that's chicory is almost done, and the part that's plain bean is doing."

Benton looked at the two who were sleeping in the sun. They were mere boys. "Shall we wake them?"

"Pretty soon. They worry too much. Especially Pommy. He's afraid of being afraid."

"Sackworth doesn't. He thinks we're bloody heroes. Do you?"

"I'd feel heroic as blazes if I had a shave," Ryan said. "Funny, how you like being shaved. It sets a man up somehow."

Pommy turned over and opened his eyes. "I say, Bent? Shall I spell you a bit? You've been there hours!"

Benton looked at him, liking his fresh, clean-cut look.

"I could use some coffee. I feel like I was growing to this rock."

The young Englishman had risen to his feet.

"There's something coming down there. A man, I think."

"Couldn't be one of our men. We didn't have any over there. He's stopped—looking back."

"He's coming on again now," Sackworth said after a moment. He had joined them at the first sign of trouble. "Shall I try a shot?"

"Wait. Might be a Greek."

The sun climbed higher, and the moving figure came slowly toward them. He seemed to move at an almost creeping pace. At times, out of sight of the pass, they thought he would never show up again.

"He's carrying something," Pommy said. "Too heavy for a rifle, but I saw the sun flash on it back there a way."

The man came into sight around the last bend. He was big, but he walked very slowly, limping a little. He was wearing faded khaki trousers and a torn shirt. Over one shoulder were several belts of ammunition.

"He hasn't carried that very far," Ryan said. "He's got over a hundred pounds there."

Benton picked up one of the rifles and stepped to the parapet, but before he could lift the gun or speak, the man looked up. Benton thought he had never seen a face so haggard with weariness. It was an utter and complete weariness that seemed to come from within. The man's face was covered with a stubble of black beard. His face was wide at the cheekbones, and the nose was broken. His head was wrapped in a bloody bandage above which coarse black hair was visible.

"Any room up there?" he asked.

"Who are you?" Benton demanded.

Without replying, the big man started up the steep path. Once he slipped, skinning his knee against a sharp rock. Puzzled, they waited. When he stood beside them, they were shocked at his appearance. His face, under the deep brown of sun and wind, was drawn and pale, his nose peeling from sunburn. The rags of what must have once been a uniform were mud-stained and sweat-discolored.

"What difference does it make?" he asked mildly, humorously. "I'm here now."

He lowered the machine gun and slid the belts to the ground. When he straightened, they could see he was a half-inch taller than Benton, who was a tall man, and at least thirty pounds heavier. Through his shirt bulging muscles showed, and there was blood clogging the hair on his chest.

"My name's Horne," he added. "Mike Horne. I've been fighting with Koska's guerrillas in Albania."

Benton stared, uncertain. "Albania? That's a long way from here."

"Not so far if you know the mountains." He looked at the pot on the fire. "How's for some coffee?"

Silently Ryan filled a cup. Digging in his haversack, Horne produced some Greek bread and a thick chunk of sausage. He brushed the sand from the sausage gravely. "Want some? I salvaged this from a bombed house back yonder. Might be some shell fragments in it."

"You pack that gun over the mountains?" Ryan asked.

Horne nodded, his mouth full. "Part of the way. It was surrounded by dead Greeks when I found it. Four Italians found it the same time. We had trouble."

"Did you—kill them all?" Pommy asked.

Horne looked at him. "No, kid. I asked them to tea an' then put sand in their bearings."

Pommy's face got red; then he grinned.

"Got any ammo for a .50?" Horne looked up at Benton. "I got mighty little left."

"They put down four boxes by mistake," Benton said.

Ryan was interested. "Koska's guerrillas? I heard of them. Are they as tough as you hear?"

"Tougher. Koska's an Albanian gypsy. Sneaked into Valona alone a few nights ago an' got himself three dagos. With a knife."

Sackworth studied Horne as if he were some kind of insect. "You call that bravery? That's like animals. One can at least fight like a gentleman!"

Horne winked at Ryan. "Sure, kid. But this ain't a gentleman's fight. This is war. Nothing sporting about it, just a case of dog eat dog, an' you better have big teeth."

"Why are you here?" Sackworth demanded.

Horne shrugged. "Why am I anyplace? Think I'm a fifth columnist or something?" He stared regretfully into the empty cup. "Well, I'm not. I ran a gun in the Chaco a few years ago; then they started to fight in China, so I went there. I was in the Spanish scrap with the Loyalists.

"Hung around in England long enough to learn something about that parachute business. Now that's a man's job. When you get down in an enemy country, you're on your own. I was with the bunch that hopped off from Libya and parachuted down in Southern Italy to cut off that aqueduct and supply line to the Sicily naval base. Flock of spiggoties spotted me, but I got down to the water and hiked out in a fishing boat. Now I'm here."

He looked up at Benton, wiping the back of his hand across his mouth. "From Kalgoorlie, I bet. You got the look. I prospected out of there once. I worked for pearls out of Darwin, too. I'm an original swagman, friend."

"What's a swagman?" Pommy asked.

Horne looked at him, smiling. Two of his front teeth at the side were missing.

"It's a bum, sonny. Just a bum. A guy who packs a tucker bag around looking for whatever turns up."

Horne pulled the gun over into his lap, carefully wiping the oil buffer clean. Then he oiled the moving parts of the gun with a little can he took from his hip pocket and slowly assembled it. He handled the gun like a lover, fitting the parts together smoothly and testing it carefully for head space when it was ready for firing.

"That a German shirt you have on?" Sackworth asked. His eyes were level, and he had his rifle across his knees, pointed at Horne.

"Sure," Horne said mildly. "I needed a shirt, so I took it out of a dead German's outfit."

"Looting," Sackworth said with scorn. There was distaste and dislike in his gaze.

"Why not?" Horne looked up at Sackworth, amused. "You're a good kid, so don't start throwing your weight around. This sportsmanship stuff, the old school tie, an' whatnot—that's okay where it belongs. You Britishers who play war like a game are living in the past. There's nothing sporting about this. It's like waterfronts or jungles. You survive any way you can."

Sackworth did not move the rifle. "I don't like him," he said to Benton. "I don't trust him."

"Forget it!" Benton snapped. "The man's all right, and Lord knows we need fighting men!"

"Sure," Horne added quietly. "It's just you an' me are different kind of animals, kid. You're probably Eton and then Sandhurst. Me, I came up the hard way. A tough road kid in the States, then an able seaman, took a whirl at the fight game, and wound up in Chaco.

"I like to fight. I also like to live. I been in a lot of fights, and mostly I fought pretty good, an' I'm still alive. The Jerries use whatever tactics they need. What you need, kid, in war is not a lot of cut-an'-dried rules but a good imagination, the ability to use what you've got to the best advantage no matter where you are, and a lot of the old moxie.

"You'll make a good fighter. You got the moxie. All you need is a little kicking around."

"I wish we knew where the Jerries were," Ryan said. "This waiting gets me."

"You'll see them pretty quick," Horne said. "There's about a battalion in the first group, and there's only one tank."

Benton lowered his cup, astonished. "You mean you've actually seen them? They are coming?"

Horne nodded. "The main body isn't far behind the first bunch."

"Why didn't you say so?" Sackworth demanded. His face was flushed and angry. "We could have warned the troops behind us."

"Yeah?" Horne did not look up from wiping the dust from the cartridges. "Well, we couldn't. You see," he added, looking up, "they broke through Monastir Pass two days ago. Your men back there know more about it than we do. This is just a supporting column to polish off any leftovers like us."

"Then—we're cut off?" Pommy asked.

Horne nodded. "You have been for two days. How long you been here?"

"Just three days," Benton said. He studied Horne thoughtfully. "What are you? A Yank?"

Horne shrugged. "I guess so. When I joined up in Spain,

they took my citizenship away. It was against the law to fight fascism then. If it was wrong then, it's wrong now. But me, I feel just the same. I'll fight them in China, in Spain, in Africa, or anywhere else.

"In Spain when everything was busting up, I heard about this guy Koska. One of his men was with us, so when he went back, I trailed along."

"They're coming," Sackworth said. "I can see the tank."

"All right," Benton said. He finished his coffee.

"Did you fight any Germans in Spain?" Pommy asked.

"Yeah." Mike Horne brushed invisible dust from the gun and fed a belt of cartridges into it. "Most of them aren't much better than the Italians. They fight better—the younger ones try harder—but all they know how to do is die."

"It's something to know that," Sackworth said.

"Nuts. Anybody can die. Everybody does. And dead soldiers never won any battles. The good soldier is the one who keeps himself alive and fighting. This bravery stuff—that's for milksops. For pantywaists. All of us are scared, but we fight just the same."

"The tank's getting closer," Sackworth said. He was plainly worried and showed it.

"I got the .50," Horne said. He settled himself comfortably into the sand and moved his gun on the swivel. "Let it get closer. Don't fire until they are close up to us. I'll take the tank. You take the first truck with the other gun, I'll take the second, an' so on. Get the drivers if you can."

They were silent. The rumble of the tank and heavy clank of the tread drew nearer. Behind them rolled the trucks, the men sitting in tight groups. They apparently expected no trouble.

"I'd have expected them to send a patrol," Benton said, low-voiced.

"They did," Horne replied.

They looked at him, startled. His eyes were on the gray-green column. He had sighted the .50 at the gun aperture on the tank.

"All right," he said suddenly.

His gun broke into a hoarse chatter, slamming steel-jacketed bullets at the tank. Then its muzzle lifted suddenly and swept the second truck. Soldiers were shouting and yelling, spilling from trucks like madmen, but the two first trucks were smashed into carriers of death before the men could move. The Germans farther back had found their enemy, and gunfire smashed into the parapet. Pommy felt something like a hot whiplash along his jaw.

They were above the column and out of reach of the tank. Mike Horne stood up suddenly and depressed the gun muzzle. The tank was just below. The gun chattered, and the tank slewed around sideways and drove full tilt into the rock wall as though to climb it.

Horne dropped back. "The older ones have a soft spot on top," he said.

The men of the broken column ran for shelter. Some of them tried to rush the steep path, but the fire blasted them back to the road, dead or dying. Others, trying to escape the angry bursts from the two guns, tried to scramble up the walls of the pass but were mowed down relentlessly.

It had been a complete and shocking surprise. The broken column became a rout. Horne stopped the .50 and wiped his brow with the back of his hand. He winked at Ryan.

"Nice going, kid. That's one tank that won't bother your pals."

Ryan peered around the rocks. The pass was empty of life. The wrecked tank was jammed against the rock wall, and one of the trucks had plunged off the precipice into the ravine. Another was twisted across the road.

A man was trying to get out of the first truck. He made it and tumbled to the road. His coat was stained with blood, and he was making whimpering sounds and trying to crawl. His face and head were bloody.

"Next time it'll be tough," Horne said. "They know now. They'll come in small bunches, scattered out, running for shelter behind the trucks."

Rifle fire began to sweep over the cup. They were low behind the parapet and out of sight. It was a searching, careful fire—expert fire.

Benton was quiet. He looked over at Horne. Officially in charge, he had yielded his command to Horne's superior knowledge.

"What d'you think?" he asked.

"We'll stop them," Horne said. "We'll stop them this time, maybe next time. After that—"

Horne grinned at Pommy. "First time under fire?"

"Yes."

"Take it easy. You're doing all right. Make every shot count. One cinch is worth five maybes."

Pommy crowded his body down into the gravel and rested his rifle in a niche in the rocks. He looked at Mike Horne and could see a thin trickle of fresh blood coming from under his bandage. The wound had opened again.

Was it deep, he wondered, or just a scratch? He looked at the lines about Horne's mouth and decided it was deep. Horne's sleeve was torn, and he had a dragon tat-tooed on his forearm.

They came with a rush. Rounding the bend, they broke into a scattered line; behind them, machine guns and ri-fles opened a hot fire to cover the advance.

They waited, and just before the men could reach the trucks swept them with a steel scythe of bullets that mowed them down in a row. One man tumbled off the brink and fell into the ravine; then another fell, caught his fingers on the lip, and tumbled head over heels into the ravine as the edge gave way.

"How many got there?" Horne asked.

"A dozen, I think," Ryan said. "We got about thirty."

"Fair enough." Horne looked at Sackworth. The young Englishman was still resentful. He didn't like Horne. "Doing all right?" Horne asked.

"Of course." Sackworth was contemptuous, but his face was drawn and gray.

"Ryan," Horne said, "you and Pommy leave the main attack to the machine guns. Watch the men behind the trucks. Pick them off as they try to move closer. You take the right, Pommy."

The German with the bloody face had fallen flat. Now he was getting to his knees again.

Then, suddenly, three men made a concerted rush. Ryan and Pommy fired instantly, and Ryan's man dropped.

"I missed!" Pommy said. "Blast it, I missed!"

There was another rush, and both machine guns broke into a clattering roar. The gray line melted away, but more kept coming. Men rounded the bend and split to the right and left. Despite the heavy fire a few of them were getting through. Pommy and Ryan were firing continuously and methodically now.

Suddenly a man broke from under the nearest truck and came on in a plunging rush. Both Ryan and Pommy fired, and the man went down, but before they could fire again, he lunged to his feet and dove into the hollow below the cliff on which their pit rested.

"He can't do anything there," Sackworth said. "He—"

A hurtling object shot upward from below, hit the slope below the guns, rolled a few feet, and then burst with an earth-shaking concussion.

Horne looked up from where he had ducked his head. Nobody was hit.

"He's got grenades. Watch it. There'll be another in a minute."

Ryan fired, and a man dropped his rifle and started back toward the trucks. He walked quite calmly while they stared. Then he fell flat and didn't get up.

Twice more grenades hit the slope, but the man was too close below the cliff. They didn't quite reach the cup thrown from such an awkward angle. "If one of those makes it—" Benton looked sour.

Pommy was shooting steadily now. There was another rush, and Benton opened up with the machine gun. Suddenly another grenade came up from below, traveling an arching course. It hit the slope, too short. It rolled free and fell. There was a terrific explosion.

"Tough," Ryan said. "He made a good try."

"Yeah," Horne said. "So have we."

Hours passed. The machine guns rattled steadily now. Only at long intervals was there a lull. The sun had swung over and was setting behind the mountain.

Horne straightened, his powerful body heavy with fatigue. He looked over at Ryan and grinned. Ryan's face was swollen from the kick of the rifle. Benton picked up a canteen and tried to drink, but there was no water.

"What now?" Pommy said.

Horne shrugged. "We take it on the lam."

"What?" Sackworth demanded. "What does that mean?"

"We beat it," Mike Horne said. "We get out while the getting is good."

"What?" Sackworth was incredulous. "You mean— *run?* Leave our post?"

"That's just what I mean," Horne said patiently. "We delayed this bunch long enough. We got ours from them, but now it doesn't matter anymore. The Jerries are behind us now. We delayed them for a while. All around through these hills guys are delaying them just for a while. We've done all we could here. Now we scram. We fight somewhere else."

"Go if you want to," Sackworth said stubbornly. "I'm staying."

Suddenly there was a terrific concussion, then another and another.

"What the deuce?" Benton exclaimed. "They got a mortar. They—"

The next shell hit right where he was sitting. It went off with an ear-splitting roar and a burst of flame. Pommy went down, hugged the earth with an awful fear. Something tore at his clothes; then sand and gravel showered over him. There was another concussion and another.

Somebody had caught him by the foot. "Come on, kid. Let's go."

They broke into a stumbling run down the slope back of the nest, then over the next ridge and down the ravine beyond. Even then they ran on, using every bit of cover.

Once Pommy started to slow, but Horne nudged him with the rifle barrel.

"Keep it up," he panted. "We got to run."

They slid into a deeper ravine and found their way to a stream. They walked then, slipping and sliding in the gathering darkness. Once a patrol saw them, and shots rattled around, but they kept going.

Then it was night, and clouds covered the moon and the stars. Wearily, sodden with exhaustion, they plodded on. Once, on the bank of a little stream, they paused for a drink. Then Horne opened the old haversack again and brought out the remnants of the sausage and bread. He broke each in half, and shared them with Pommy.

"But—"

Pommy's voice caught in his throat. "Gone?" he said then.

Horne nodded in the darkness. "Yeah. Lucky it wasn't all of us."

"But what now?" Pommy asked. "You said they were behind us."

"Sure," Horne agreed. "But we're just two men. We'll travel at night, keep to the hills. Maybe they'll make a stand at Thermopylae. If not there, they might try to defend the Isthmus of Corinth. Maybe we can join them there."

"But if they don't? If we can't?"

"Then Africa, Pommy, or Syria or Suez or Russia or England. They'll always be fighting them somewhere, an' that's where I want to be. It won't stop. The Germans win here, they win there, but they got to keep on fighting. They win battles, but none of them are decisive. None of them mean an end.

"Ever fight a guy, kid, who won't quit? You keep kicking him, and he keeps coming back for more, keeps trying? You knock him down, but he won't stay down? It's hell, that's what it is. He won't quit, so you can't.

"But they'll be fighting them somewhere, and that's where I want to be."

"Yeah," Pommy said. "Me, too."

THE CROSS AND THE CANDLE

WHEN IN PARIS, I went often to a little hotel in a narrow street off the Avenue de la Grande Armée. Two doors opened into the building: one into a dark hallway and then by a winding stair to the chambers above, the other to the café, a tiny bistro patronized by the guests and a few people of the vicinity.

It was in no way different from a hundred other such places. The rooms were chill and dank in the morning (there was little heat in Paris; even the girls in the Folies Bergère were dancing in goose pimples); the furnishings had that added Parisian touch of full-length mirrors running alongside the bed for the obvious and interesting purpose of enabling one and one's companion to observe themselves and their activities.

Madame was a Breton, and as my own family were of Breton extraction, I liked listening to her tales of Roscoff, Morlaix, and the villages along the coast. She was a veritable treasure of ancient beliefs and customs, quaint habits and interesting lore. There was scarcely a place from Saint-Malo to the Bay of Douarnenez about which she didn't have a story to tell.

Often when I came to the café, there would be a man seated in the corner opposite the end of the bar. He was somewhat below medium height, but the thick column of his neck spread out into massive shoulders and a powerful chest. His arms were heavy with muscle and the brown hands that rested on the table before him were thick and strong.

Altogether, I have seen few men who gave such an impression of sheer animal strength and vitality. He moved in leisurely fashion, rarely smiled, and during my first visits had little to say.

In some bygone brawl his nose had been broken, and a deep scar began over his left eye and ran to a point beneath the left ear, of which half the lobe was gone. You looked at his wide face, the mahogany skin, sun polished over broad cheekbones, and you told yourself, "This man is dangerous!" Yet often there was also a glint of hard, tough humor in his eyes.

He sat in his corner, his watchful eyes missing nothing. After a time or two, I came to the impression that he was spinning a web, like some exotic form of spider, but what manner of fly he sought to catch, I could not guess.

Madame told me he was a *marin*—a sailor—and had lived for a time in Madagascar.

One afternoon when I came to the café, he was sitting in his corner alone. The place was empty, dim, and cold. Hat on the table beside him, he sat over an empty glass.

He got up when I came in and moved behind the bar. I ordered vin blanc and suggested he join me. He filled the two glasses without comment, then lifted his glass. *"À votre santé!"* he said. We touched glasses and drank.

"Cold, today," he said suddenly.

The English startled me. In the two months past, I had spoken to him perhaps a dozen times, and he replied always in French.

"You speak English then?"

He grinned at me, a tough, friendly grin touched by a

sort of wry cynicism. "I'm an American," he said, "or I was."

"The devil you say!" Americans are of all kinds, but somehow . . . Still, he could have been anything.

"Born in Idaho," he said, refilling our glasses. When I started to pay, he shook his head and brought money from his own pocket and placed it under an ashtray for Madame to put in the register when she returned. "They call me Tomas here. My old man was an Irish miner, but my mother was Basque."

"I took it for granted you were French."

"Most of them do. My mother spoke French and Spanish. Picked them up around home from her parents, as I did from her. After I went to sea, I stopped in Madagascar four years, and then went to Mauritius and Indochina."

"You were here during the war?"

"Part of the time. When it started, I was in Tananarive; but I returned here, got away from the *Boche*, and fought with the Maquis for a while. Then I came back to Paris."

He looked up at me and the slate-gray eyes were flat and ugly. "My girl was dead."

"Bombs?"

"No. A Vichy rat."

He would say nothing more on the subject and our talk drifted to a strange and little-known people who live in and atop a mountain in Madagascar, and their peculiar customs. I, too, had followed the sea for a time so there was much good talk of the ways of ships and men.

Tomas was without education in the accepted sense, yet he had observed well and missed little. He had read widely. His knowledge of primitive peoples would have fascinated an anthropologist and he had appreciation and understanding for their beliefs.

After talking with him, I came more often to the café, for we found much in common. His cynical toughness appealed to me, and we had an understanding growing from mutual experiences and interests. Yet as our acquaintance grew, I came to realize that he was a different man when we talked together alone than when others were in the room. Then his manner changed. He became increasingly watchful, talked less and only in French.

The man was watching for someone or something. Observing without seeming to, I became aware the center of his interests were those who came most often to the café. And of these, there were four that held his attention most.

Mombello was a slender Italian of middle years who worked in a market. Picard was a chemist, and Leon Matsys owned a small iron foundry on the edge of Paris and a produce business near The Halles. Matsys was a heavy man who had done well, had educated himself, and was inclined to tell everyone so. Jean Mignet, a sleek, cat-like man, was supported by his wife, an actress of sorts. He was pleasant enough to know, but I suspected him of being a thief.

Few women came to the café. Usually the girls who came to the hotel entered by the other door and went to the chambers above, and after a period of time, returned through the same door. To us, they existed merely as light footsteps in the dark hall and on the stairs.

Madame herself, a friendly, practical Breton woman, was usually around and occasionally one of the daughters Mombello would come in search of their father.

The oldest was eighteen and very pretty, but business-like, without interest in the men of the café. The younger girl was thin, woefully thin from lack of proper food, but a beautiful child with large, magnificent dark eyes, dark wavy hair, and lips like the petals of a flower.

Someone among these must be the center of interest, yet I could not find that his interest remained long with any one of the four men. For their part, they seemed to accept him as one of themselves. Only one, I think, was conscious of being watched. That one was Jean Mignet.

On another of those dismal afternoons, we sat alone in the café and talked. (It always seemed that I came there only when the outside was bleak and unhappy, for on the sunny days, I liked being along the boulevards or in St. Germain.) The subject again arose of strange superstitions and unique customs.

There was a Swede on one of my ships who would never use salt when there was a Greek at the table, an idea no more ridiculous than the fear some people have of eating fish and drinking milk in the same meal.

Tomas nodded. "I've known of many such ideas," he said, "and in some of the old families you will find customs that have been passed along from generation to generation in great secrecy for hundreds of years.

"I know of one"—he hesitated, describing circles on the dark tabletop with the wet bottom of his glass—"that is, a religious custom followed so far as I know by only one family."

He looked up at me. "You must never speak of this around here," he said, and he spoke so sharply and with so much feeling, I assured him I'd never speak of it anywhere, if he so wished.

"In the family of my girl," he said, "there is an ancient custom that goes back to the Crusades. Her ancestor was a soldier with Saint Louis at Saint-Jean d'Acre; no doubt you know more of that than I do. Anyway, when his brother was killed in the fighting, there was no shrine or church nearby, so he thrust his dagger into a log. As you know, the hilts of daggers and swords were at that time almost always in the form of a cross, and he used it so in this case, burning a candle before the dagger.

"It became the custom of a religious and fighting family, and hence whenever there is a death, this same dagger is taken from its wrappings of silk and with the point thrust into wood, a candle for the dead is burned before it.

"Marie told me of this custom after her mother's death when I came hurriedly into her room and surprised her with the candle burning. For some forgotten reason, a tradition of secrecy had grown around the custom, and no one outside the family ever knew of it.

"That night in the darkened room, we watched the candle slowly burn away before that ancient dagger, a unique dagger where on crosspiece or guard was carved the body of Christ upon the cross and the blade was engraved with the figure of a snake, the snake signifying the powers of evil fallen before God.

"I never saw the dagger again while she lived. It was put away among her things, locked carefully in an iron chest, never to be brought out again until, as she said, she herself died, or her brother. Then, she looked at me, and said, 'Or you, Tomas, for you are of my family now.'"

He looked at me, and underneath the scarred brows, there were tears in his eyes.

"She must have been a fine girl," I said, for he was deeply moved.

"She was the only thing in my life! Only a madman, a

mad American, would return to France after the war broke out. But I loved her.

"Look at me. I'm not the kind of man many women could love. I'm too rough, too brutal! I'm a seaman, that is all, and never asked to be more. A good man at sea or in a fight, but I have no words with which to say nice things to a woman, and she was a beautiful girl with an education."

Tomas took out his wallet and removed a worn photograph. When I looked at it, I was frankly astonished. The girl was not merely a pretty girl, she was all he had said, and more. She *was* beautiful.

Furthermore, there was something in her eyes and face that let you know that here was a girl who had character, maybe one who knew what loyalty was.

"She is lovely," I said sincerely. "I never saw anyone more beautiful!"

He was pleased, and he looked at me with his face suddenly lighter. "She was magical!" he said. "The best thing in my life. I came first to her house with her brother, who had been my shipmate on a voyage from Saigon. She was a child then, and I thought of her as nothing else.

"So, when next I came to the house, I brought her a present from Liverpool, and then others from Barcelona and Algiers. Simple things, and inexpensive, the sort of things a sailor may find in almost any port, but they had romance, I suppose, a color.

"I gave them simply because I was a lonely man, and this family had taken me as one of them, and because the giving of things is good for a lonely heart.

"One day—she was twelve then, I think—she had gone to a theater in the Boulevard de Clichy with her brother, and when they came out, she saw me with a girl, a girl from a café in the Pigalle. She was very angry and for days she would not speak to me.

"Her brother teased her, and said, 'Look! Marie thinks already she is a woman! She is jealous for you, Tomas!'"

He smiled at the memory. "Then, I was gone again to sea, and when I came again to the house, Marie was fourteen, taller, frightened, and skinny. Always she stared at me, and I brought her presents as before. Sometimes I took her to the theater, but to me she was a child. She was no longer gay, full of excitement and anger. She walked beside me very seriously.

"Four years then I was gone, and when I returned . . . you should have seen her! She was beautiful. Oh, I tell you, she was a woman now, and no doubt about it.

"I fell in love! So much that I could not talk for feeling it, but never did I think for a moment that it could matter.

"But did I have a choice? Not in the least! She had not changed, that one. She was both the little girl I knew first and the older one I knew later, and more besides. She laughed at me and said that long ago she had made up her mind that I was to be her man, and so it was to be whether I liked it or not! Me, I liked it. She was so much of what I wanted that she frightened me.

"Can you imagine what that did to me, m'sieu? I was a lonely man, a very lonely man. There had been the girls of the ports, but they are not for a man of soul, only for the coarse-grained who would satisfy the needs of the moment. Me, I wanted love, tenderness.

"I know." He shrugged. "I don't look it. I am a sailor and pleased to be one, and I've done my share of hard living. More than once, I've twisted my knife in the belly of a man who asked for it, and used my boots on them, too. But who is to say what feeling lives in the heart of a man? Or what need for love burns inside him?

"My parents died when I was young and the sea robbed me of my country. In such a life, one makes no close friends, no attachments, puts down no roots. Then, this girl, this beautiful girl, fell in love with me.

"Fell in love? No, I think the expression is wrong. She said she had always loved me even when she was a child and too young to know what it meant.

"Her mother and brother approved. They were good people, and I had lived long among them. Then the mother died, Pierre was away in the colonies, and Marie and I were to be married when he returned. So we lived together.

"Is this wrong? Who is to say what is right and what is wrong? In our hearts we understood and in France, well, they understand such things. What man is to live without a girl? Or a girl without a man?

"Then away I went to sea on my last trip, and while I was gone, the war came, and with it the Germans. When I returned, I joined the Maquis to get back into France. Her letters were smuggled to me.

"Marie? She was a French girl, and she worked with the underground. She was very skillful, and very adept at fooling the *Boche*. Then, something happened.

"One of the men close to her was betrayed, then another; finally, it was her brother who was killed. The Gestapo had them, but they died without talking. One night I came to her to plead that she come away with me. It had been three years that I had fought in the underground; for her, almost six. But she told me she could not go, that someone close to her was working with the Nazis, someone who knew her. She must stay until she knew who it was.

"Yet try as she could, there was no clue. The man was shrewd, and a very devil. He finally came to her himself, after her brother was caught. He told her what he knew of her underground activities and of mine. He told her unless she came to live with him that I would be tortured and killed.

"He had spied upon her. He had even discovered her burning the candle before the dagger for Pierre after he was killed. He told her of it, to prove how much he knew—to prove he knew enough to find me—and she had admitted the reason.

"In the letter in which all this was told, she could not tell me who he was. He had friends in the underground, and she was fearful that learning who she was writing about, they would destroy the letter if they saw his name, and then she would be cut off from me and from all help.

"She would give me his name, she said, when I came next to Paris. He had not forced himself on her, just threatened. We had to plan to do away with him quickly. Marie said, too, that she was afraid that if the invasion came, he would kill her, for she alone could betray him; she alone knew of his activities for the Nazis.

"The invasion a secret? Of course! But when orders began to come for the underground, come thick and fast, we knew it was coming. Then, the landings were made, and for days we were desperately busy.

"We rose in Paris, and they were exciting, desperate days, and bitter days for the collaborators and the men of Vichy. Their servitude to the Nazis had turned to bitterness and gall; they fled; and they begged, and they died.

"When I could, I hurried to the flat where Marie lived.

It was near here, just around the corner. I found her dying. She had been raped and shot by this collaborator two days before and she had crawled to her apartment to wait for me. She died telling me of it, but unable before her last breath to give me his name."

"And there was no way you could figure out who he was?" I asked.

"How?" He spread his hands expressively. "No one suspected him. His desire for her was such that he had threatened her, and in threatening her he had boasted of what he had done. That was a mistake he rectified by killing her.

"Only one thing I know. He is one of our little group here. She said he lived in this neighborhood, that he was waiting here more than once when he accosted her. He thinks himself safe now. My girl has been dead for some time and her body buried. She is never mentioned here.

"Mombello? He is an Italian. Picard is a chemist, and has had traffic with Germany since the twenties. Matsys? An iron foundry owner who retained it all through the war, but who was active in the underground, as were Picard and Mignet."

We were interrupted then by some others coming into the café, yet now the evening had added zest. Here was a deadly bit of business. Over the next two hours, as they trooped in, I began to wonder. Which was he?

The slender, shrewd Mombello with his quick, eager eyes? That lean whip of a man, Mignet? The heavy Matsys with blue and red veins in his nose, and the penchant for telling you he'd seen it all and done it all? Or was it dry, cold Picard who sipped wine through his thin lips and seemed to have ice water for blood?

Which man was marked to die? How long would Tomas

sit brooding in his corner, waiting? What was he waiting for? A slip of the tongue? A bit of drunken talk?

None of these men drank excessively. So which one? Mombello whose eyes seemed to gloat over the body of every woman he saw? Mignet with his lust for money and power and his quick knife? Or big affable Matsys? Or Picard with his powders and acids?

How long would he wait? These five had sat here for months, and now . . . now there were six. I was the sixth. Perhaps it was the sixth to tip the balance. Here they were caught in a pause before death. Yet the man who killed such a girl, and who betrayed his country, should not go free. There was a story in this, and it had an ending, somewhere.

Over the following gray days, several in a row, the conversation ebbed and flowed and washed around our ears. I did not speak privately to Tomas again but there seemed an ongoing, silent communication between us. Then, in a quiet moment of discussion, someone mentioned the bazooka, and it came to me then that another hand had been dealt . . . mine.

"A strange weapon," I agreed, and then moved the tide of conversation along the subject of weapons and warfare. I spoke of the first use of poison gas by soldiers of Thebes when they burned sulfur to drive defenders from the walls of Athenian cities, then to the use of islands of defense, a successful tactic by the Soviets in this war, previously used by the Russians defending themselves against Charles XII of Sweden.

Then other weapons and methods, and somehow, but carefully, to strange knives.

Tomas ignored me, the spider in his web, but he could hear every word and he was poised, poised for anything.

Mignet told of a knife he had seen in Algiers with a poisoned barb in the hilt near the blade, and Mombello of a Florentine dagger he had once seen.

Tomas stayed silent, turning his glass in endless circles upon the table before him, turning, turning, turning. We locked eyes for a moment and before he looked away he seemed to sigh and give a nearly imperceptible nod.

"There was a knife I saw once," I said suddenly, "with engraving on it. A very old knife, and very strange. A figure of Christ on the cross rose above a fallen snake. The religious symbolism is interesting. I'd never seen its like before, the worksmanship was so finely wrought."

A moment passed, a bare breath of suspended time. . . .

"It was not the only one, I think," Leon Matsys said. "Odd things; they were used in some custom dating back to the Crusades."

He looked up, about to say more, then slowly the life went from his face. He was looking at Tomas, and Tomas was smiling.

Jean Mignet's eyes were suddenly alive. He did not know, but he suspected something. He was keen, that one.

Leon Matsys's face was deathly pale. He was trapped now, trapped by those remarks that came so casually from his lips. In the moment he had certainly forgotten what they might imply, and could not know that it would matter. He looked to one side and then the other, and then he started to take a drink.

He lifted the glass, then suddenly put it down. He got up, and his face was flabby and haunted by terror. He seemed unable to take his eyes from Tomas.

I glanced at Tomas, and my muscles jumped involuntarily. He had the ancient knife in his hand and was drawing his little circles with its point.

Matsys turned and started for the entrance, stumbling in his haste. The glass in the tall door rattled as it slammed closed, leaving only a narrow view of the dimly lit street.

After a moment Tomas pushed his chair back and got up and his step was very light as he also went out the door.

A FRIEND OF THE GENERAL

While I was in France, my company was stationed for a while in a château not far outside Chartres. The girl who owned the château, a countess, was living in the gardener's cottage. Which, if you had it in Beverly Hills it would sell for half a million dollars anyway and probably more. It was a beautiful place. She had quite a bunch of friends around, an international group, you know, and a very exciting crowd.

One day I had to go up to Paris and I commented on the fact that I'd like to get a good meal. Well, the only good meals you could get in Paris at the time because of the rationing of food was in black-market restaurants. I didn't know any of them and you had to have somebody to introduce you or you couldn't get in. Toni told me . . . she said, "I'll tell you what to do, you go to this restaurant," and she described where it was, it was a little restaurant in a cul-de-sac and, "you go in there and take a seat at the table furthest from the door, you'll see which one it is right away when you get there. Sit down and don't look at the menu at all. When the waiter comes to you just tell him you are a friend of the general and you'll get the greatest meal in the world."

THEY KNEW EACH other by name and sometimes by sight. Occasionally those who were in the city would have a drink together at the Astor Bar or a lesser-known place, off the beaten track, called the International. In the years from 1920 until the beginning of World War II it was the place to which they came. The warlords were hiring men who had specialties, although it was the flyers who were most in demand. Some of their names became legend; some were never known but to each other and those who hired them. There were others who never came to Shanghai but whose names were known, for they were men of a kind. One-Arm Sutton, General Rafael de Nogales, Ignaz Trebitsch-Lincoln, and, of course, their long-dead predecessor, General Frederick Townsend Ward, commander of the "Ever-Victorious Army," to whom the Chinese raised a statue.

They were soldiers of fortune, men who made their living by their knowledge of weapons and tactics, selling their services wherever there was a war.

The munitions dealers were there, also, mingling with diplomats and officers of a dozen armies and navies. Thirteen flags, it was said, floated over Shanghai, but there were always visiting naval vessels from still other countries.

The terrorist tactics that have become so much a part of world news in these later years were an old story in Shanghai. Korean, Chinese, and Japanese gunmen killed each other with impunity, and if one was discreet, one avoided the places where these affairs were most likely to take place. There were a few places frequented by each group, and unless one enjoyed lead with one's meals, it was wise to go elsewhere. The Carlton, fortunately, was not one of these places, and they had boxing matches as part of the floor show. A fighter who did not become too destructive too soon could make a decent living there and at a few other spots. The secret was to win, if one could, but not so decisively as to frighten possible opponents, for there were not too many fighters available.

When I first met the general, I had no memory of him, but a chance remark brought it all back. He had been a regular, always sitting close to the ring and giving the fights his full attention. My time in Shanghai was too brief to really know the place, although some of my friends knew it about as well as one could. From them I learned a great deal, and with some small skill I had for observing what goes on, I learned more.

IT BEGAN QUITE casually as such things often do, with a group of people conversing about nothing in particular, all unsuspecting of what the result might be.

My company was quartered in the château of the countess, as during the war she had moved into what had once been the gardener's cottage. It was the sort of place that in Beverly Hills would have sold well into six figures, a warm, cozy place with huge fireplaces, thick walls, and flowers all about.

The countess was young, very beautiful, and clever. She had friends everywhere and knew a bit of what went on anywhere you would care to mention. I was there because of the countess, and so, I suppose, was everybody else.

Her sister had just come down from the Netherlands, their first visit since the German occupation. There was a young American naval attaché, a woman of indeterminate age who was a Russian émigré, a fragile blond actress from Paris who, during the war, had smuggled explosives hidden under the vegetables in a basket on her bicycle. There was a baron who wore his monocle as if it were a part of him but had no other discernible talents and an American major who wanted to go home.

The war was fizzling out somewhere in Germany, far from us, and I wondered aloud where in Paris one could find a decent meal.

They assured me this was impossible unless I knew a good black-market restaurant. Due to the war there was a shortage of everything, and the black-market cafés had sprung up like speakeasies during the Prohibition era in the States—and like them you had to know somebody to get in.

Each had a different restaurant to suggest, although there was some agreement on one or two, but the countess solved my dilemma. Tearing a bit of note paper from a pad, she wrote an address. "Go to this place. Take a seat in a corner away from the windows, and when you wish to order, simply tell the waiter you are a friend of the general."

"But who," somebody asked, "is the general?"

She ignored the question but replied to mine when I asked, "But suppose the general is there at the time?"

"He will not be. He has flown to Baghdad and will go from there to Chabrang."

I could not believe that I had heard right.

"To *where?*" the naval attaché asked.

"It is a small village," I said, "near the ruins of Tsaparang."

"Now," the Russian woman said, "we understand everything! Tsaparang! Of course! Who would not know Tsaparang?"

"Where," the naval attaché asked, "are the ruins of Tsaparang?"

"Once," I began, "there was a kingdom—"

"Don't bother him with that. If I know Archie, he will waste the next three weeks trying to find it on a map."

"Take this"—she handed me the address—"and do as I have said. You will have as fine a meal as there is in Paris, as there is in Europe, in fact."

"But how can they do it?" Jeannine asked. "How can any café—"

"It is not the restaurant," the countess said, "it is the general. Before the war began, he knew it was coming, and he prepared for it. He has his own channels of communication, and being the kind of man he is, they work, war or no war.

"During a war some people want information, others want weapons or a way to smuggle escaped prisoners, but the general wanted the very best in food and wine, but above all, condiments, and he had them."

The general, it seemed, had served his apprenticeship during Latin American revolutions, moving from there to the Near and Middle East, to North Africa, and to China. Along the way he seemed to have feathered his nest quite substantially.

A few days later, leaving my jeep parked in a narrow street, I went through a passage between buildings and found myself in a small court. There were several shops with artists' studios above them, and in a corner under an awning were six tables. Several workmen sat at one table drinking beer. At another was a young man, perhaps a student, sitting over his books and a cup of coffee.

Inside the restaurant it was shadowed and cool. The floor was flagstone, and the windows were hung with curtains. Everything was painfully neat. There were cloths on the tables and napkins. Along one side there was a bar with several stools. There were exactly twelve tables, and

I had started for the one in the corner when a waiter appeared.

He indicated a table at one side. "Would you sit here, please?"

My uniform was, of course, American. That he spoke English was not unusual. Crossing to the table, I sat down with my back to the wall, facing the court. The table in the corner was but a short distance away and was no different from the others except that in the immediate corner there was a very large, comfortable chair with arms, not unlike what is commonly called a captain's chair.

"You wished to order?"

"I do." I glanced up. "I am a friend of the general."

"Ah? Oh, yes! Of course."

Nothing more was said, but the meal served was magnificent. I might even say it was unique.

A few days later, being in the vicinity, I returned, and then a third time. On this occasion I was scarcely seated when I heard footsteps in the court; looking up, I found the door darkened by one who could only be the general.

He was not tall, and he was . . . corpulent. He was neatly dressed in a tailored gray suit with several ribbons indicative of decorations. The waiter appeared at once, and there was a moment of whispered conversation during which he glanced at me.

Embarrassed? Of course. Here I had been passing myself as this man's friend, obtaining excellent meals under false pretenses. That I had paid for them and paid well made no difference at all. I had presumed, something no gentleman would do.

He crossed to his table and seated himself in his captain's chair. He ordered Madeira, and then the waiter crossed to my table. "Lieutenant? The general requests your company. He invites you to join him."

A moment I hesitated, then rising, I crossed over to him. "General? I must apolo—"

"Please be seated." He gestured to a chair.

"But I must—"

"You must do nothing of the kind. Have they taught you nothing in that army of yours? Never make excuses. Do what has to be done, and if it fails, accept the consequences."

"Very well." I seated myself. "I shall accept the consequences."

"Which will be an excellent meal, some very fine wine, and I hope some conversation worthy of the food and the wine." He glanced at me. "At least you are soldier enough for that. To find a very fine meal and take advantage of it. A soldier who cannot feed himself is no soldier at all."

He filled my glass, then his. "One question. How did you find this place? Who told you of me?"

Of course, I could have lied, but he would see through it at once. I disliked bringing her into it but knew that under the circumstances she would not mind.

"It was," I said, "the countess—"

"Of course," he interrupted me. "Only she would have dared." He glanced at me. "You know her well?"

It was nobody's business how well I knew her. "We are friends. My company is quartered in her château, and she is a lovely lady."

"Ah? How pleasant for you. She is excellent company, and such company is hard to come by these days. A truly beautiful woman, but clever. Altogether too clever for my taste. I do not trust clever women."

"I rather like them."

"Ah, yes. But you are a lieutenant. When you are a general, you will feel otherwise."

He spent a good deal of time watching the court, all of which was visible from where he sat. He had chosen well. The court had but one entrance for the public, although for the fortunate ones who lived close there were no exits, as I later discovered.

Not only could he not be approached from behind, but anyone emerging from the passage was immediately visible to him, while they could not see him until they actually entered the restaurant.

On our second meeting I surprised him and put myself in a doubtful position. I was simply curious, and my question had no other intent.

"How did you like Chabrang?"

He had started to lift his glass, and he put it down immediately. His right hand slid to the edge of the table until only his fingertips rested there. His tone was distinctly unfriendly when he replied, "What do you mean?"

"When I asked the countess if you would be here, she said you were in Baghdad—on the way to Chabrang."

"She said *that*? She mentioned Chabrang?"

"Yes, and I was surprised. It isn't the sort of place people hear of, being in such an out-of-the-way place, and only a village—a sort of way station."

His right hand dropped into his lap, and his fingers tugged at his trouser leg, which clung a bit too snugly to his heavy thigh. "You know Chabrang."

It was not a question but a statement. His right hand hitched the pant leg again. Suddenly I realized what was on his mind, and I almost laughed, for I'd been away from that sort of thing too long and had become careless.

The laugh was not for him but simply that it seemed like old times, and it was kind of good to be back.

"You won't need the knife," I told him. "I am no danger to you."

"You know Chabrang, and there are not fifty men in Europe who know it. Am I to believe this is pure coincidence?"

He had a knife in his boot top, I was sure of that. He was a careful man and no doubt had reason to be, but why that was so I had no idea and told him as much.

"It was my only way out," he said. "They found me, but they were looking for a man who was carrying a great lot of money, and I had nothing but food, weapons, and some butterflies. They let me go."

"I believed it was a way out for me, too," I said, "but I was not so lucky. I had to turn back."

He turned to look at me. "When were you in China?"

"It was long ago." I have never liked dates. Perhaps because I have a poor memory for dates in my own life. "It was in the time of the warlords," I said.

He shrugged. "That's indefinite enough."

We talked of many things. He gestured widely. "This is what I wanted," he said. "I wanted time—leisure. Time to read, to think, to see. Some people make it some ways, some another. Mine was through war."

"It is no longer regarded with favor," I suggested.

He shrugged again. "Who cares? For ten thousand years it was the acceptable way for a man to make his fortune. A young man with a strong arm and some luck could go off to the wars and become rich.

"All the old kingdoms were established so. All the original 'great families' were founded in just such a way. What else was William the Conqueror? Or Roger of Sicily? Or their Viking ancestors who first conquered and then settled in Normandy? What does 'Norman' mean but 'Northmen'? Who were Cortés and Pizarro? They were young men with swords."

"Ours is a different world," I suggested. "Our standards are not the same."

"Bah!" He waved his fork. "The standards are the same, only now the fighting is done by lawyers. There is more cunning and less courage. They will sell you the arms—"

"Like Milton," I said.

He stopped with his fork in the air and his mouth open. "You know about Milton," he said. "I am beginning to wonder about you, Lieutenant."

"Everybody in China knew that story. Perhaps I should say everybody in our line of business or around the Astor Bar. It was no secret."

"Perhaps not. Perhaps not."

Such stories are repeated in bars and tearooms, over bridge tables as well as in the waterfront dives. Milton had been a well-set-up man in his early forties, as I recall him. A smooth, easy-talking man, somewhat florid of face, who played a good game of golf, haunted the Jockey Club, and owned a few good racehorses, Mongolian ponies brought down for that purpose. He had been a dealer in guns, supplying the various warlords with rifles, machine guns, mortars, and ammunition. As a machine gun was worth its weight in gold and as some European nation was always liquidating its stores to replace them with more modern weapons, Milton did well.

He reminded me of a first-class insurance salesman, and in a sense that was what he was. The weapons he sold were the kind of insurance that was needed.

He might have become enormously wealthy, but he had an urge to gamble, and he had a blonde. The blonde, some said, was none too bright, but she had other assets that were uniquely visible, and nobody really inquired as to her intelligence, least of all Milton.

A day came when too much blonde and too much gambling left him nearly broke, and she chose that moment to say she wanted to go to Paris. She pleaded, she argued, and he listened. He was willing enough, but the problem was money.

At that moment an order came for six thousand rifles, some machine guns and mortars, with ammunition for all. Milton had only six hundred rifles on hand and insufficient cash. Such deals were always cash on the barrelhead. He agreed to supply what was needed.

Long ago he had arranged a little deal with the customs officials to pass anything he shipped in a piano box, and as a piano salesman he seemed to be doing very well indeed.

Knowing the kind of people with whom he dealt, he also knew the necessity for absolute secrecy in what he was about to do, so with one German whom he knew from long experience would not talk, he went to his warehouse, and locking the doors very carefully, he proceeded to pack the cases with old, rusted pipe and straw. Atop each case, before closing it, he put a few rifles to satisfy any quick inspection. Yet the greatest thing he had going for him was his reputation for integrity. He supervised the loading of the piano boxes on a Chinese junk and collected his down payment of three hundred thousand dollars.

He had taken every precaution. Through a closemouthed acquaintance he had bought two tickets on a vessel that was sailing that very night.

"Pack an overnight bag for each of us," he said. "Nothing more. And be ready. Say nothing to anyone and I'll buy you a completely new wardrobe in Paris."

Now, his rifles loaded on the junk, he drove at once to his apartment on Bubbling Well Road. He ran lightly up the steps carrying the small black bag. "Come! We've got to move fast! There's not much time to catch the boat!"

This, you must remember, was before World War II, and there were no airlines as such.

"Where are the tickets?" he asked.

She came to him, her blue eyes wide and wonderful. "Oh, Milt! I hope you're not going to be angry, but the Funstons are having a party tonight, and they are always such *fun!* Well, I turned in our tickets and got tickets on another boat, a much faster one, that leaves tomorrow!"

No doubt there was a moment of sheer panic; then what he hoped was common sense prevailed. It would take that junk a week to get to its destination. Well—four days at least. There was nothing to be done, and why not one more night?

The next morning was one I would never forget. I'd known Milton only to speak to, although we did have a drink together once. When a friend banged on my door at daybreak and told me he had something to show me, I went along.

What he showed me was what Milton might have expected, for the men with whom he did business did not play games.

There, standing upright in the parking lot outside his place on Bubbling Well Road, was a piece of the rusty pipe he had so carefully packed. On top of it was Milton's head. His complexion was no longer florid.

"Everybody knew that story," I repeated. "At least everybody of our sort. I heard it again a few days ago in the Casual Officers' Mess on Place St. Augustine."

"But you know about Chabrang," the general said.

The wine was excellent. "I see no connection," I said.

He gave me a sidelong glance, filled with suspicion. Why the mention of Chabrang disturbed him, I could not guess, as it was but an unimportant village on one of the routes out of Sinkiang to Ladakh. It was in no way note-worthy except that it was near the ruins of Tsaparang. The ruins represented about all that remained of a long-ago kingdom.

"Did you know Milton?" I asked.

"I knew him. If the Chinese had not killed him, I would have. Those munitions were consigned to me."

"To *you?*"

"They were consigned to me for the warlord, and the fraud put my head on the block. I was suspected of com-plicity."

"What happened?"

"I acted. Perceiving that I was suspected, and knowing the gentleman concerned was not one to dilly-dally, I made my move. You see, he already owed me money, a considerable sum. By disposing of me, he could make somebody atone for the fraud and liquidate his debt at the same time."

He fell silent while the waiter brought a steaming plat-ter of seafood. When he had gone, the general resumed. "It was the time to move, so I acted. Remember that this is the first principle—*act!* Remember that, my young friend! Do not deliberate! Do not hesitate! Do not wait upon eventuality! *Act!* It is always better to do something, even if not quite the right thing, than to do nothing. *Action! Decision!* Only these are important!"

He toyed with an oyster, glancing from under his brows. "My mind, at such times, works quickly. He needed a scapegoat to save face. Not in Shanghai but there, before his men! At once! Instantly I perceived it was I who must pay."

He ate the oyster, and taking a bit of bread, buttered it lavishly. Many of the good people of France had not seen so much butter in months.

"You see, the commander himself did not yet know of the fraud, but immediately the discovery was made, an officer had left to report to him. He could reach him in not less than an hour, then an hour to return.

"The captain of the junk had seen none of what went on, so I went to him immediately, put money in his hand, and told him to sail to such and such a point up river. The cargo would be received there.

"Then I went to the telegraph station, which was closed. I broke into it and sent a message to another, rival warlord up the river, offering the guns to him for a fancy price. He was desperately in need of them, and I told him I could promise delivery if the money was paid to me in gold. A place of payment was mentioned.

"There was a charter plane at the field. You knew him, I think? Milligan? He would fly you anywhere for a price and land his plane on a pocket handkerchief if need be. Moreover, he could be trusted, and there were some, in those days, who could not. I placed five hundred dollars in his hand and said I wished to leave for Shanghai at once.

" 'After I gas up,' he said.

" 'Now,' I told him. 'Right now. There is petrol at . . .' I took his map and put my finger on the place. 'And you can land there.'

" 'If you say,' he replied doubtfully. 'I never heard of—'

" 'The petrol is there,' I promised him. 'I had it placed there for just such an emergency.' "

The general looked around at me. "You are young, Lieutenant, and wise as you may be, you are still learning, so remember to trust no one! Prepare for every eventuality no matter how remote! Not even a mouse trusts himself to one hole only. That is an old saying, but it has remained in my mind, and can I be less wise than a mouse?

"We took off at once. Within twenty minutes of my realization I *acted!* And that night I was in Shanghai with *her!*"

"Her?" He had lost me.

"Of course! With Milton's blonde. What was her name? I've forgotten. No matter. I was there, consoling her.

"Of course"—he glanced at me—"I was younger then and not so—so well, I am a little overweight now. But then, ah, I was handsome then, Lieutenant! I was handsome, and I was, of course, younger.

"I found her in tears. She was weeping for him. For Milton. Or perhaps she was weeping for that lost trip to Paris. About women, Lieutenant, one never knows. No matter.

"There on the floor was the black bag. It was out of the way, back against the sofa's end, but I recognized it at once. True, I'd never seen it before, but I'd seen others of the kind. In it would be the money! All that delightful, beautiful money! And she was crying? Well, as I have said, she was a woman, and about women one never knows.

"I consoled her. What else could I do? What does one do with a pretty woman who is sad and has a quarter of a million dollars, give or take a few? I told her she must not worry, that I—*I* would take her to Paris! And who knew Paris better? Who knew the night spots, the cafés, the bordel— Well, who knew the town better than I? Even its history!

"Oh, I was marvelous that day! I told her exciting and glamorous tales of what the city was like, of living there, and I dropped names, names of all the famous and infamous. As a matter of fact, I actually did know some of them.

"She was consoled! She rested her head on my shoulder. As you have seen, they are very broad. She dried her tears; then she smoothed her dress, she touched up her makeup, and she said, 'I still have the tickets. We could go at once. I—there is nothing more for me here! Nothing!'

"'I know.' I took her two hands. 'It is tragic. But in Paris, my dear, you can forget. In Paris there is music, there is dancing, there is love, and there is beauty! And we shall be there—together!'"

He paused, refilling his glass. "She listened, her blue eyes very wide and wondering. She was a dear girl, no question of it. The black bag was at my feet. 'Look!' I took from my pocket a packet of bills and stripped off several of the thousand-dollar denomination. 'Take this! I shall meet you in Paris! Go to this place'—I wrote out the name of a small, discreet hotel—'and wait for me. I shall not be long.'

"Then I picked up the black bag and walked out. Once beyond the door with the bag I did not wait for the lift, but ran down the stairs. I had it, did I not? I had the black bag with the quarter of a million, and more to come from my own sale of the munitions! Ah, it was exciting, my friend, most exciting! It is always exciting when one is making money! And such delightful sums! Into my car then and away to the field where Milligan awaited me.

"Racing out on the field, I leaped from the car. Milligan was there, beside his plane, but he was not alone.

"Three men were with him, and one of them was the old marshal. He was the last person I expected in Shanghai, where he had many enemies, but here he was. One of the men stood guard over Milligan, and the other had a pistol directed at me.

"My eyes caught those of Milligan. He was a man I knew—a tough man, a ready man. Did I tell you that he was from Texas? Anyway, a lift of the brows, a small hand gesture—he knew what was coming. There was no doubting that he wished to be away as much as I.

" 'Ah, Marshal Chang! How delightful to see you! And what a surprise to find you in Shanghai of all places! Once I knew what happened I flew here at once! At once, Marshal. It was my duty as your aide, your confidant, and your friend to rectify this error!'

"You see, one does what one can, and I had already given up on this money. True, what I was about to do would *hurt!* Hurt, Lieutenant! But it was my only way out. The old marshal would be in no mood for games, and every second here was filled with danger for him, so he was desperate. As for me, it is a wise soldier who knows when to retire from the field.

"Anyway, did I not have money awaiting me at the other end? From my sale of the arms?

" 'When I realized what had happened, Marshal, I flew

to recover your money! It was the least I could do for one who has been my friend, my adviser, almost a second father!'

" 'Recover?' he asked, puzzled.

" 'Of course! It is here! In this bag! Now if you would like to fly back with me?'

" 'Let me see the money,' he demanded.

" 'Of course,' I said, and yielded the bag to his grasp. Yielded it reluctantly, you understand, for I had hoped to have that money somehow, someway. If I could just get the marshal into the plane—

"He gestured to one of his men, he who had been covering me, to open the bag. He did so. The marshal leaned over and peered inside; then he looked up at me, and his face was dark with anger.

"Looking into the bag, I knew why, knew that we had been cheated, that—

"The bag was filled with old newspapers, and there was a novel there to give it weight. And *that* novel? How could it have had weight enough? It was by a writer I have never liked—never!

"The old marshal was trembling with anger. 'You!' he shouted. 'You—!'

"It was a time, Lieutenant, a time for decision! Never have I been more pleased with myself than what I did then! In an instant I should have been killed! And Milligan, also! It was a time for *action*, and like the old soldier I was, I *acted*!

"He who guarded me had lowered his pistol while he opened the bag, and for that reason he was holding the pistol but loosely. I struck down at the base of his thumb with the edge of my hand, and as the pistol fell from his hand, I seized it and fired!

"Not at the man I had disarmed but at the man guarding Milligan.

"Turning swiftly, I shoved the old marshal. He was a heavy man, and he tottered back off balance and fell. Milligan had leaped into the plane, and the man I had disarmed leaped at me. My pistol exploded, and he fell; then I leaped into the plane, and we were off—gone!

"Once again, Lieutenant, I had snatched victory from the jaws of defeat. I do not wish to appear smug, but it is only the truth.

"In Kansu I received payment for the guns and told them where the junk would be. Then once more we took off. In the air I changed clothing, changed to such a costume as an English scientist might wear in the field. I had it always with me, for you know how the English are—one is apt to find them anywhere, in any out-of-the-way, godforsaken place, doing God knows what.

"I was to be a hunter of butterflies and a bit vague about all else. You see? It was an excellent cover.

"We landed—I shall not say where, for it is a field I have often used and may well use again. I have such places here and there. One never knows, does one?

"There I paid Milligan. Ten thousand dollars, more than he had ever seen before at one time, and there I left him, but with regret. He was a man, that one!

"I bought horses, and in a small town I found some equipment abandoned at some time by a scientific scholar before he attempted the Karakoram Pass. Have you tried it? If not, do not. It is—anyway, there is another older pass not far from there that is useful if one does not mind swinging bridges over gorges with roaring water beneath.

"It is a very remote country, yet it seemed by far the best and far from troublesome officials. Who would expect to find anyone in such a place. Yet when we reached Chabrang—"

"Yes?"

"We went to a place where we might find food, and I heard a merchant, a Kirghiz, complaining in a loud voice against the government! He had been stopped, searched, questioned. It seemed there were soldiers there looking for someone with a great deal of money. As if any merchant dared carry any money at all in such a place!

"You can see my problem. But again I refused to be defeated! It is my decision that counts! I decided, and I acted! Promptly!

"I inquired, and in a voice just loud enough that all might hear, as to the ruins of Tsaparang and which road must I take?

"I knew the road, and I had seen the ruins. Who could forget them, high in that yellow cliff? Built into the very face of it like some of your cliff dwellings.

"Of course I knew where the ruins lay, and we went to them. The men I had hired to travel with me and who owned the horses were only too glad to lie in the shade and rest. I took a pack from a horse, some scientific instruments, and of course the money. Then I made my way up the steep slope. One too curious fellow chose to follow me, but I found heavy stones that must be moved from my path, so he soon lost interest.

"I hid the money, hid it securely, in a place only I shall find, and in its place I packed some broken bits of pottery, a few blue beads, bits of carnelian and such. I took measurements, and took pictures with an old camera I had wheedled from Milligan, and then returned to my horses.

"We were stopped, of course, and questioned. We were

searched, and they found the shards of pottery, some but-terflies collected long ago by that traveler, whoever he was, and some very smelly bottles.

"I had donned thick-lensed glasses with which I peered at them—I had to peer to see anything at all—and there, where they think much of the evil eye, they were pleased to be rid of me."

"And now you have been back? Did you pick up the money?"

He smiled. "One does what one must, Lieutenant. Now I live here in Paris, and, I might say, I live well." He patted his stomach affectionately. "Even very well."

He sipped his wine. "Of course one must be careful when one has enemies. The old marshal—yes, he is alive and well—too well, altogether. He dislikes me for some reason. He would have me shot if he could. And regret-tably there are others."

"What of the blonde? Milton's girlfriend? Did you ever see her again?"

"See her?" He smiled complacently. "In fact, I shall see her tonight. I see her quite often, in fact."

"And the money? Milton's money?"

"She had taken it out of the black bag and hidden it. But she was a fool! Did she spend it on beautiful clothes? Did she buy jewels and wine? She did not. She *invested* it, every centime! Invested it, can you imagine?"

He emptied his glass. "She invested in the black market. Somewhere she found truckloads of American cigarettes and tanks of petrol."

"So the quarter of a million is forever beyond your reach?"

"Did you say a quarter of a million? It is more than a

million now, and only the good Lord knows where it will end! Given time, that stupid girl will own half of Paris."

I stood up. After all, I had things to do even if he did not, and as I turned to pick up my cap from an adjoining chair, there was a spiteful little snapping sound from beside me and a loud report from the door. Turning quickly, I saw the student, he who had been drinking coffee and working his sums at the outside table. The student had a Luger pistol that was slipping from his fingers, and as if by magic, the gendarmes were running into the court.

"Sit down, Lieutenant." The general caught my arm, and holding it out from my body a little, guided me to a chair. "You cannot leave now. There will be questions."

Glancing out the door, I saw the student, or whatever he was, lying as he had fallen. Evidently he had spun when hit, for he lay facedown almost in the doorway but headed the other way.

"Relax, Lieutenant. It is nothing. The poor man! It is terrible, the kind of help one gets today! So inefficient!"

The police were there, questioning everybody, but of course nobody knew anything. We were the last.

The general spoke excellent French. "I am General—"

"We know, *mon général,* we know. Did you, by any chance, see what took place?"

"I did not, but you know how it is. The Free French are still finding pockets of resistance, and of course they are hunting collaborators. When they find them—" He held up his forefinger and thumb like a pistol. "When they find them—*ping!* And they deserve no better."

He stood up. "If you would like to search—?"

"Oh, no!" The gendarme was appalled. "Of course not, *mon général!* Of course not!"

When I reached my quarters that night, it was with

some relief that I pulled off my tie and then started to shed my trench coat. Something bumped my side, and I slid my hand into the pocket—an automatic, small, neat, and very deadly.

It was not easy to be a friend of the general.

AUTHOR'S TEA

Actually to make a success, I had to succeed at least three times. I worked for a long time writing short stories while I was knocking around and the stories came back like homing pigeons and I didn't make any sales for a long time. Finally, I did and I built myself to a point in the pulps where I was one of the top pulp writers, drawing as much money as anybody, which wasn't much, but I was selling a lot of stories each year. One year I wrote forty-eight stories, some of them magazine-length novels, some of them novelettes.

I wrote for a group called the Thrilling or Standard magazines. I sold them a couple of hundred stories over a few years. And then all of a sudden, television came in and the paperback book came in and the pulps went out.

———

"I'VE BEEN READING your work, Mr. Dugan, and like it tremendously! You have such *power,* such *feeling!*"

"Thank you," he heard himself saying. "I'm glad you liked it." He glanced toward the door, where several women were arriving. They weren't young women. He sighed and glanced hopelessly toward the table, where one of those faded dowagers who nibble at the crusts of culture was pouring tea. Now if they only had a steak—

"Mr. Dugan," his hostess was saying, "I want you to meet Mrs. Nowlin. She is also a writer."

She was so fat she had almost reached the parting of the stays, and she had one of those faces that always reminded him of buttermilk. "How do you do, Mrs. Nowlin?" He smiled in a way he hoped was gracious. "It is always a pleasure to meet someone in the same profession. What do you write?"

"Oh, I'm not a *regular* writer, Mr. Dugan, but I do so love to write! Don't you find it simply fascinating? But I just never have been able to get anything published. Sometimes I doubt the publishers even read my manuscripts! Why, I believe they just *couldn't!*"

"I imagine they are pretty busy, Mrs. Nowlin. They get so many stories, you know."

"Why, I sent one of my poems away not long ago. It was a poem about James, you know, and they wouldn't take it. They didn't even *say* anything! Just one of those rejection slips. Why, I read the poem at the club, and they all said it was simply *beautiful!*"

"Was—was James your husband?" he asked hopefully, glancing toward the tea table again. Still no steak.

"James! Oh, goodness no! James is my dog! My little Pom. Don't you just *adore* Poms, Mr. Dugan?"

Then she was gone, fluttering across the room like a blimp escaped from its moorings.

He sighed again. Every time chance caught him at one of these author's teas, he would think of Frisco Brady. He could imagine the profane disgust of the big Irish longshoreman if he knew the guy who flattened him in the Harbor Pool Room was guest of honor at a pink tea.

Dugan felt the red crawling around his ears at the thought, and his eyes sought the tea table again. Someday, he reflected, there is going to be a hostess who will serve real meals to authors and achieve immortality at a single stroke. Writers would burn candles to her memory, or better still, some of those shadowy wafers that were served with the tea and were scarcely more tangible than the tea itself.

He started out of his dream and tried to look remotely intelligent as he saw his hostess piloting another body through the crowd. He knew at a glance that she had written a book of poetry that wouldn't scan, privately published, of course. Even worse, it was obvious that in some dim, distant year she had seen some of Garbo's less worthy pictures and had never recovered. She carried her chin high, and her neck stretched endlessly toward affected shoulders.

"I have so *wanted* to meet you! There is something so deep, so spiritual about your work! And your last book! One feels you were on a great height when you wrote it! Ah! . . ."

She was gone. But someone else was speaking to him, and he turned attentively.

"Why do so many of you writers write about such *hard* things? There is so much that is beautiful in the world! All people aren't like those people you write about, so why don't you write about *nice* people? And that boy you wrote about in the story about hunger, why, you know perfectly well, Mr. Dugan, that a boy like that couldn't go hungry in this country!"

His muscles ached with weariness, and he stood on the corner staring down the street, his thoughts blurred by hunger, his face white and strained. Somehow all form had become formless, and things about him took on new attitudes and appearances. He found his mind fastening upon little things with an abnormal concentration born of hunger and exhaustion. Walking a crack in the sidewalk became an obsession, and when he looked up from that, a fat man was crossing the street, and his arms and legs seemed to jerk grotesquely. Everything about him seemed to move in slow motion, and he stopped walking and tried to steady himself, conscious it was a delirium born of hunger.

He had been standing still for a moment trying to work his foot free from the sock where it was stuck with the dried blood from a broken blister, and when he moved forward suddenly, he almost fell. He pulled up sharply and turned his head to see if anyone noticed. He walked on then with careful attention.

He was hungry.

The words stood out in his consciousness, cold and clear, almost without thought or sensation. He looked at them as at a sign that had no meaning.

He passed a policeman and tried to adopt a careless, confident air but felt the man looking after him. As he passed a bakery, the smell of fresh pastry went through him like a wave, leaving a sensation of emptiness and nausea.

"You've had such an *interesting* life, Mr. Dugan! There must have been so many adventures. If I had been a man, I would have lived just such a life as you have. It must have been so *thrilling* and romantic!"

"Why don't you tell us some of the *real* stories? Some of the things that actually happened? I'll bet there were a lot you haven't even written."

"I'm tellin' you, Dugan. Lay off that dame, see? If you don't, I'll cut your heart out."

The music moved through the room, and he felt the lithe, quick movements of the girl as she danced, and through the smoky pall he heard a chair crash, and he looked down and smiled at the girl, and then he spun her to arm's length and ducked to avoid the first punch. Then he struck with his left, short and hard. He felt his fist thud against a jaw and saw the man's face as he fell forward, eyes bulging, jaw slack. He brought up his right into the man's midsection as he fell toward him and then stepped away. Something struck him from behind, and it wasn't until he got up that the blood started running into his eyes. He knew he'd been hit hard, and heard the music playing "In a little Spanish town 'twas on a night like this, stars were shining down. . . ."

He was speaking then, and he heard himself saying, "There is only the personal continuity. The man we were yesterday may not be the man we are tomorrow. Names are only trademarks for the individual, and from day to day that individual changes, and his ways and thoughts change, although he is not always himself aware of the change. The man who was yesterday a soldier may be a seller of brushes tomorrow. He has the same name, but the man himself is not the same, although circumstances may cause him to revert to his former personality and character. Even the body changes; the flesh and blood change with the food we eat and the water we drink.

"To him who drifts about, life consists of moving in and out of environments and changing conditions, and with each change of environment the wanderer changes, also. We move into lives that for the time are very near and dear to us, but suddenly all can be changed, and nothing remains but the memory.

"Only the innocent speak of adventure, for adventure is only a romantic name for trouble, and when one is having 'adventures' one wishes it were all over and he was elsewhere and safe. 'Adventure' is not nice. It is more often than not rough and dirty, cruel and harsh. . . ."

Before they screwed on the copper helmet, Scotty stopped by, his features tight and hard. "Watch yourself, kid, this is bad water and too many sharks. Some say there are more octopi and squids here than anywhere else, but usually they're no trouble. We'll try to hold it down up here." He slapped his waistband as he spoke. Scotty moved, and Singapore Charlie lifted the helmet.

"Don't worry, Skipper, I'll keep your lines clear, and I can handle any trouble." Then Dugan was sinking through the warm green water, feeling it clasp him close so that only the copper helmet protected him. Down, down, still farther down, and then he was standing on the sandy floor of the ocean, and around him moved the world of the undersea. There was silence, deep, unfathomable silence, except for the soft hiss of air. He moved forward, walking as though in a deep sleep, pushing himself against the water, turning himself from side to side like some unbelievable monster that haunted the lower depths.

Then he found the dark hull of the old ship and moved along the ghostly deck, half shrouded in the weed of a hundred years, moving toward the companionway where feet no longer trod. He hesitated at the door, looking down into darkness, and then he saw it moving toward him, huge, ominous, frightening. He tucked his warm-blooded hands into his armpits to leave only the slippery surface of the canvas and rubber suit. It came toward him, only vaguely curious, and inquiring tentacles slipped over and around him . . . feeling . . . feeling . . . feeling.

He sipped his tea and avoided the eyes of the woman who had the manuscript she wanted him to comment on, nibbled impotently at those infinitesimal buttons of nourishment, and listened to the ebb and flow of conversation about his ears. Here and there a remark swirled about, attracting his momentary attention. He heard himself speaking, saying how pleasant it had been, and then he was out on the street again, turning up his collar against the first few drops of spattering rain.

LET ME FORGET. . . .

Let me forget the dark seas rolling,
The taste of wind, the lure and lift
Of far, blue-shrouded shores;
No longer let the wild wind's singing
Build high the waves in this
My heart's own storm;
Now let me quietly work, for I have songs.

Let not my blood beat answer to the sea. . . .
The beaches lie alone, so let them lie.
Let me forget the gray-banked distant hills,
The echoing emptiness of ancient towns;
No longer let the brown leaves falling
Move me to wander. . . . I have songs to sing.

WHAT IS LOUIS L'AMOUR'S
LOST TREASURES?

L ouis L'Amour's Lost Treasures is a project created
to release some of the author's more unconventional
manuscripts from the family archives.

Currently included in the series are *Louis L'Amour's
Lost Treasures: Volume 1*, published in the fall of 2017,
and *Volume 2*, which will be published in the fall of 2019.
These books contain both finished and unfinished short
stories, unfinished novels, literary and motion picture
treatments, notes, and outlines. They are a wide selection
of the many works Louis was never able to publish during his lifetime.

In 2018 we will release *No Traveller Returns*, L'Amour's
never-before-seen first novel, which was written between
1938 and 1942. In the future, there may be a selection of
even more L'Amour titles.

Additionally, many notes and alternate drafts to Louis's
well-known and previously published novels and short
stories will now be included as "bonus feature" postscripts within the books that they relate to. For example,
the Lost Treasures postscript to *Last of the Breed* will
contain early notes on the story, the short story that was
discovered to be a missing piece of the novel, the history
of the novel's inspiration and creation, and information
about unproduced motion picture and comic book versions.

An even more complete description of the Lost Treasures project, along with a number of examples of what

is in the books, can be found at louislamourslosttreasures .com. The website also contains a good deal of exclusive material, such as even more pieces of unknown stories that were too short or too incomplete to include in the Lost Treasures books, plus personal photos, scans of original documents, and notes.

All of the works that contain Lost Treasures project materials will display the Louis L'Amour's Lost Treasures banner and logo.

LOUIS L'AMOUR'S LOST TREASURES

POSTSCRIPT

By Beau L'Amour

This collection of short stories, *Yondering,* has gone through a number of changes over the years. Like a theory based on growing archeological evidence, its contents have shifted and been refined, but now, after finally cataloging and studying all of my father's manuscripts, I'm convinced that this Lost Treasures edition is its final form.

Though my father had long planned to publish these stories in one volume, the idea of *Yondering* finally coalesced only once he began to seriously consider writing an autobiography. In the late 1950s and early '60s Dad had painfully learned that it was going to be hard for him to expand his writing outside the Western genre. In the '70s he executed a careful plan to write a number of books, utilizing some of his more popular characters, which stretched back in time to the era of the colonial frontier. His hope was that this would slowly alter the type of writing people expected of him. The plan worked, and in the 1980s he had great success with a previously rejected historical adventure, then a cold war thriller and a work of science fiction. In the same time period Dad was also enacting a similarly cautious approach to writing about himself. In 1981 Louis wrote the following to Candace Klaschus, a doctoral student at the University of New Mexico:

> . . . once one acquires a
> reputation, and has proved himself

by his sales, nobody wants to
interfere. Before that I had people
warning me away from the things I do
now. Even Bantam was, at first, very
wary about me deviating in any way
from the straight western. Even
YONDERING was at first published
largely to humor me and to mark that
period of my sales. . . .

The comment about sales refers to the moment when Bantam figured Louis had sold around a hundred million copies of his many works. Conveniently, Dad used their interest in celebrating that threshold to justify the release of *Yondering*. He followed up a few years later with the next step in his plan: his ode to the books that shaped his life, *Education of a Wandering Man*.

While my father didn't live long enough to write his own life story, the Louis L'Amour's Lost Treasures series is my unconventional first step toward writing a biography. The whole Lost Treasures project, both the new titles and the postscripts added to many classics like *Yondering,* are my father's "professional biography." A more personally focused version of his long and eventful life is yet to come. But, for now, back to *Yondering* . . .

Below is a letter written to Marc Jaffe, the editorial director at Bantam, in which Dad outlines some of his reasons for putting this collection together. It's also likely that he was practicing, consciously or unconsciously, his responses to anyone who might insist that he just stick to writing Westerns:

Dear Marc:

As you know, I have for some time
considered publishing some of my
earlier stories, partly because
many of those who read my books
have asked for them, but partly
because they are to some extent
autobiographical. They are glimpses
of what my life was like during the
years when I was just wanting to
become a writer. They weren't easy
years. Often I was hungry, often out
of work, often facing situations
such as I have since written about.
The stories in this group are either
based on experiences of my own or of
acquaintances along the way.

They were rough years. I rode
freight trains, worked in lumber
and mining camps, went to sea, and
generally did whatever I could do to
make a buck and do it honestly. It
was a time when I met all kinds and
varieties of people, moving in and
out of their lives as they moved in
and out of mine.

Yet hard as they were they were
ripe, rich years in both experiences
and learning, and in the fo'c'sles
of merchant ships, in bunk-houses on
ranches, in mining and lumber camps
I heard stories of which I have

since written. As every writer must do, I have taken the raw stuff of listening and experience and fashioned it into stories. No story is found as written. Life is a huge block of raw stuff in which the writer sees the idea or the motive he wishes to illustrate. Then he must cut away and discard all the extraneous material and keep only that which is essential. The essence of writing is the ability to perceive the story; all men look, but few men see.

None of these stories have anything to do with the West, as such. Yet they are stories of people, and stories lived under conditions not too dissimilar from the way they might have been lived on the frontier.

Where do stories come from? Where does a writer get his ideas? The stories and the ideas come from the stuff of his own life and the material that is the source of his stories, and these few stories came from a period that demanded much of me but gave much in return.

Sincerely,
Louis L'Amour

Typically, my father was highly disciplined but not all that well organized. He had a plan for what he wanted to accomplish, but in all the tottering pyramids of paper that littered his office floor he was unable to find every one of the stories that fit the *Yondering* mold. Even I, who got things fairly well organized after his death, missed some material when I published *Yondering: The Revised Edition* in 1989. On the other hand, as he prepared the original book, Dad was able to drop right back into the *Yondering* style and write the one story that he felt was missing from the group, "A Friend of the General." Initially, I'd have sworn he'd created it in the late 1940s, but evidence suggests it was written in just a day or two in the late 1970s.

Placing all of Louis's "semiautobiographical short fiction" in one volume is especially important now because of the release of my father's first novel, *No Traveller Returns*, which is the final piece of the *Yondering* series. I will discuss the connections as I comment on the contents of this version of *Yondering*. . . .

"Somewhere my love lay sleeping," the opening line of the four-line poem that begins this collection, was once the beginning to a novel. That beginning appears in *Louis L'Amour's Lost Treasures: Volume 2* in the section labeled "Shanty," but it was also likely that Dad had originally planned to title that novel *Yondering*. It was set in the nineteenth century and had no relationship to this collection other than a vague suggestion that my father was considering aspects of his own life as he wrote the first chapter or so. Within a few years that attempt was abandoned, but the title and a new version of the lyrical first line had been recycled to become elements in this book of short stories. The poem is a haunting fragment, looking back on a deep nostalgia for a home and family that its author had yet to find.

"Death, Westbound" is the earliest example we have of Louis's short fiction—but for a long time its existence was shrouded in mystery. In *Education of a Wandering Man* Dad wrote:

> I placed my first story for publication. It was a hobo story, submitted to a magazine that had published many famous names when they were starting out. The magazine paid on publication, but that never happened. The magazine folded after accepting my story and that was the end of it.

This was interesting, yet not exactly true. Carefully examining his correspondence, I discovered that in February of 1933 he wrote the following to a girlfriend of his in Oklahoma:

> I have . . . managed to have one short story accepted by a small magazine one finds on the newsstands. It pays rather well but is somewhat sensational. The magazine . . . is generally illustrated by several pictures of partially undressed ladies, and they are usually rather heavily constructed ladies also. It is called "10 Story Book." My story was

a realistic tale of some hoboes
called "Death, West-bound."

So, late in life, Louis mentioned an unnamed "hobo story" in an unnamed magazine, a story that supposedly went unpublished. Yet fifty-five years earlier there is the suggestion that a similar story *was* published. A check of Louis's list of submissions for the early 1930s shows that he continued to send stories to *10 Story Book* for the next several years. That's not the behavior you'd expect if it had actually folded before the publication of his 1933 story.

I began to suspect that Dad had misdirected people for a long time—telling them that his first sale was the short story "Anything for a Pal" in 1935—because he was concerned about the risqué content of *10 Story Book*. We'll never know if his appearing in this publication embarrassed friends or family at the time, or if he became concerned later, maybe in the 1950s, as he became more well known.

Times and attitudes change, however. By the 1960s Louis was considering submitting both fiction and articles to *Playboy,* a magazine with a very similar format. Like *Playboy, 10 Story Book* had published work by some well-known authors, including my father's hero, Jack London, though I sincerely doubt that it paid even a fraction as much as Hugh Hefner's magazine.

After years of scrounging at antique shows and contacting collectors of vintage pornography (an "interesting" subculture to say the least), my dogged researcher Charles Van Eman finally located a copy of "Death, Westbound" by "Louis D'Amour." While the pictorial content of the magazine isn't something I'd leave lying around the house, to a modern audience I doubt it would be very challenging. Regardless of the racy reputation of its publisher and the fact that the story is little more than a "slice of life," "Death, Westbound" does document Louis's first successful attempt at authorship and the fact that he was planning to try and tell a particular type of story.

In some ways my father's vision for his *Yondering* material was similar to the concept he later used with his Sackett, Talon, and Chantry series. He wanted to create a cycle of stories documenting the life he had witnessed in his years on the road and in different cities around the world: San Pedro in the 1920s ("Old Doc Yak," "It's Your Move," "And Proudly Die," "Survival," "Show Me the Way to Go Home"); Shanghai in the 1930s ("The Admiral," "The Man Who Stole Shakespeare," "Shanghai, Not Without Gestures"), and Paris in the 1940s ("The Cross and the Candle," "A Friend of the General"). Other stories would examine the colorful characters, the ships and crews, and the roads and rails that connected these locations.

Dad was never a cowboy; his Western experiences tended to be related to farming, logging, and, in particular, mining. "Dead End Drift" is an extrapolation of the fears of every miner, but the mention in this story of "The Big Stope" indicates that it was specifically related to his time working at the Katherine Mine in Arizona.

"Dead-End Drift" was written in the summer of 1939 and, typically, Louis did not think it was very good. Relatively quickly, however, it was picked up by a New Mexico literary journal. It was also listed in the 1941 edition of *The Best American Short Stories,* rated with two out of three stars. It was the third year that Louis had made it into *Best American,* but this time he was rewarded with the attention of a prestigious literary agent. Though the man turned out to be a notorious scoundrel and was initially little help, a dozen years later, when Dad was on the edge of failure, the agent managed to sell "Gift of Cochise" to *Collier's* magazine, and started a chain reaction that within a few years led Louis to some modest fame writing paperback Westerns.

In the mid-1920s, after a successful string of boxing matches but an unsuccessful hunt for steady work in central Arizona, Dad left his parents and hoboed his way to Los Angeles, hoping to go back to sea. The employment situation in San Pedro (the Port of Los Angeles) was, however, a disaster. My father estimated there were over seven hundred seamen "on the beach"—out of work. He lived hand to mouth for three months until a lucky break gave him a ship.

"Old Doc Yak" is a story directly lifted from my father's life in that period. The somewhat pretentious gentleman got his nickname from a portly, goatlike character in a popular newspaper comic strip. The shack in the story was rented with money borrowed from a friend, Jimmy Eads, whom Dad rescued from being robbed by a group of rough characters from "Happy Valley."

This gang of misfits, along with their run-down lair, are depicted in the novel *No Traveller Returns.* Eads is most likely the guy in "Old Doc Yak" who remarks that the old man talked like someone had "thrown a dictionary at him and he got all the words but none of the definitions." The story won the full three stars in the *Best American Short Stories* index in 1942. The 1942 index was notable because the new editor, Martha Foley, greatly reduced the number of mentioned titles. It was the fourth consecutive year for Louis.

Dad said "Old Doc Yak" taught him a good deal about writing, significantly that he must love all his characters whether they be represented as good, bad, or indifferent. Relaying that lesson, he wrote:

It was written about a man I profoundly disliked as did most of those around me, but when I wrote a story about him suddenly he became alive and I understood him better and no longer disliked him.

And then, specifically discussing his goals for the future and what would become of the *Yondering* stories in particular, he wrote the following to Oklahoma friend Betty Brown:

It was pleasing to me that OLD DOC YAK won the attention it did. A minor thing, of course, and yet, the story is my best effort at presenting human nature, and handling the case of a cold, unliked man in a sympathetic and understanding manner. . . . I cannot condemn anyone for anything. I do not believe in sin. There is no such thing. There is wrong and right, and those in my conception are simple enough. If you injure another person, you are wrong. Otherwise all

is well. What I want to do is write
of people so well that when I have
gone on those who read my work will
understand them better. I want to
interpret people, the unfortunate,
the lost, the lonely, misunderstood
and shiftless. I want others to
know how they feel. I never,
intentionally, nor do I think
unintentionally, did anyone a wrong
or injured anyone. I would go far to
avoid anything of the kind.

"It's Your Move," another *Best American Short Stories* selection, was the first of the San Pedro stories to be written and published. This story, and a few others that I will note in this postscript, have a direct link to other works in the Louis L'Amour's Lost Treasures series. The environment of San Pedro prior to World War II appears over and over in the novel *No Traveller Returns,* but the more interesting connection is that of the character of Sleeth, who shows up in the "Samsara" chapter of *Louis L'Amour's Lost Treasures: Volume 1.* "Samsara" is a mysterious story of reincarnation, and Sleeth plays the role of a man who is just enough aware of his past lives to be tormented by that knowledge. He informs the young hero that there may be a hidden library, constructed to help the "arrived" incarnations recover their memories, somewhere in Central Asia.

It's an idea that also may have inspired the final story in *Lost Treasures: Volume 1,* "Journey to Aksu." For photographs of San Pedro at the time and more information related to all of the *Yondering* stories, a reader might enjoy taking a look at the "Louis' Adventures" section of the louislamourgreatadventure.com website.

"Survival" is literally a chapter out of *No Traveller Returns*. *No Traveller* is a book that, among other things, deals with the mysterious connections between people. The events leading up to the moment when each of the major characters join the crew of the SS *Lichenfield* are detailed in separate chapters. "Survival" follows Tex Worden and features another character from my father's first novel, Shorty Conrad. Louis supposedly knew the real-life versions of these two men. In Shorty's case, they met when he was shipping off the Gulf Coast, a few years earlier than the San Pedro era. In the case of Tex, he claimed he actually sailed with the man *after* his 'Pedro days, but I have always gotten the feeling that Dad also knew him during his time "on the beach" in Southern California.

Unlike the suave protagonist of "Show Me the Way to Go Home," Louis actually had no idea when he would be shipping out of San Pedro. As you can tell from that story's introduction, the opportunity came up at the last second; if he had any possessions that weren't in his pockets, he left them behind.

"Thicker Than Blood" is one of several stories that came from that voyage; the names have been changed ever so slightly, but even the ending—where the character who is a stand-in for my father encounters the hated first mate "Duggs" on the Columbia River waterfront—is likely true, rather than a fictionalized or poetic resolution. I have followed the career of "Duggs," and he and Louis were indeed both in Portland at the same time.

"Thicker Than Blood" also relates directly to the one voyage through Asian waters I can prove my father took.

This is the reason all the *Yondering* stories, whether related closely to Dad's actual experiences or not, have been arranged in the rough order of that journey.

"The Admiral" was published in *Story* magazine, possibly the most exclusive short story publication of the 1930s. Saul David, my father's first editor at Bantam Books, confirmed that fact for me in an interview just before his death: "*Story* magazine?" he said. "That was the apex. . . . If you were . . . aiming for the big time, for the Hemingway/Faulkner/Scott Fitzgerald league, that was the way in."

"The Admiral" was the first of Dad's Shanghai stories. In his journal in 1964, he wrote: "Long ago [I] planned a series, like O. Henry on N[ew] Y[ork], but the town [Shanghai] died. I knew too little of the place, but for my time there, a good deal."

The only time that I know for certain that Louis was in Shanghai was just for three or four days, so possibly he's not kidding about having rapidly taken in the atmosphere of the place. On the other hand, I have shown all of Dad's Shanghai writings, many more than are presented here, to a number of experts, one of them being Victor Krulak, an author and retired Marine Corps lieutenant general who, as a young officer, was stationed as a military observer in Shanghai prior to World War II. All swore that my father had the measure of the place and they could hardly believe the sum total of his days there was little more than seventy-two hours. Perhaps he returned. Dad's commentary suggests that this is the case, but the evidence I currently possess does not support that theory.

"Shanghai, Not Without Gestures" and "The Man Who Stole Shakespeare" both take advantage of Louis's knowledge of Shanghai, no matter where it may have come from. They also introduce us to Haig, a mysterious character who has an apartment on an alley off of Avenue Edward VII where Louis or his fictional alter ego may have stayed. Haig is doubly mysterious because he also shows up in the obviously fictional story fragment "Journey to Aksu" and in his presumably nonfiction memoir *Education of a Wandering Man*!

In *Education,* Louis describes "the old crowd" as a type whose "ranks are thinning" and can be found "in every large seaport city." These men were smugglers, dealers in information, and those who wanted to "avoid the eyes of officials." Dad claimed a man named Oriental Slim (mentioned elsewhere in this volume), whom he met while "on the beach" in San Pedro, first put him in touch with this group:

> My first contact in Shanghai came in a sailors' joint called, if I remember correctly, The Olympic, having nothing to do with the games--although games of other kinds were played there.
>
> It was a perhaps-accidental meeting with a Scotsman, a former British-India Army officer named Haig. He had left the service and become a Buddhist, but I always suspected he was with British Intelligence.

Also mentioned in "The Man Who Stole Shakeseare" is underworld figure Dou Yu-seng. Dou was a real character, though not well known outside of China. He was the leader of the Green Circle Society (one of the infamous

"Tongs") and controlled a great deal of Shanghai's French Concession. He joined with Chiang Kai-shek to fight both the Communists and the Japanese when they attempted to take over his city. The story suggests that Dou was the owner of the Edward VII apartment building, and, of course, he would be exactly the sort of contact that a man like Haig would want to have. He was also the sort who might have set up Paul Medrac, the would-be mercenary of "Journey to Aksu," or the Louis-like narrator of "The Man Who Stole Shakespeare" with a dangerous assignment either "up the river" or in China's Far West.

Moving on from China, at least for the moment, "Off the Mangrove Coast" introduces us to four desperate characters and a story that Dad claimed was based on truth. In the summer of 1939 Louis related a similar tale to columnist Roger Devlin of the *Tulsa Tribune:*

Louis condensed four thrilling weeks of treasure hunting into a few agonizingly casual sentences. Happened up in the Malay States, he recalled. Some native ruler had fled a rovolution a few years before, loading all his gold and jewels on a river boat. Hurricane came up, ship sank.

"It was believed to be several million dollars of treasure in the ship's strong room," Louis said. "A bunch of [us] obtained a boat and with four weeks' supply of food aboard, we set out to be wealthy.

"We charted the currents of the river, figuring just where the ship might have drifted. That took time. But finally, in diving outfits, we found a sunken vessel, and we were fairly certain it was the right one.

"The only trouble was that it was half drifted over with sand, and it took us a long time to clear that off. Then we found the ship was made of teak, just about the hardest wood going, and even harder after its long immersion. Took a long time to break through the side of the vessel. By then, too, we were running short of food. Had to live on the few fish we could catch.

"At last we were just about ready to break into the strong room. We felt we already had the treasure in our hands, when--" He paused. . . .

"When another hurricane came up. We managed to live through it, but by the time it quieted down the treasure ship was completely buried in the sand. Far's I know she's still there."

Now, I'm not sure that I really believe all that. Louis himself noted in his journal that there were some mistakes in Devlin's retelling of the story. But while Dad did spend some time, even longer than four weeks, in both the Federated Malay States and the Netherlands East Indies (today's Malaysia and Indonesia), and while he did sail past Darvel Bay, the location of the wreck in "Off the Mangrove Coast," it is highly unlikely he was able to take time off for treasure hunting. However, and regardless of its fictional aspects and whatever inconsistencies may have been added by the reporter, this story does form a sort of "first draft" or inspiration for "Off the Mangrove Coast."

If there are any autobiographical qualities included in "The *Dancing Kate*," they may come from stories Dad used to tell of sailing with the Captain Douglas mentioned in his introduction. That said, there are a number of suspicious aspects to these tales. The first is that I can't track down even a hint of when they could have occurred. There are several notable "dark periods" in Louis's young life, times when I have no idea what he was up to. However, as with China, none seem long enough to have included travel time to the Far East and then the months necessary for significant adventures. The second is that Douglas, depicted in this version of "The *Dancing Kate*" as a man who claims to have been sailing in Asian waters for nearly fifty years, is described as being a virile man in his mid-thirties in my father's correspondence from the 1930s. Lastly, a pulpier take on the same story was published in *Thrilling Adventures* magazine in 1941. The *Yondering* version seems to have been created, and toned down, specifically for the 1980 edition of *Yondering*.

However, my father's including this story was not just a case of his searching for additional material for *Yondering* or seeking to further establish some fictional alter ego in Indonesian waters; he included a modified and possibly more realistic iteration of this adventure in the background of Fritz Schumann, one of the characters in

No Traveller Returns. On top of that he wrote the following story fragment, which is a bit like a sequel to "The *Dancing Kate*," sometime after the mid-1950s. Given the way my father could turn out new story ideas, it seems odd he would become so preoccupied with this one unless it had some significance to him that I have yet to fathom.

He was a big man in a sweat-stained khaki shirt and he came to the door mopping his face with a rumpled handkerchief. His hair was uncombed and there was a two-day stubble of black beard on his swarthy face.

He was big-boned and powerful, the white-blue of his eyes startling against the dark skin.

He squinted his eyes against the glare from sea and sand, and leaned against the post that supported the porch roof. The house was old and shabby; no coat of paint had ever graced the gray, weather-beaten boards. There were three rooms, the living room that extended across the front of the house, and behind it the bed-room and kitchen.

The big man studied the sea through his squinted eyes, and recognized the meaning of the slow, heavy swell. He watched the curl of the surf at the water's edge. He had learned to know the moods of the sea by watching the way the surf came up on the sand.

His name was Tanner Malloy and he had been four years in this house, on this beach. Sometimes he fished. Sometimes he patrolled the long stretch of beach for what drifted ashore. He had managed to get along almost without money.

He mopped under his arms and across the back of his neck. God, was it hot! He knew the feeling in the air. It was heavy, like that swell out there, and it was slow, like the curl of the surf. This one would be bad.

Tanner Malloy had lived through many storms in his four years on the beach, and he had lived through many other storms elsewhere. He considered briefly the cave in the coral ridge behind the house . . . that might be the place to spend the night. The sea had never come this high since the house had been built, at least thirty years before. But it might. Tanner Malloy never questioned what the sea might do.

He had turned to go back inside when he heard the muffled beat of the motor from beyond the sand-spit. The boat was beyond the spit and so out of sight, but he did not need to guess who it was.

He only needed to wonder why Frank Myers was coming around the island. Tanner Malloy did not like Myers and he was not one to conceal his feelings. He knew his own faults, and one of them was a sharp impatience with people he did not like. He knew there were many who did not like him, and cared less, although respecting their privilege. He had a brusque, hard-heeling way of going through life, which was one reason why he was here.

Only it was not the only reason.

The boat was rounding the spit now, a long, graceful motor ship displacing about a hundred tons. That boat had cost a lot of money, but Malloy had no respect for the boat, its owner, nor even for money.

Only of late had he begun to think about money. Strangely, he had awakened several times thinking about home.

Not that he had a home anywhere, but home meant the town from which he had come, back in the States. At last he had decided he wanted to go back. And for him it was a strange decision.

Malloy walked back into the bed-

room and lifted the lid of the
trunk. From it he took a .44 magnum
Smith & Wesson, a heavy gun with
enormous shooting power. Into his
pocket he dropped a double handful
of cartridges, first tucking the
pistol behind his waistband. Pulling
off the torn shirt, he donned a
light cotton jacket that covered the
pistol but left it ready to hand.

He did not trust Frank Myers now
and had never trusted him, nor did
he need a pistol to handle him. The
pistol was insurance against whoever
Myers had with him. He was not
likely to come alone.

He waited on the porch, making no
move to greet the visitor at the
pier. As he waited he thought about
the arrival. It was thirty miles to
the port where Myers had his store
and his home. Myers would come here
for no trivial reason.

Frank Myers was a large man, an
inch taller and thirty pounds
heavier than Malloy. There was a
little extra bulk at his waist-line.
Two men accompanied him.

Leaving these two in the shade of
the palms, Myers walked up to the
house alone.

"Hello, Tan."

"Hiya." Malloy did not move his

shoulder from the post, and over the head of Myers he could watch the two men under the palms. Tanner Malloy was not a trusting man.

Myers wasted no time. "Do you know where Pocklington Reef is?"

"You know damned well I do."

"You can land on it?"

Malloy regarded Myers with cynical distaste, but curiosity was stirring within him.

Pocklington Reef was a lonely, desolate, God-forgotten coral reef some twenty miles long and two to three miles wide out in the Coral Sea. It was eighty-odd miles from the nearest land, and someday it would be an island. There were a few rocks projecting well above the sea; some stretches of the reef were drying, some breaking. Much of it was still underwater.

There were, at times, a few skimpy stretches of sand, and there was some wreckage. There was the rusting hull of an ancient iron ship which Tanner Malloy would not soon forget. It had been his home for three miserable months after his ketch piled up there during a hurricane.

"You don't want to go to Pocklington Reef."

"Is there an anchorage?"

"Properly speaking . . . no."

"But a boat could anchor there? It is possible?"

Tanner Malloy straightened up and tucked his thumbs behind his belt. "If the wind was right. If there wasn't much of a sea, and if you didn't stay long."

"Will you come with us?"

Malloy's laugh held no humor. "Myers, I don't have any notion of going anywhere near Pocklington. And if you're smart, you won't either."

"I'll pay you."

Malloy merely looked at him.

"I mean it. I'll pay you well."

"No."

Myers was growing angry. Malloy could see it and was not displeased. "I'll give you two hundred dollars."

"No."

Myers was really angry now. "Tanner, what's wrong with you? Don't you care about money at all? How can you live like this?" He gestured angrily at the lonely beach and the sea. "I don't understand you."

"Let it go at that, Myers. You don't understand me. You think I'd rather live close to you? I like the sea and the sky. I don't like your stinking gin mills. I don't like

you. I don't like the way you do
business."

Myers hesitated. Suddenly, he
looked up. "Malloy, there's a woman
on Pocklington Reef."

Tanner Malloy just looked at him.
He was stunned. Then he relaxed.
Myers was lying. Of course, he was
lying.

"So?"

"We've got to get her off. She's
there alone, Tan, she's stuck
there."

Malloy studied Myers, suddenly
impressed. Suppose he was telling
the truth? His eyes lifted to the
sea. That was an ugly swell. The air
had that tight, close feeling that
came before a storm, and with a
coldness that struck deep within
him, he remembered the terror of a
storm on Pocklington Reef. He
remembered those nightmares where
the enormous waves crashed over the
reef, the wind howling and filling
the air with tremendous sound.

Malloy lifted his eyes to those of
Myers. He searched the big man's
hard eyes carefully. "Since when are
you so worried about somebody else?"
he asked. "I've never known you to
give thought to anything but money."

"The Navy," Myers said, "they put

word out to get her off that ship.
They can't make it in time themselves.
She's on the rocks there at
Pocklington, all stove up and in a
sinking condition, but the girl
won't leave her."

It made sense, put that way. Frank
Myers had reason to want to stay
on the good side of the authorities,
for they had been showing a good
deal of interest in some of his
activities. Anyway, if word got out
that nothing had been done . . . As
for himself, he wouldn't see a wharf
rat left to Pocklington in a storm.

He glanced at the sky, which was
blue and quiet, then at the sea,
which had a greasy look. No breaking
waves, nothing like that at all,
just a long, deep swell and the
heaviness in the air.

He studied the sea and considered
the distance. The *Coral Queen* could
make good time, but it was over
eighty miles to the reef. Not less
than seven hours with good luck, and
very likely as much as eleven or
twelve. They would reach the reef
with a tremendous storm building,
and to even approach it under the
circumstances was a fool's trick.

But a girl . . .

"Who's there with her?"
"That's just it. She's alone."

The sky was gray with torn clouds as they began the last hour of the drive to Pocklington Reef. There were whitecaps now, and the seas were slate gray and heavy with power.

Tanner Malloy lounged in the stern, nursing a cup of steaming coffee, liking none of his surroundings.

Myers had five men aboard the *Coral Queen* aside from the cook and the engineer, and the cook doubled as cabin boy and when the situation demanded, on deck as a seaman. And none of the five men were the sort Tanner Malloy would have selected for company, and he was not a choosy man.

In his oilskin coat he stared at the sea, feeling a tightness in his scalp as they drew nearer and nearer to the reef. There was nothing about Pocklington he liked. The roughly oval reef was a nightmare in which he had lived for three months, of starvation, struggle and sleeplessness. He had ripped shell-fish from the rocks, caught other fish with his hands or with a hook and line, and he had trapped a couple of sea birds, one of which he had eaten raw.

His drinking water had come from pools left from the rain, or rain-water caught in a ragged piece of tarpaulin. And throughout the tropical storms for which the Coral Sea was a breeding ground, he had clung with bloody hands to the broken coral knobs, filled with a wild despair. Somehow he had survived, more an animal than a man when finally picked up by an astonished marine survey ship.

He sipped his coffee, staring into the distance where the reef would first appear. He was afraid of it. He admitted it wryly, and without shame. A man who was not afraid of the sea was a fool. You could live on the sea, you could live with it, you could learn to understand it . . . and then it would suddenly become monstrous. There were frightful storms . . . such as the typhoon that struck down upon the American Navy during World War II . . . perhaps it was the worst storm in history. But there had been other storms, and he knew that no ship could survive when the sea was at its worst.

He also knew the jagged teeth of

Pocklington, the broken molars
hidden beneath the turbulent waters,
baring themselves through the foam
of the white water. It was a
trap . . . he knew it well, and
feared it from knowledge.

"We'd better go in from the south,
Myers," he said, when the owner of
the ship came back to him. "We won't
have much time. We will have to get
in, get the girl and get out. I'd
say we'd be fools to be there more
than fifteen minutes."

Myers avoided his eyes. Then he
said, "It may not take longer than
that."

Malloy was uneasy. He had a
restless, irritable feeling of some
undercurrent of which he was
unaware.

The nagging doubt returned in full
force. What had happened to Myers
that he would risk his ship and his
life to rescue a girl? True, if it
was realized that he could have done
it and had not, he would be despised
all over the Pacific. Yet such
things had not been known to weigh
very heavily with Frank Myers
before.

Malloy could feel the hard weight
of the Smith & Wesson under his
coat. Now the oilskin was over it,

but he had left a snap unfastened to get his hand to the gun.

He straightened suddenly, balancing to the movement of the boat. He could see the bulk of the grounded ship, a big, old freighter of some five thousand tons displacement, canted sharply over, her funnel demolished, and one mast broken sharply off.

At a glance he could see that the freighter would never be refloated. There was no need to examine her position, for he had been over every foot of the reef while there. The present storm would batter her into junk . . . and there was little time.

He walked to the wheel and took it in his hands. The man turned to glance at Myers, and Myers nodded, but watched the progress of the *Coral Queen* with care.

The sea was picking up, the air had grown colder. The storm had been farther away than he had suspected, but it was coming now. He eased her past a coral head, slid through a break in the reef and called out, "Let go forward!"

He heard the anchor splash in the water and several fathoms of chain ran out.

And then he saw the girl.

She was standing, a small, pitiful figure on the canted deck of the freighter. Now he could see the freighter was already almost broken in half, for she was twisted hard so that the foredeck and fo'c'slehead were on an even keel, while the after end of the freighter was canted sharply over.

"Better hurry," he said, "there's mighty little time."

They got the boat over quickly. The sea had an ugly look and the swells coming in over the outer reef were tremendous.

Malloy got into the boat and they shoved off. Even here, under the protection of several sections of the reef, the sea was lifting and plunging.

They moved in swiftly, and he sprang to the rock. On the reef, the water was washing over the coral, several inches deep. Myers and two other men followed, while one remained in the dinghy.

Malloy led the way along the reef, but only at a place or two was the coral above water. At times they splashed through knee-deep, and once a wave reached them nearly waist-high.

Malloy was in the lead when they
reached the crushed hull. The bottom
was ripped open, and she was badly
canted over. He yelled at the girl,
"Come on! Hurry!"

She did not move. He could see her
face was pale and she was obviously
frightened, yet she was looking past
him. And then suddenly he was
shouldered aside and two of the men
rushed for the freighter, leaping to
catch the rail and pull themselves
to the deck, which was at this point
scarcely seven feet above the water.

He sprang for the rail himself and
was struck a wicked blow across the
shoulder from behind. He tried to
turn, and another glancing blow from
a pistol barrel slammed alongside
his head.

He went down, falling on his face
in the water. A heavy boot caught
him in the ribs and he looked up
into the contorted, triumphant face
of Frank Myers.

"I'd kill you," Myers said, "but I
want you to die slow. You and that
girl. You'll never be so lucky as to
get off here again."

From the deck above he heard an
anguished scream, and then the two
men leaped from the deck and started
for the dinghy.

One of the men held a small black waterproof bag.

Tanner Malloy struggled to get up. His head was spinning and he could feel the sticky wetness of blood on his face. He was almost to his knees when the wave hit him and he went down, gasping for breath under the drenching of icy water.

He got to one knee, then heaved himself erect. Fumbling with the front of his slicker, he got his hand inside and came out with the Smith & Wesson.

He lifted the gun and fired. Even in the howling wind he heard the hoarse bark of the gun, but his aim was off. He distinctly saw chips leap from the gunwale of the dinghy, and then it was alongside and the men were springing aboard. At the same time, he heard in a momentary lull the sound of the anchor chain being heaved in.

He steadied himself and fired, but this time he fired at the hull itself, aiming at the engine. He knew the terrific penetrating power of the pistol. His second shot was at the man at the wheel, partly concealed behind the deckhouse.

He saw splinters fly, heard a yelp,

and the *Queen* yawed sharply. Then it
was moving away.

He started to fire again, but a
heavy sea drenched him, almost
knocking him down. For a minute or
more the ship was lost in blown
spray and when he saw it again, he
fired again. Then he reloaded the
gun.

Somebody was firing at him, but by
then the range was more than four
hundred yards, and they were coming
nowhere near. He took careful aim at
the hull and squeezed off a tight
bunch of four shots.

Reloading the gun, he thrust it
back into his waistband holster, and
jumping, he caught the rail and
climbed aboard. The girl was
sprawled upon the deck. He bent over
her quickly, and as he lifted her,
she stirred in his arms and looked
up, then tried to twist away from
him, her eyes wild.

"It's all right," he said, "they've
gone!"

She stared at him, as if trying to
collect her wits, then sat up.
Turning, she looked toward the *Queen*
and could see it pulling away.

"You came with them," she accused.

"Myers told me it was to rescue
you before the storm broke. I should

have known something was wrong,
because I know him."

The clouds were low now, and the
waves lifted with power and smashed
down over the outer reef. He got to
his feet and took careful stock of
their situation.

Better than any man alive, he knew
what they could expect. The
freighter had been driven through a
partial gap in the outer reef,
probably ripping open her bottom in
the process.

The part of the reef where the
freighter lay was barely above
water; most of it in the vicinity
was just near enough to the surface
to cause the waves to break. It was
true that the force of the waves
would be broken by the outer reef,
but the freighter would take a
tremendous pounding, and would very
likely go to pieces.

He explained this as he looked
around, taking stock. From
skepticism, the girl began to watch
him in fascinated horror. He glanced
aside and caught her expression, and
then he said, more quietly, "You
see, I know how it is. I was wrecked
here . . . three months of hell."

"Three months?"

"I was lucky," he said. "An oceanic

survey ship happened by, otherwise I might have been here yet. Most ships come nowhere near this place."

For the first time the impact of what he was saying made an impression. Slowly, she looked around. As far as her eyes could reach the sea was a snarling mass of white water, broken only here and there by the blackened stumps of the broken teeth of the reef. In the distance she could see some larger rocks.

"There used to be an old, rusting wreck further along," he said, "a ship wrecked here many years ago. And there are quite a few areas above water when it is calm."

He looked at her. "What was it they took?"

"They took seventy thousand dollars," she said quietly, "and half of it belonged to me. Half was to go to the other stockholders. We had sold our equity in some property, and were settling my father's estate."

There was little time. Comber after comber was thundering on the outer reef, and the storm was not far off. With the seas mounting, there would be little time to plan.

Swiftly, he searched the ship,

gathering food, clothing, and
oilskins against the coming storm.
No boats were left, and no rafts.
The after hatches were stove in, and
several hatch covers were adrift.
Working with a boat hook, he snared

As I say so often regarding the unfinished material included in Louis L'Amour's Lost Treasures: "Yes, that's
really how it ends."

On top of this Tanner Malloy–Pocklington Reef sequel, Dad also wrote up a rough draft for a movie project
that was somewhat similar. This likely dates from the
mid to late 1950s and seems intended for one of the low–
budget productions of the era:

Characters:

'Bastien McTeague, a successful
Basque-Irish playwright who began
life as a fisherman, sailor and
soldier. Handsome, but rugged and
tough, a man fitted by physique
and disposition for survival, he
learned his fighting the hard way
along the waterfronts. Self-educated
he has not softened in three years
away from the sea.

Lisa Fairman: Beautiful, voluptuous
and tricky. She married Fairman for
his money and he knows it. He wanted

her and she wanted the money and up to now both are satisfied with the deal. Selfish, but a wench. She has her own method of survival: to attach herself to the man who can best provide for her.

Taylor Fairman: Extremely rich and always has been, a man of the cities who is helpless when away from places where money is useful. Cynical, he has a perfect understanding of the woman he married, knowing her better than she knows him. He is thirty years older than she is, a slender man, sharp and ironic. Perfectly aware of his abilities and deficiencies.

Cris Romano: Skipper and owner of the *Dancing Lady,* a two-mast, auxiliary schooner. Once a gun-runner he is now a trader and poacher of pearls. Big and a scrapper, he could cut your throat without malice if there was money in it. Respects nothing but strength, has a sort of harsh good humor that carries nothing of mercy in it. Survival to him is based on strength and he will stop at nothing to get what he wants.

Lucas: His saturnine, sadistic mate and companion in trade or crime.

Pinto: A half-caste who functions as auxiliary engineer, cook and cabin boy.

Big London: A powerful young native who has been shanghaied aboard the schooner but seems content. He does not talk. Could be either Negro or Kanaka.

The story opens on an immense expanse of sea and sky with:

McTeague afloat on some wreckage. A few storm clouds are lingering in the sky but this storm is over. McTeague had been sailing on a chartered yacht from Hawaii to Tahiti when they were struck by a hurricane. McTeague has survived by clinging to the wreckage which consists of the mast, yard and part of a sail.

He has neither food nor water and knows he is on the edge of one of the loneliest expanses of water in the world. West, there are scattered islands, east there is nothing for two thousand miles. He manages to get water, to catch fish, and to make his wreckage into a crude raft. He knows that clouds gather over islands; the proximity to land can be told by the birds seen and fish seen, and eventually he gets to an island.

The island is a mere sandbar with a few palms, at no place as much as a dozen feet above the sea. There is wreckage along the reef, and some on the beach of the island itself. There is also a wrecked lifeboat and two other passengers, Taylor and Lisa Fairman. Neither of them has the faintest idea of how to exist in such a place; Fairman has failed after many attempts to open a coconut, to take off the outer husk and then crack the nut itself. McTeague does know how, and the three manage to survive. Their island is far from any steamer lanes and they realize from the start that their chance of being rescued is slight. There is every chance they may be there for the rest of their lives.

Lisa develops a lively interest in McTeague and has words with Fairman. There is a good bit of biting

sarcasm tossed back and forth
between them that carries a good
deal of humor as well as some
underlying viciousness. The
situation develops along with their
struggle to live, and then the
Dancing Lady arrives.

Cris Romano takes them aboard and
then discovers that Fairman has a
metal box containing a considerable
sum of money that he had managed to
lay hands on before the yacht went
down. Additionally, of course, there
is Lisa--a welcome sight to the eyes
of any sailor.

Romano can see nothing in the way
of doing whatever he wishes. A hard
character, he will stop at nothing.
McTeague has already recognized him
and guesses their situation. As
nobody knows the three are alive,
Romano tells Lucas they can kill the
two men and take the money, and they
then can keep Lisa around only as
long as she can keep them amused.

McTeague manages a few words with
the Kanaka, Big London, but he does
not talk, just listens and will not
commit himself. Nevertheless,
McTeague hopes he will remain

neutral, at least. McTeague keeps
with him a small waterproof bag that
contains a number of other things:
some fish hooks, line, etc. It was a
sack he always carried fastened to
his belt when at sea and contained
articles necessary for survival.

Lucas suggests it would be a simple
matter to get the two men into a
poker game and trim them but good.
They play, and the two are cheating,
but after winning at first, they
begin to lose. Meanwhile, Fairman
wins a good deal and McTeague wins a
little; he is a skillful card
mechanic and succeeds in trimming
Lucas and Romano. However, Romano
tells him it makes no difference--
they are on his boat, and he wins
anyway, and they won't get off it
alive. McTeague replies that he
still holds the best hand--it is
under the table pointed at Romano's
stomach. He has a .380 Colt taken
from the waterproof bag.

Later, Romano succeeds in
surprising McTeague and he loses
hold on the gun. There is a battle
to end all battles, and McTeague
wins.

During all this time, beginning shortly after his arrival on the island, Lisa has been trying to attach herself to McTeague. From the beginning it looks as if he is listening to her and perhaps falling for her wiles. But she does not know who he is, believes him to be merely a rugged sailor. Her husband does know, and McTeague knows he knows. Now, with land in view and the schooner moving up to the harbor, it suddenly becomes apparent to Lisa that she has been backing the wrong horse.

Once they get ashore Fairman will be able to spend money. . . . She moves over to him again. Her character by this time has been well established. Beautiful, but a selfish, sexy, wench. She is the kind of woman that nine out of ten women will enjoy seeing get dumped, and she does.

As the gangway goes down, she remarks to Fairman that they will soon be ashore, and how wonderful it will be to be home again, and he turns and looks past her to McTeague and with an exchange of comments, they go ashore together, Fairman

slapping the playwright on the back,
and thanking him for saving his
life.

Lisa, her feet apart and her hands
on her hips, looks after them
thinking you can imagine what.

Getting back to the more typical *Yondering* stories, it
would seem "Glorious! Glorious!" is not something that
my father could have experienced firsthand but may have
heard about in Egypt during his ship's slow transition of
the Suez Canal. On the way from there to New York he
also sailed the North African coast during the last days
of Abd el-Krim and the Republic of the Rif.

"By the Ruins of El Walarieh" was later updated to
form the beginning of the 1960s-era thriller "The Golden
Tapestry," which can be found in *Louis L'Amour's Lost
Treasures: Volume 1*. Exactly how Dad decided that this
minor-key story about the meeting of two young men
from vastly different cultures was the appropriate beginning for a novel that feels like it might have been adapted
into a movie by Alfred Hitchcock is a complete mystery,
but many drafts were written in an attempt to get the first
few chapters just right. The short story takes place in
Morocco, while the location of the unfinished novel is
Istanbul, Turkey. The following fragment is Louis's first
attempt to fuse "By the Ruins of El Walarieh" into the
plot of the more extensive adventure story "The Golden
Tapestry":

Twice in the first days that I
waited near the ruins of El Walarieh,

the black car went by, and each time it passed slowly. A man who lives by his wits, by his knowledge of the ways and customs of men, you might say, observes such things. He is careful to observe them if he wishes to prosper . . . and at times if he wishes to remain alive.

From the hillside above the ruins one could watch the surf breaking along the shore below the cliffs, and although the grass was at times sparse, thin goats grazed among the occasional clumps of brushwood high on the long slope behind me. It was a lonely coast, south of Casablanca, but possessed of its own wild beauty.

Three times I had been there before the boy approached. He was a thin boy with large, dark eyes and brown skin. He squatted on his heels behind me, his shins brown and dirty, and he looked curiously toward the sea, where I was looking.

"You sit here often," he suggested tentatively.

"Yes, very often."

"You look at something?"

"I look at the sea, sometimes at the shore and the clouds. They are very beautiful."

"Beautiful?" He was astonished. "The sea is beautiful?" He looked again to be sure if I was, as he was now certain, mildly insane.

"I find the sea beautiful," I insisted, "and I like the ruins, and sometimes I try to picture the people who lived among them and what their lives were like."

He did not even glance toward the time-blackened ruins. "They are no good, not even for goats. The roofs have fallen in. Why do you look at the sea and not at the goats? I think the goats are more beautiful than the sea. Look at them!"

There were at least fifty goats browsing along the hillside, which stretched back a long mile to meet the sky. The goats were white and brown against the green of the young grass. Yes, there was beauty there, too. He seemed pleased that I agreed with him.

"They are not my goats," he explained, "but someday I shall own goats. Then you will see beauty. They shall be like small white clouds upon the green sky of the hillside." He studied the camera at my feet. "You have a machine. What is it for?"

"To make pictures. I shall make pictures of the ruins."

"Of the goats, too?"

To please him I agreed. "And of the goats, too."

The reply did please him yet he seemed restless and puzzled. Something was here that he did not understand. He broached the idea, as one gentleman to another. "You take pictures of the sea and the ruins. Why do you do this?"

"To catch their beauty. To look at them."

"But why a picture? They are here! You can see them without a picture."

"They are here for you," I explained, "because you are here. But I shall go away and it is good to remember beauty. I shall look at them many times."

"You need the machine for that?" He was astonished. "I can remember without a machine. I can remember the goats, each of them as they are today, and as they were last year." He paused, considering. "Ah, then. The machine is your memory. It is very strange to remember with a machine." Neither of us spoke for several minutes and then he said, "I have heard of this, but I did not believe. It is said that you have machines for everything."

The following day I returned to the hillside. It had not been my

plan to come but somehow the
conversation left me unsatisfied.
I'd a feeling somehow that I'd been
bested . . . and there was also the
matter of the curious black car.

When he saw me he joined me where
I sat and gravely accepted a
cigarette. "You have a woman?" he
asked.

"No."

"What? You have no woman? It is
good for a man to have a woman."

"No doubt." He was very wise for a
man of thirteen. "Do you have a
woman?" I asked, in all seriousness.

He accepted the question in the
same manner. "No . . . I am young
for a woman. They are much trouble.
And I must work with the goats."

"They are no trouble?"

He shrugged his thin shoulders.
"Goats are goats."

He smoked in silence and then said,
"If I had a woman I would beat her.
Women are good when beaten . . . but
they are not so productive as goats."

It was a question I had no wish to
debate for he undoubtedly knew goats,
and spoke of women with profound
wisdom, while I understood neither
women nor goats.

The black car rolled slowly along
the road below the ruins and I

watched it with interest. I believed
I knew who was in that black car and
why they were here.

"If you like the hillside, why do
you not stay? The picture is no
good. It will remember the sea and
the ruins at only one time and they
are never twice the same."

When I made no reply, watching the
black car, he asked, "Have you goats
at home?"

"No." I was ashamed, feeling the
confession would lower me in his
esteem. "I have no goats."

"A camel, perhaps?" He was giving
me every chance.

"No," I admitted reluctantly, "I
have no camel." Inspiration came to
me. His esteem was more important
than the truth. "I have horses."

He pondered the matter. "It is good
to have horses, but a horse is like
a woman. It is unproductive. If you
have a horse or a woman you must
also have goats."

"If one has a woman," I ventured,
"one must have many goats."

He was watching the car also.
"I think," he said, "they look for
the woman with the rug."

Ah . . ! "She sits on a rug?"

"She looks at it. She sits on the
grass . . . or sometimes on the

stones of the ruin." He paused. "She is a very beautiful woman . . . and not old." Reluctantly, he added, "She is more beautiful than the goats."

It was a compliment of the highest order. "How could a woman be more beautiful than goats?"

"It is difficult to believe," he admitted. "She is a woman who looks at a rug. . . . It is very strange."

There are rugs and there are rugs . . . and mine is a nose sensitive to the smell of money . . . however, I had expected the rug, with or without the woman.

"She is there now?"

"I will show you."

The ruins of El Walarieh lie something beyond thirty miles south of Cape Blanco, and roughly southwest from Casablanca. Nearer are the smaller port of Mazagan and the town of Safi. The ruins are unimpressive in themselves, but for me all ruins hold a fascination, and a ruin where a beautiful woman looks at a rug . . . I went down the slope with Rashid after the car was out of sight.

You wonder why I, a man of many countries and no profession, am interested in a rug? Naturally. In

the modern American home a rug has
no distinction. It is simply a
manufactured substance that covers a
floor, and of a nondescript shade.
It has no imagination, it has no
story, it has no color and no
vitality.

In Persia, in Turkey, in China, a
rug is a dream captured in thread,
it is a voice speaking beyond the
time of the weaver, it can be a
masterpiece, like a great painting.

She was seated on a gray stone with
the rug in her lap, and at once I saw
this was a rug of great beauty. . . .
It was also *the* rug . . . a rug of
legend.

Her hair was dark and her eyes were
long, almond-shaped and green. Her
cheekbones were high, which is a
good thing in a woman, yet the bones
of her face had delicacy.

"This is Rashid, a keeper of goats,
and he has told me of a beautiful
woman who sits among the ruins and
looks at a rug. I have come to be of
service."

She regarded me with her long green
eyes, and she said, "Do you know
something of rugs?"

Rashid squatted on his thin heels
and looked at me with cool regard.

He looked at me as if to say "You know nothing of goats. Let us see how you do with women."

"A rug needs examination. There is much to know of rugs." I paused. "As much as there is to know of men or jewels."

When she lifted her lashes to look at me her eyes were no longer green, but hazel . . . almost yellow. "Do you know me, then?"

"My life is to know beauty, Madam, and who can forget such beauty as yours? The first time was at an inn . . . the Inn of the White Horse, in Honfleur. You had been motoring along the coast, and the food is quite good there.

"The second time was in the Mosky, that charming market of odds and ends and strange things in Cairo. The first time I sat at an adjoining table listening to your voice and watching your profile. . . . The Marquis was quite annoyed."

"And the third time?"

"You bought from me an antique ring . . . with a green stone."

Her eyes darkened. "I remember the stone. It was false."

"Many things are, Madam, but at the time it was all I had to sell, and a man must live. And on you, Madam, who would suspect it of being false? Madam lends all thing beauty."

"I believe you are a thief . . . perhaps worse."

"One lives as one can. . . . The falseness or the purity of things are relative, and few things are coincidence. For example, some might believe my presence here an accident, but by now you know it is by intention. You have the rug, Madam, but I have the knowledge."

Her hand-bag, a large white one, lay open on the wall beside her, facing away from me so its contents were invisible, but I knew there was a gun.

"Those others," I said, "the ones who drive by in the car. It is you they look for."

"Who are you?" she asked.

"It is a question, Madam. Sometimes I wonder if I remember who I am myself. Identities are, you understand, a matter of convenience, but I seem to remember that my name is Ali O'Mara. The name is from my father . . . the O'Mara is. He was from Tipperary. My mother was a Circassian, and I was born in Istanbul. I am a man of several passports, Madam, and no loyalties."

"You will have no money from me," she replied coolly. "I am broke."

"Who is not, Madam? Even you, the incomparable Villette, can be broke. There is always another gentleman. . . . Of course, the Marquis was scarcely worthy of you, but the Maharajah! Ah, there was a man!"

Pausing slightly, I said, "You say you are broke, but you cannot be. You have the rug . . . a gift from the Maharajah, I believe . . . and now you have my friendship."

Taking the rug from her hands I spread it atop the ruined wall. It was a Ghiordes prayer rug. The shape of the Prayer Arch with its high central spire and strongly defined shoulders were a distinctive feature of its design. The elegance of design and the beauty of color were typical of the Middle Period, but all that was obvious. What was obvious also was the masterful workmanship that had gone into the making of this rug. . . . It was by no means an ordinary rug, by no means even a special rug of the period . . . it was a masterpiece, and it was unique.

"It is superb," I said quietly. "I have seen no rug like it." As I

spoke my eyes were eagerly tracing
out the design, searching for the
clue. Here, within my hands, I held
the clue to the burial of a vast
treasure of gold and jewels, for if
the legends were true the secret was
woven into this rug.

Yet the rug itself fascinated me.
Typical of the Ghiordes prayer rugs,
the nap brushed toward the top of the
arch, and that arch pointed toward
Mecca when the rug was placed on the
ground. The Ghiordes rugs were made
of wool through which a little cotton
had been woven. A rug entirely of
wool would be perfect, and by mixing
the cotton the weaver symbolized his
humility before Allah.

Scanning the rug quickly, I
searched for a clue, knowing the
opportunity might never be mine
again. The spandrel, or that area
directly above the arch, was of deep
blue, symbolizing the vault of the
heavens, and there could be no clue
there. The clue must therefore be in
the border, the panel, or the
supporting pillars of the arch . . .
or, and I glanced searchingly, the
temple lamp suspended from the peak
of the arch. Only in this case, as
in some others, the lamp hung free
in the arch.

"They come." It was Rashid, who had watched us with interest.

Our eyes turned toward the road. The black car was there again, and several men were getting out. It was the first time the car had stopped. . . . It was three hundred yards off down the hill, and there was little time.

"They must not find you." I caught Villette's arm quickly. There was no hiding place among the ruins, and the hillside was totally without cover. The grass was short and there were only the scattered goats. . . .

There was a slight depression in the face of the slope down which run-off water had found a way. "Go up there," I said to her, "with Rashid, and lie down among the goats, your back down slope, knees drawn up. And whatever you do . . . don't move!"

She quickly understood, and as quickly disappeared. Shallow as the depression was, it gave them cover for the space of time necessary for them to mount the slope. There was an instant when she might have been seen for what she was, and then she was lying down, looking but little different than the goats, some of which were lying down, some grazing, the nearest of them more than a hundred yards up hill.

As for me, I opened my camera, checked my light meter, and gave the camera the proper setting. A camera, I have observed, offers concealment for a multitude of sinful plans. A man with a camera might be photographing anything . . . in those nations accustomed to tourists a man with a camera might be anywhere, even among the ruins of El Walarieh.

There were four men, and two were dark, sallow men with suspicious eyes. One was a European, the last an American. It was this one about whom I worried for of them all he was the only one who might know me. . . . He was an ex-G.I. who had remained behind in Europe, buying and selling on the black market, smuggling a little, dealing in contraband.

"Good afternoon," I said cheerfully, and checked my light meter again.

They looked at me suspiciously, and then they looked around, their eyes searching every nook and cranny of the ruins.

"It isn't much of a ruin," I said, "but against the green hillside, with the sea beyond and the white clouds on that sky . . . I'll get some good color shots."

"There was a girl here?" The American's name was Butler.

"A girl?" I winked at him. "Ah, now that would be something. Were you expecting a girl?"

Butler was staring at me, and under the stare I grew uneasy. If he knew me by sight or name, I did not know, but the others did not. Seeing them now at close range, I recognized them all, and they were trouble, real trouble. These men were not casual thieves following up a rumor from the bazaar, they were as dangerous as any men in North Africa or Europe.

"If you want a good shot," I ventured, "there's a place with a great view of the cliffs, the hillside and the sea with the white line of the surf breaking."

They ignored me. One of the Greeks, for such he was, prowled among the ruins and finally returned. "Nobody here," he said, with disgust. "Probably mistook that goat-herd for a woman."

Walking away, toward their car, Butler turned and glanced back at me. Something was riding his memory, and I was worried. There was one thing to do: study the rug, discover its secret, find the cache of jewels and get away. And the quicker the better.

When the car had gone I strolled up the hillside toward the goats, occasionally stopping for a picture.

Villette lay still, and I admired her. She'd done what was necessary with no questions. A moment of hesitation or panic might have been disastrous.

She sat up when I spoke to her. "It was Hans Butler," I said, "and Armand Vico and that scarred Greek. Do you know them?"

"I know them," she said, and from her tone I surmised she knew them well enough.

"The rug," I said, and sat down beside her. "We must do what we can, at once."

Rashid came to join us. He had been seated with his goats higher on the hill.

Seated on the wall of the ruin in the light of a fading afternoon, I studied the rug. The border offered nothing. Each design on such a rug has meaning, or once had meaning; much knowledge is required to comprehend the designs used in rug design. Jewish and Christian symbols

may be found as well as Moslem, and
many a pagan symbol has held over,
but there was once a group of
Chinese weavers who settled in the
Middle East and wove rugs there, and
their dragon symbols, altered but
recognizable, can often be found.

The temple lamp . . . it always
came back to that in the end. The
design of the lamp was simple but
unlike any I had ever seen. The
pattern was geometrical, but broken
and distorted. Study it as I would,
it made no sense.

The story of the Weaver of El
Walarieh was a strange one, although
in North Africa the weird and
unusual is so common as to be almost
the usual.

The Weaver had been friend and
adviser to Moulay Ismail, a powerful
prince who at one time wished to
join with Queen Elizabeth and divide
the empire of Spain. The Weaver had
been just that--a weaver of rugs in
Turkey, a wanderer in Persia, a
shrewd and cunning man wherever he
was. Above all he was the most
trusted adviser to Moulay Ismail,
and as such he gathered wealth.

Moulay Ismail himself was one of
the most fabulously rich rulers who
ever lived, but the amount of the

Weaver's wealth was never known.
The truth of the matter was, that
the Weaver was a

Yes, again . . . that *is* where it ends. There is a great
deal more information about how this story eventually
developed in my comments in "The Golden Tapestry"
chapter of *Louis L'Amour's Lost Treasures: Volume 1*—
more on Villette Mallory, more on her late husband the
Maharajah, and more on the secret of the rug and the men
who want to possess it.

Next we look at "The Cross and the Candle" and the
out-of-the-way Paris café featured in it. The place seems
to be a quainter and quieter version of the nightclub
owned by the notorious Suzy Solidor. Here are a couple
of bits extracted from letters Louis wrote to his parents
from France during the waning days of the war:

There seems some evidence that
part of the family [the L'Amour
family] either were connected with
Surcouf, the corsair and great
Breton hero, or were with him on his
ships. So, I'm going down tomorrow
evening to see Suzy Solidor, a great
grand daughter of his who owns the
Chez Suzy, a night club on the Rue
St. Anne, near the Louvre. . . . It
seems she was a few years ago one of
the great beauties of Europe; that
she was also a famous model;
that she is still striking and
attractive. . . . I dropped by the

> night club last night but it was
> full to the doors and not a place
> anywhere, but I told the doorkeeper
> I was a writer, and came of an old
> Breton family. . . . So I have an
> appointment with Suzy tomorrow night
> at ten.

And...

> The place has over a hundred
> portraits of her done by all the
> famous artists of the past thirty
> years. She is about fifty, or
> perhaps a few years younger, and
> still something of a woman.

It is well known that many of these portraits were indeed created by significant painters like Picasso, Braque, and Tamara de Lempicka. If Solidor's "nightclub" and the "café" Louis describes in "The Cross and the Candle" are the same place, its formal name was La Vie Parisienne.

Ironically, given the subject of Louis's story, Suzy herself was eventually convicted of being a collaborator. I am unaware of the exact charges, but no doubt this was more related to the popularity of her club with Nazi officials than to her having possibly betrayed beautiful resistance fighters or secret societies of crusaders.

For any students of writing who may be reading these Lost Treasures postscripts, it is worth noting my father's ability to manipulate actual events into various story lines. These stories were "inspired by" real life but not, with a few exceptions, intended to be exact depictions of it. However, if you look closely, you can see how the addition or subtraction of an element or two can turn an event, like visiting Suzy Solidor's café, into a complete and satisfying short story about family histories, Nazi collaborators, and ex-sailors who have fallen in love with aristocratic Frenchwomen.

One of my favorites of all Dad's short stories is "A Friend of the General." It ties together Paris and Shanghai and joins the two extremes of my father's possibly true or possibly mythical lives. I can remember hearing the story of Milton, originally named Mason, long before Louis actually wrote this story. As I've said before in this postscript, I have no evidence that Dad returned to Shanghai, or if he made up these stories, remembered others telling them, or read them in the newspapers of the era. It is slightly possible that he witnessed Milton's fate, but more likely that he heard about it . . . providing he didn't just make it all up.

But what I do know is that the countess who lived in the lavish gardener's cottage while troops (first German, then American) were quartered in her husband's château was a real person, actually an American married to a Frenchman. While I corresponded with her prior to her death, she claimed not to remember my father or to be aware of any of the events in this story. She did, however, affect a very French weariness with life and, while very willing to talk to me, was unwilling to take my questions very seriously. . . . I don't know if that means anything or not. There is also a bit of Countess Marguerite "Guitou" de Felcourt in this character. Guitou was a wonderful lady whom my father was engaged to for much of the war and its aftermath and whose family is still friends with ours.

The "old marshal" is probably based on Chang Tso-lin, or in its more modern version, Zhang Zuolin. Chang was a warlord and *tuchun* (governor) of Manchuria for a dozen or so years. However, he died when a Japanese agent planted a bomb in his train in June of 1928 and so, in reality, would not have been alive at the end of World War II.

Tex Milligan, the old China hand who rents out his services as a pilot, also appears in the "Journey to Aksu" chapter of *Lost Treasures: Volume 1*. Additionally, some of the discussion that the lieutenant and the general have about Chabrang and the ruins of Tsaparang in Central Asia (especially the moment where the lieutenant says, "I believed it was a way out for me, too . . . but I was not so lucky. I had to turn back") may have been Dad trying to have some fun by hinting that the two stories, the unfinished "Journey to Aksu" and "A Friend of the General," were part of the same continuum.

The last story in the collection, "Author's Tea," humorously draws on my father's experience at the many poetry and writers' society meetings he attended from the 1930s into the 1950s. Unlike the somewhat jaded character of "Dugan," I believe that Dad enjoyed these get-togethers. Among the Oklahoma writers, he got the opportunity to market his book of poetry, spend time with many different types of authors, including old ladies who wrote about their dogs, and establish some support for his budding career. Later, in Los Angeles, he made connections that helped him make his way through the byzantine environment of Hollywood. I imagine there were plenty of times that he did feel like a wolf strolling through a herd of sheep, but there were always a few successful professionals at these affairs who could both teach him a thing or two and help keep his ego in check.

The poem "Let Me Forget. . . ." was written in 1942, three years too late to be included in *Smoke from This Altar*. Along with the short piece created for the beginning of this volume, it forms a wonderful bookend for *Yondering*, and also celebrates a line of demarcation in my father's life: the wanderer becoming a storyteller. More than anything else, what he wanted in the early 1940s was to be allowed the time to perfect his craft and to set the foundations of a successful career. But all the literary potential of that period was snatched away on the first Sunday of December 1941.

Reading that last poem with fresh eyes, I found myself wondering if the reason he had included it didn't contain a double layer of nostalgia: first and foremost for his *Yondering* past, but also for the poor but comfortable existence he had enjoyed as a struggling artist living with his parents in rural Oklahoma.

Within a year he would be thrown back into a world of foreign travel, high adventure, and epic violence. Dad had always found his own personal meaning in Shakespeare's line "No traveller returns." To him it suggested not only the one-way journey into death that every human will experience, but the fact that none of us return to the places, people, and situations we once knew without all having undergone significant change. Indeed, in 1942, my father could never have guessed at the joys and heartaches to come. Like all of us, he ventured into the future, never to return. . . .

Beau L'Amour
November 2018

ABOUT LOUIS L'AMOUR

*"I think of myself in the oral tradition—
as a troubadour, a village taleteller, the man
in the shadows of the campfire. That's the way
I'd like to be remembered—as a storyteller.
A good storyteller."*

IT IS DOUBTFUL that any author could be as at home in the world re-created in his novels as Louis Dearborn L'Amour. Not only could he physically fill the boots of the rugged characters he wrote about, but he literally "walked the land my characters walk." His personal experiences as well as his lifelong devotion to historical research combined to give Mr. L'Amour the unique knowledge and understanding of people, events, and the challenge of the American frontier that became the hall marks of his popularity.

As a boy growing up in Jamestown, North Dakota, he absorbed all he could about his family's frontier heritage, including the story of his great-grandfather who was scalped by Sioux warriors.

Spurred by an eager curiosity and a desire to broaden his horizons, Mr. L'Amour left home at the age of fifteen and enjoyed a wide variety of jobs, including seaman, lumberjack, elephant handler, skinner of dead cattle, miner, and officer in the Transportation Corps during

World War II. He was a voracious reader and collector of books. His personal library contained 17,000 volumes.

Mr. L'Amour "wanted to write almost from the time I could talk." After developing a widespread following for the many frontier and adventure stories he wrote for fiction magazines, Mr. L'Amour published his first full-length novel, *Hondo*, in the United States in 1953. Every one of his more than 120 books is in print; there are more than 300 million copies of his books in print worldwide, making him one of the bestselling authors in modern literary history. His books have been translated into twenty languages, and more than forty-five of his novels and stories have been made into feature films and television movies.

His hardcover bestsellers include *The Lonesome Gods, The Walking Drum* (his twelfth-century historical novel), *Jubal Sackett, Last of the Breed*, and *The Haunted Mesa*. His memoir, *Education of a Wandering Man*, was a leading bestseller in 1989. Audio dramatizations and adaptations of many L'Amour stories are available from Random House Audio.

The recipient of many great honors and awards, in 1983 Mr. L'Amour became the first novelist ever to be awarded the Congressional Gold Medal by the United States Congress in honor of his life's work. In 1984 he was also awarded the Medal of Freedom by President Ronald Reagan.

Louis L'Amour died on June 10, 1988.